WIRED FOR
MURDER

Previously published Worldwide Mystery title by
KAREN McCULLOUGH

A GIFT FOR MURDER

WIRED FOR MURDER

KAREN McCULLOUGH

WORLDWIDE®

TORONTO • NEW YORK • LONDON
AMSTERDAM • PARIS • SYDNEY • HAMBURG
STOCKHOLM • ATHENS • TOKYO • MILAN
MADRID • WARSAW • BUDAPEST • AUCKLAND

Author's Note: I try to produce as clean a work as possible. This book has been through several rounds of editing in an effort to eliminate errors of grammar, usage, and consistency. However I realize that even multiple editors will overlook some things, so I ask that if you find any errors in this book, you let me know. You can email me at karen@kmccullough.com.

Recycling programs for this product may not exist in your area.

Wired for Murder

A Worldwide Mystery/March 2018

First published by CreateSpace Independent Publishing Platform

ISBN-13: 978-1-335-50651-1

Printed in U.S.A.

CAST OF CHARACTERS

Market Center Personnel:

Heather McNeil: assistant to the director of the Washington DC Commerce and Market Center

Janelle Addison: the Commerce and Market Center's director and Heather's superior

Scott Brandon: former police officer, security officer for the center

Craig Vincelli: head of security

Jo Sterling: marketing director

Tina: receptionist

Mark Templeton and Sam Boresi: maintenance

Howie Harper: security officer

Carl Roney: executive vice president, Market Centers and Events Inc., MCEI, owner of the Commerce and Market Center. Janelle Addison's superior.

Exhibitors:

MegaComp: Thomas Hovey, founder and CEO; Jim Driscoll, chief technology officer; assorted bodyguards and assistants

RTX Inc.: Drake Galloway, owner and president; Sandy Pangborn, marketing manager; Chase Markham, chief engineer

Gryphon-Loyal Enterprises: Ross Campbell, CMO;
Jennifer Martinez, account support manager;
Ted Hanford, technical support manager;
Larry Barnes, account support manager

SteadySafe: Frank Merrimon, president; Dean Lee,
account coordinator; Shawn Kelly, account coordinator;
Joel Halloway, temp

Schwartz-Mann GmbH: Dieter Gebhardt, sales
representative

Others:

Detective Peter Gilmont: the police detective assigned
to the murder investigation

ONE

Monday

JUST TWO HOURS into setup day of the annual Business Technology Show at the Washington, D.C., Commerce and Market Center, I was struggling to keep from screaming at an exhibitor. That was so not me. I was cool, calm, collected Heather McNeil. The person who could handle even the most troublesome people. Most of the time.

Dieter Gebhardt was pushing my buttons and he knew it.

"I do not understand vy you say ve cannot do this." A hint of smirk leaked onto his face. The tiny curl of his lip belied his pretended ignorance of my meaning, much less the authority behind the words. The sales representative for Schwartz-Mann GmbH was playing me, and I couldn't tell if he really thought he could get his way by feigning stupidity or if he was trying to score some machismo points. I didn't care about the points, but he damned well wasn't going to win the argument.

The whine of an electric screwdriver a couple of booths away almost drowned me out as I explained yet again why the Market Center couldn't allow the huge, powerful, multi-colored strobe lights they'd set up on poles around their booth to flash *all* the time. If those weren't bad enough by themselves, a set of sirens went along with them, blaring every few minutes. No way that could continue.

The complaints had started flooding in after the first blare shrieked around the show floor. I was dispatched to have a talk with the perpetrators.

When Gebhardt finally got the message that pretending stupidity wasn't going to win the argument, he tried a different tactic, waving a piece of paper in my face. "Ve haf planned lights and display many months ago. Rules say ve can haf the lights and sound. This is not so?"

I stared at him for a moment, irritated again by the smarmy smile that leaked past his attempt to maintain a straight face. *Asshole.* He was too good-looking for his own good, but too much of a jerk to be attractive. I was willing to bet his English was a lot better than he let on.

While I grappled with my temper, I looked around at the piles of crates and cartons littering their booth. Judging by the pictures on some of those boxes, Schwartz-Mann sold industrial-sized printers and copiers. But the apparatus a pair of other guys wrestled together right then wasn't any kind of printer. In fact, it looked like a cross between a giant roulette wheel and that spinner thing they use on *Wheel of Fortune*.

Finally, I drew a long breath and turned my attention back to the man in front of me. *Stay calm.* I could do this. "As long as your actions don't interfere with other exhibitors' displays or business," I reminded him, citing the rest of the line in the agreement. I've done it so often I can say it from memory and point to its exact location on the contract. "The lights you've got on the strings between the poles are okay as long as we don't get any complaints about them, but the strobe lights are annoying everyone in the neighboring booths and the sirens are so loud they drown out all conversation on the floor. I'm sorry, but those are not within the rules. The smaller lights should be okay and we'll make an exception for occasional use of the strobes, as long as we don't get complaints about them. The noise, no."

The man's wrinkled brow and narrowed eyes tried to suggest he hadn't understood half the words but got the drift anyway and wasn't happy about it. I still wasn't buying it, and that faint gleam in his eyes indicated he knew it. He glanced again at the business card I'd handed him. "You are… Miss Heather McNeil. You are in charge here?"

He knew I wasn't. The title was on the card, right beneath my name. "I am Heather McNeil, and I'm *assistant* to the director. I represent her." *And she wouldn't be nearly as patient with you as I'm being.*

He drew a breath and considered. "I vill talk to your… to the person at the top," he said after a moment. "This is not right." I'm sure it was meant to intimidate me, but he didn't know my boss either. Still, this was his last, desperation shot, and it wasn't going to work.

"Fine. But meanwhile, no more loud noise. No sirens. Use the strobe lights no more than once an hour." I tried to keep it to words of one syllable and almost succeeded. "And the director—the person at the top—will say the same thing I'm telling you." A loud, metallic bang from across the aisle punctuated my words.

"Not goot." He shook his head in exasperation, gave me a curt nod, and turned to a man standing nearby who carried a roll of wire and had a pair of pliers sticking out of his shirt pocket. The dismissal was clear, if not polite. A string of angry-sounding German spilled from Gebhardt. The other one nodded and shrugged.

I hoped a return visit wouldn't be necessary, but I wasn't betting money on it. Given that I already had a long list of other complaints to attend to, I really didn't need another patience-stretching interlude with Mr. Gebhardt.

Ninety-nine days out of a hundred I love my job as assistant to the director of the Washington, D.C., Commerce and Market Center. That particular Monday morning, however, I had a hard time remembering why. Setup day before the start of the Washington, D.C., Business Technology Show had already staked its claim as the one in the current hundred that made me want to re-examine my career choice.

Whatever my title might indicate, I spend most of my time as liaison between the exhibitors and the director, being general troubleshooter and flak-catcher. That part of the job I usually don't mind so much. I'm good at listening and staying calm and finding ways to make things better. I keep my head when everyone around me is losing theirs. In general, anyway. But dealing with a list of problems growing faster than I could possibly handle them set my nerves on edge.

On the plus side, the exhibition starting the next day meant I had to be down on the show floor rather than at my desk dealing with the mountain of paperwork that filled my inbox, the gazillion phone messages, and an email box that beeped and glared at me, sulking because I'd neglected it for so long. Of course that just delayed tackling the mess, which would only grow bigger and be even harder to face later.

On the down side, by ten-thirty in the morning I already had a full day's worth of aggravations to deal with. Plus, setting up for a trade show creates a huge, headache-inducing racket. Several hundred booths being assembled at the same time in an echoing, cavernous space could make an aircraft carrier sound peaceful by comparison. Metal clanged against metal as structures were put together and pieces whacked into place; voices called back and forth; boxes were ripped open; hand trucks squealed on constant rushes back and forth from the loading dock; and footsteps tromped relentlessly.

The buzz of an electric screwdriver rasped my nerves again while my temples throbbed in time to the pounding of a hammer on steel joints. One of the rental bucket-lifts chirped a grating counterpoint to the banging as it backed up.

My throbbing head demanded a couple of ibuprofens before I tackled the next item on the list. I headed for the elevator to go back upstairs, but no such luck. A pair of men approached at a run, their eyes focused on me. I sighed and waited. I didn't recognize them, but their intent gaze said they knew who I was. *Next crisis,* I thought.

"Miss McNeil?" The man in the lead stopped and huffed in a sharp breath. "I think you might want to do something. A couple of guys are…"

"What?"

"Fighting," the second one, older and a bit pudgy, said. His face was red and pulled into a worried frown.

"Really more of an argument," the first one elaborated. "A loud one."

Great.

I followed them around the corner and down two aisles into the midst of the largest and most elaborate booths in the hall, the ones belonging to the biggest players in the electronics and technology industries. The setting made it more shocking to see two men standing in the middle of the aisle shouting at each other. A crowd had begun to form around them.

I debated a moment, then called for security. It might not be needed, but I wanted someone close at hand just in case. While I waited, I pushed my way to the front of the group of gawkers, listening to the increasingly loud exchange and studying the two men.

Probably everyone there recognized the taller man. As the CEO of one of the largest computer companies in the world, Thomas Hovey's face had stared from hundreds of magazine covers and newspapers. He had to be in his mid-fifties but was still handsome in a quirky way. The casual clothes he favored suited his long, lean, gym-honed frame. Expensively cut and styled silver hair and sharp, hard features made an interesting counterpoint to the black jeans and his usual green polo shirt.

I've never been quite sure just what charisma is, but Thomas Hovey oozed it out of every pore. It wasn't his looks, which were fair but not spectacular, nor anything else physical you could point to. But it almost seemed like something within him vibrated on a higher or faster level than anyone else. You couldn't see it, but you could almost hear it and sort of feel it, like an electrical charge that radiated from him.

At the moment, his hair bristled as if he'd run his hands through it, and a deep flush tinted the fake-bake tan to an unbecoming maroon. His voice was a deep, carefully modulated baritone, the syllables tight and clipped with an apparent effort to hold onto his temper as he told the other man, "I'm not even sure what you're talking about. We've had engineers working on that interface design for years now."

"And gotten nowhere with it," his opponent shouted. "Until I developed the exo-phase receiver." The younger man's voice echoed down the aisles, drawing an ever-growing crowd. He was only slightly shorter than the other man, but he had a weedy build, thinning dark brown hair, and blazing blue eyes. The anger gave his face a glow that made it more attractive rather than less. With all that, though, he still came across as more of a whiny child or hollow windbag next to Hovey's fierce, controlled energy.

Hovey drew a deep breath, though it wasn't obvious that he was particularly upset or concerned. "You're dreaming." He tried to brush past his opponent, but the younger man grabbed his arm to hold him in place.

"No, I'm not. You stole the methodology of the receiver. I can prove it."

The largest of three dark-suited men who'd stayed close to Hovey stepped forward to intervene, but the man in charge shook his head and the other halted.

I stepped forward, too, but stopped and waited to see what would happen next.

The older man turned to stare at the younger again. "Take it to court, then," he said.

"You know I don't have the resources to fight all your high-priced lawyers."

"There are plenty who'll work on contingency. But you don't want to just go flinging around accusations like that in public. That kind of mud splatters everyone, not just the target. A lot of it ends up on the one throwing it." Hovey's dark eyes were hard and tiger-bright behind his wire-rimmed glasses, his lips clenched as he pushed the words out. He shook himself loose from the other's hold.

"It tends to cling more when it finds mud in its target," the young man shot back. "Or other dirty dealing."

Hovey drew a sharp breath. "You're skating close to the edge, son."

The younger man flushed even redder. "I'm no 'son' to you."

"No. Probably just as well for you. Now quit wasting time. I'm sure we both have better things to do."

"Yeah, you're going to make your big splashy announcement this afternoon. A product you developed with stolen technology. Don't think you're going to get away with it."

Hovey's eyes narrowed. "Be careful what you say. And what you *do*," he warned.

I'd gotten so caught up in the interplay between the two men that I jumped when someone touched my shoulder. I turned sharply to stare up into Scott Brandon's oddly-colored eyes. They were neither blue nor green nor gray, but some combination of all three. Scott works security for the Center. He's also just about the hottest guy I've ever met.

"We need to intervene?" he asked, quietly, close to my ear.

I shook my head and put a hand on his arm as I leaned toward him to answer. "Not yet."

Scott nodded, but snapped into an alert stance. His tall, lean body went stiff as muscles tensed. Eyes narrowed, shoulders squared, jaw hardened into "cop" mode. Even his short blond hair seemed to bristle in readiness for action. It was impressive, if a bit intimidating to watch.

"This isn't over," the younger antagonist said. "You're

not getting away with stealing my work. No one can. I made sure of it. And others are going to know."

The older man had started to walk away, but swung back, his raised brows and narrowed eyes showing a mix of surprise and perplexity. He hesitated a moment, staring hard, before he drew a breath and said, "If you could manage that, then more power to you. I might even hire you myself."

"You had your chance and you blew it. You'll be sorry." After those furious and petulant words, the younger man hesitated, mouth open, as though he drew a blank on what to say next.

"Perhaps, but I wouldn't advise you to make a scene this afternoon." Hovey's amused condescension turned abruptly into warning. Serious warning. Almost scary warning.

The younger man had run out of words. Instead of responding, he turned sharply on his heel and marched off, pushing his way through the crowd that had gathered.

Hovey watched him for a moment more before he shrugged and turned to walk off in the other direction. His three companions flanked him as they strode down the aisle toward the steel and plastic castle that was the MegaComp booth. The onlookers scattered, with lots of commentary.

Scott sighed and eased out of his battle-ready stance. "What was that all about?" he asked. "I came in on the end. Was that—what's his name, the computer honcho?"

"Thomas Hovey. Yup." I told him what he'd missed— or as much of it as I'd seen. "Hovey and MegaComp are the ones putting on the show this afternoon for their big product announcement."

"You don't know the other guy?"

"No."

"Be good to know who he is and who he's with. We probably want to keep an eye on this."

"We'll need everyone on deck at the announcement ceremony this afternoon," I said, thinking about the kinds of disruption an angry young man might attempt.

Scott nodded but continued to stare after the man who had stalked off. I wondered what he was thinking. Scott is a former D.C. cop who doesn't talk much about why he isn't still on the force. He's suggested that he had some differences with his superiors and failed to keep his mouth shut when it would have been a better strategy, but he won't say anything about it beyond that. Even to me. Even though we're kind of dating. The schedules we work here at the Market Center are hectic and erratic, which makes it hard to find time when we're both free and not exhausted. Plus I've only known him for a few weeks. The signs have been encouraging, but after only four dates it's hard to say anything more than that we like each other and get along well. Oh, and there's the chemistry factor. My insides start sizzling whenever he's near.

"I'll see if I can find out who he is," I told him, distracted by the sight of more trouble approaching. This time it took the form of one of our maintenance guys, Mark. This could be double layers of trouble. Mark eyed Scott with unconcealed loathing. I had a harder time reading Scott's reaction to Mark, but it wasn't friendly.

Mark has had a crush on me for most of the year and some he's been working here. I've never done anything to encourage it, but I've tried to deal gently with his feelings. Maybe too gently. I think he's harbored an illusion that I secretly returned the affection but didn't feel I could act on it. When Scott began working here a couple of months ago and we began dating shortly thereafter, Mark's illusions suffered a nasty collision with my reality.

Mark's a few years younger than Scott's thirty-one, a little shorter and quite a bit broader and heavier. I'm not sure which one I'd back to win a fight, and I never want to find out.

Some women like to be the bone of contention between two men. I'm not one of them. To me, it's just sad and kind of stupid. Not that these two men were likely to fight openly over me. Mark values his job too much and Scott has too much control. Still, they regarded each other with the wary hostility of a pair of dogs circling a juicy piece of steak. Damn. Bad metaphor.

Mark kept an eye on Scott, but gave most of his attention to me once he came close. "The Gryphon-Loyall guys are having problems with their something-or-others interfering," he said to me. "Or maybe something's interfering with them? I don't even understand what they're talking about, but you better come and talk to them."

I sighed. I really needed those ibuprofens. "Where are they?" I asked.

"Twenty-two ten, twenty-two eighteen."

"I'm on the way."

I turned to Scott, but he forestalled any requests. "Do you need me for this?"

"Does it look like anyone's going to come to blows over it?" I asked Mark.

He glanced quickly at Scott before he said, "Don't think so. They're frustrated but not ready to fight about it yet."

"Good," Scott said. "I've got a meeting with the Nova-

Cyn people over security for their celebrity guest, and then I need to do a pre-check on A and B." That was ballrooms A and B, the two largest areas outside the main show floor. The big announcement would be held there later.

I nodded to him. He gave me a very private smile and I returned it. That was almost as good as the missing ibuprofen, for a while at least. I turned to follow Mark.

TWO

Monday

OUR DESTINATION WAS only a couple of aisles away, so it was a short walk, though we had to pick our way around forklifts, wooden pallets, and piles of boxes clogging the aisles. At the corner, I almost got blind-sided by a hand-truck bearing a crate so large the person behind it had to keep peering around the side to be sure of his path.

The Gryphon-Loyall booth seemed relatively peaceful, if you can use that term where seas of cardboard, plastic, and packing foam swirled in every direction, people raced back and forth with piles of papers and equipment, voices called questions and orders, and the general background racket still clanged away. Mercifully, nobody looked hostile or even angry except for one young man performing screwdriver surgery on an uncooperative…something. I had no idea what it actually was, other than a small box leaking wires out its sides and top.

I grinned as the guy shook it, slapped it, and said, "Blasted 57-60." He swung it around by a dangling wire, looked up at a nearby coworker and added, "This thing's a piece of junk."

"Don't say that too loud. The Swiftfire people are three aisles over." The speaker pushed back a wayward lock of bright red hair before he ripped open a cardboard box and withdrew another unidentifiable gizmo.

The guy with the screwdriver rolled his eyes. "Ask me if I care. This thing's a mess. Whoever had the brilliant idea to *glue* all the ribbon cables to the housing deserves to be wrapped in fifty feet of Cat 5 and tossed in the river. I know they don't expect you to take it apart, but when they've barely soldered the chips into the board at all and they shake loose in every breeze, what do they think you're going to do?"

The other man laughed. "What most sensible non-geeks do. Throw it away and buy a new one. From some *other* vendor."

"Hey, I wear my geekhood proudly."

"I'll say. All that tee shirt needs is a pocket—complete with protector, of course—big enough to hold your pens and your phone."

The geek stood up and tossed the screwdriver aside. "Don't diss the shirt. I got it at Dragoncon last year. I hope Jenny remembered to bring the back-up 680 unit."

"Jen never forgets anything."

The young man with the tee shirt turned enough to let me see what was on the front. Under an image of a swooping dragon, it read, "Mess not in the affairs of dragons, for you are crunchy and taste good with ketchup."

I didn't realize I'd stopped to watch the interplay until Mark called, "Heather?"

That snapped me out of it.

"Coming," I said and followed him past the two men and into an area partitioned off by canvas sheets, each swath of heavy fabric bearing a huge version of the company logo, a green and white striped gryphon. A man and woman waited inside.

The man was probably in his mid-forties, going round at the middle and thin on top, but he had a nice smile and friendly manner. "Ross Campbell," he said, holding out his hand, "CMO of Gryphon-Loyall. This is Jennifer Martinez."

Jennifer was about my age, pretty, with lively brown eyes and glossy brown hair that had me dying to ask what she used on it.

"Heather McNeil," I said, shaking hands with each of them. "Assistant to the director of the Market Center. Mark said you have some kind of problem?"

Campbell nodded. "I'm not sure I understand the details." He held up a finger and went to the canvas flap, looked out and said, "Ted? Can you come here a sec?"

"It has something to do with interference with our electronics from somewhere else in the building," Jennifer added.

Ted proved to be the brown-haired young man wearing the dragon tee-shirt. He came in still twirling the wire-shedding thingamajig and said, "What's up?"

"Can you explain the communications problem we're having to this lady in terms a lay person can understand?"

"Hi. Ted Hanford." Ted gave a wry grin that showed a cute dimple as he shook my hand. His hazel eyes sparkled with good humor, lighting his otherwise plain face, making it much more interesting. "Explain in layman's terms? Probably not, but I'll give it a try." He shrugged. "Basically someone in here is using some kind of equipment that's generating electro-magnetic waves that are sometimes interfering with the wireless communication. It's not constant, but sporadic, which makes it really hard to trace. When it's on, it's messing up the back and forth between our devices and the WiMax system. And since communication systems *are* our business, it's going to make us look really bad when they don't work right. A lot of the exhibitors in here are using wireless-based systems. It may not interfere with all of them, but it's certainly going to disrupt quite a few." He looked at Campbell and then at me. "Was that comprehensible?"

I nodded. "Mostly. So I guess the question is, what can we do about it?"

"Yeah, easy question, not an easy answer. First thing is to figure out where it's coming from and what's causing it. Then you have to convince whoever owns the cause to shut it down or fix it so it's shielded."

"I'll ask our director to get our tech people in here to investigate, but they tend to be slow. It can take them two or three days just to respond. I hate to let it go on that long. Do you have a way to figure out where it's coming from? And what's causing it?"

Ted chewed on his bottom lip. "Yeah, maybe. The thing is, it takes time and some luck. I can trace the interfering EMFs, but when it's sporadic, it can be a real bit—, sorry, a real bear to track it down. Takes time and work, and we don't really have the time or manpower here either. If some of your security people could help…" He paused to give me a hopeful look.

I hated to disillusion him, but I winced just thinking about Craig Vincelli's likely reaction if I asked him. I shook my head. "We're short-handed as it is and our security people have all they can do to keep up with crowd control and maintaining order."

"There are probably going to be others with the same

problem," Ted added. "Anyone using wireless relays around the seven point two megahertz bandwidth."

"Okay, now you've lost me."

"That's not unusual." Another voice spoke up and I realized the red-headed man who'd been kidding with Ted earlier had followed him and stood just inside the entrance to the back area. "Ted can speak English when he wants to, but his native tongue is Geek."

Ted didn't even blink. "Says the guy who speaks Salesman in his sleep."

"Gentlemen," Ross said, though neither man seemed bothered by the teasing. "Focus."

"Oh, right," the redhead said. "Ross, if you can take care of the rest of the booth setup, maybe Jen, Ted, and I could spend a couple of hours trying to track it down." He looked at me. "If we can find the source, would your people help us convince whoever was responsible to shut off the offending equipment?"

I hesitated. Without even thinking too hard, I could come up with several potential pitfalls. What if the offending equipment belonged to the biggest, most influential exhibitor in the place? Or some small company that would be out of business if they had to shut down their whatever it was? And how many others were actually affected by it? "I'm not sure. All I can say is that we'll try, but a lot depends on circumstances."

I expected an argument, but he just nodded. "Guess that's the best we can expect. I'm Larry Barnes, by the way." He held out a hand and I shook it. He was a squeezer, but I managed to rescue my fingers before he crushed them. "I saw you over by the Quan-tex booth earlier, watching that argument between Tom Hovey and Chase Markham."

"You were there?"

"Yeah, I was coming back from getting some stuff at the loading dock and heard the ruckus, so I stopped to watch. Chase is always entertaining in his delusions, but I can't figure out what he was doing, tackling Hovey like that."

"You know him?"

"Tom Hovey? Only by reputation. He doesn't mix with hoi polloi like me." He said that with so much self-deprecating humor I had to grin.

"Actually I meant the other guy."

"Oh. Chase? Yeah. I worked with him at Timmer for a while. We meet up at events like this sometimes, so we've kept in touch. He can be amazingly brilliant one minute and totally off the wall the next."

"How so?"

"Well, the brilliance part is easy. I'm not an engineer, but all the engineers I know—" he glanced over at Ted, who still twisted the useless box "—say he's the go-to guy if you need to do something everyone else thinks is impossible. At Timmer, he figured out a way to solve a wiring problem no one else could. Among other things."

His smile lit up his eyes, a brilliant green, in an otherwise lean, plain face. "On the other hand, he can be kinda weird. He has a sort of tenuous grip on reality sometimes."

"'Tenuous grip on reality'? Ha," Jennifer scoffed. "He's a major nutjob with an ego even bigger than his brain."

I waited a beat or two while she decided how much to say. As I hoped, irritation won out over discretion. "To hear him tell it, half the innovations in the industry were his. People steal his best ideas all the time. He says he tries to keep his big notions secret, but he always ends up telling them to people, just to show how brilliant he is, then he wonders that others 'rip off' his ideas. He threatens lawsuits right and left, but never follows through, somehow."

"He gave you a pretty hard time, too, didn't he?" Larry suggested.

She shrugged and her pretty face twisted into an ugly frown. "Yeah, kind of. He's not real good at taking no for an answer."

"I hope that was just asking for a date," I said.

Her mouth twisted into a half-smile. "Mostly."

"You've worked with him, too?"

"Larry and Chase and I were all at Timmer at the same time."

"Is Chase still working there?"

"Nope. He's been through a couple of employers since then," Larry answered. "His technical genius tends to dazzle people, but his off-the-wall antics sour them pretty quickly. And he's always under-appreciated, if you ask him."

"Where's he working now?"

Jennifer answered. "He's with RTX now. He was actually with SiloSystems, but RTX Industries bought them out and got Chase as part of the bargain. I think they're still in the honeymoon phase."

Larry snorted. "Not anymore." He paused and various things moved on his face. I couldn't identify any of them, except maybe a touch of fear. When he started again, it was slowly, as though he chose his words with care. "I saw him earlier, before the show he put on with Hovey, and he said he was unhappy with RTX."

"There's always something," Jennifer said. "No one ever adequately recognizes the extent of his genius."

Larry gave her an uneasy glance. "True."

My headache returned with a vengeance. It looked like a talk with Mr. Markham was in my near future. Sometimes a carefully worded warning can stave off later trouble. Sometimes. "You wouldn't happen to have any aspirin or ibuprofen, would you?" I asked, since it didn't look like I was going to get back upstairs any time soon.

"I think so." Jennifer went to a pile of boxes at the far side of the area, rummaged for a moment, and came up with a container of ibuprofen tablets. While I shook two out, she got me a bottle of water and opened it. "Sorry it's not cold. We don't have the mini-fridge plugged in yet."

"No problem." I took a long gulp of the water to swallow the pills and realized I was very dry. "Can I take this?"

"Sure," Jennifer said.

I turned to go, but paused when Ted said, "We'll let you know if we can run down the source of the interference problem."

"Sounds good." I turned away, then stopped. "Do you know what booth RTX is in?"

Larry and Jennifer both gave me blank stares. "'Fraid not," she answered.

"Cell phone number for Chase Markham?"

"Which one?" Larry asked. "I think he's got three. But he keeps changing plans and phones. I don't have a current number for him." He looked around at the others, but no one offered any information.

"No problem." We exchanged cards with phone numbers and said goodbye. Once I'd left them, I pulled out my cell phone and buzzed upstairs. "Tina? Check the floor plan and tell me what booths RTX Industries is in."

Tina took longer than it should have needed to look it up, but that was nothing new. I wasn't entirely sure why Janelle put up with her, except that she did show up on time, every day, and did most of the work expected of her.

"Nine oh seven to nine-thirteen," she said, after a few minutes.

I thanked her and headed that way.

It took me a few minutes to make my way across the floor to the nine hundred aisle. RTX had a medium-sized booth, taking up four spaces on the grid. Their booth was one of those that consisted of a long wall with shelves of product, most of which seemed to be either GPS devices or pagers, in various ranges of sophistication. A desk sat at the side, but it had a small curtained-off private area at the other end.

A perky blond in tight jeans and tank top was working on stacks of boxes in front of the wall, arranging them in an elaborately designed tower already four feet high and showing no sign of being done yet. She straightened as I approached and smiled. "Hi, I'm Sandy. Can I help you?"

I introduced myself and asked for Chase Markham.

The smile faded and she shook her head. "I heard about the scene he made earlier," she said. "I told Drake we shouldn't let him come. But…"

"But?"

"Chase insisted he had to be here, and Drake wanted to show him off. The guy is brilliant."

I heard something more in her tone. "But a bit of a jerk?"

"You've heard the rumors already? Well he is…a bit."

"I need to talk to him," I said.

"He went in the back a while ago. Said he had a couple of things to check out, but he's been pretty quiet. I bet he fell asleep back there."

"Can we wake him?"

"Sure." She signed for me to follow her as she walked down the length of the wall and ducked around behind it. "Chase?"

No answer. I looked over her shoulder. The area was tiny and quite empty but for a small folding table that took up two-thirds of the space and a stack of boxes beside it.

"He must've slipped out while I was talking to Barb," she said. "Sorry."

"Do you have a cell number for him?"

Sandy pulled out her phone and pushed a couple of buttons. She read the number off to me and I pressed it in. Chase didn't answer, so I left a message telling him who I was and asking him to call me back as soon as possible.

"He's usually pretty good about returning calls," Sandy assured me. I hoped so. Worry about those threats he'd made earlier nagged at me. Not that I could do much more about it right then. There were two more messages on my phone now with requests from Janelle.

It looked like lunch was going to be a hot dog grabbed from the stand downstairs again. I spent the next hour and a half running around putting out metaphorical fires, which included settling a dispute over who could control a section of aisle, dealing with a pile of empty crates stuffed into an exhibitor's booth, and providing directions to a nearby drugstore for someone with a mercifully unspecified stomach issue.

I checked the time on my phone and was shocked to see it was already quarter to two. A rumble from my stomach reminded me I hadn't eaten yet, so I ran downstairs to grab a hot dog and took it back upstairs.

My boss, the director of the Market Center, Janelle Addison, looked up when I passed her office on the way to the soda machine and called for me to come in.

"Just a sec." I got the drink and brought it and the hot dog with me when I sat in the extra chair on the other side of her desk.

Janelle's in her mid-forties, still very attractive, straight-forward, tough, and fair. A messy divorce a few years ago left her wary of relationships, but her wry sense of humor survived it. I waved the hot dog at her. "Got to be back downstairs in twenty minutes to be sure everything's set up for MegaComp's big announcement."

"Go right ahead."

Janelle may also be the world's best boss. She hired me fresh out of college five years ago to be her assistant, but she's let me grow into taking over a significant part of her responsibilities without making me feel like she was sloughing off the parts she didn't like. She recognized pretty quickly that I work well with people, and she trained me to handle most of the minor things that happen before and during a show, and some of the major ones as well. As much as I find some aspects of it aggravating, I can't imagine finding a job I'd like more.

"There's better food in the press room, though," she reminded me. "Heck, there's better stuff downstairs even."

"Hot dogs are happy food," I told her. "Good associations. Fairs, baseball games, backyard cookouts with the family, kayak trips…"

"Oh to be young and not worrying about cholesterol." Janelle grinned, but her expression got serious again quickly. "What's up?"

I told her about the interference issue and that we were likely to continue to get complaints about it.

"I'll put in a call to the tech guys," she said, "and try to impress upon them the urgency of the situation."

"Great. A couple of exhibitors volunteered to help track it down, too."

Janelle wrote a reminder to herself on a sticky note. "They shouldn't have to be doing that. But experience says they're likely to run it down faster than our tech guys."

"I kind of think so too. And then there's the Mega-Comp announcement this afternoon."

"Is there a problem with the announcement?"

"Don't know. Maybe." I explained the situation.

"You haven't heard back from this Chase Markham yet?"

I pulled out my phone and glanced at it. "Nope."

Janelle studied my face. "You're worried. You've got security on it?"

"Scott saw the argument, too. He got the implications."

"Then he'll have it covered. So what's really bothering you?"

"Can I just say I have a bad feeling about this? Sandy said that he returns calls. I can't help wondering why I haven't heard back. I've left two messages now. What's he doing that he isn't answering or responding? Probably nothing good."

I stuffed the last of the hot dog in my mouth and

Janelle waved me away. "Go check it out. You won't settle until you do."

"I won't feel comfortable until this announcement thing is over," I said, "and has gone off without inter-ruption."

THREE

A STAGE TOOK up one end of the combined ballrooms A
and B. Rows of chairs filled the rest of the space, ready
for the grand announcement. Early arrivals had begun
filing in and staking claims to second and third row
seats, the front row having been roped off, probably for
company officials. Camera operators from a couple of
news networks were setting up equipment while some
of our support staff rolled in carts laden with ice buck-
ets, cans of soft drinks, bottled water, and plastic cups.

On the stage itself, technicians supplied by Mega-
Comp wired up sound equipment and a huge screen,
all of it supervised by one of the dark-suited men I'd
seen with Thomas Hovey earlier, during the argument.
Bodyguard or executive assistant? I was betting on assistant for this one. He didn't look large enough or tough
enough to be a bodyguard. He said little but watched everything closely.

I didn't see any of our security people other than
temps who usually manned the main entrance to prevent anyone without a show badge from crashing the
party. I looked around for Craig Vincelli, our head of
security, and Scott. At least one, but probably both, of
them should be here somewhere.

Hearing voices from behind the curtains at the back

of the stage, I mounted the three steps at the side of the platform and crossed it. Dark Suit Man watched me steadily with his hard, impassive gaze until I pushed aside a curtain, stepped behind it, and walked down the steps to the area in back.

In one corner Scott consulted with a couple of our maintenance guys, gesturing at something overhead. I looked up but didn't see anything interesting in the drapery that separated the stage area from the space behind it. I found the man doing the gesturing much more interesting. With his strong, lean build and broad shoulders, Scott looked good in the standard security officer's uniform of black pants, light blue shirt, and black belt bearing an assortment of tools. His short, blond hair gleamed in the light from the lamps on the wall behind him. I fought down an inappropriate surge of lust. I try to be professional on the job. Anyway, he was involved in the conversation and I didn't want to disturb him.

Craig spotted me from off in the other corner. He nodded for me to join him and a couple of the other security people. "Can you describe this guy you're worried about so we can keep an eye out for him?" he asked.

I gave them a description of Chase Markham as best I could remember, then the other two men with him left to spread the word around. Scott came over a moment later and said, "We've checked everywhere someone could hide or could easily hide something. So did Hovey's guys. The place appears to be clean."

"Good." Craig nodded and turned to go around the corner to come out on the side of the main area. I'd noted before that Craig trusted Scott far more than he did any of the other security people. I wondered about that. Scott had only been working here a couple of months, but he was more than just an ex-cop; he was intelligent, quick-thinking, and physically fit. Still, he'd left the D.C. police force under some kind of cloud. I felt sure Craig knew more about those circumstances than the rest of us. I have to admit I've been kind of tempted to try to sneak a peek at Scott's employment file. It wasn't worth losing my job over if I got caught, though.

The noise from the other side of the curtain swelled, and music suddenly throbbed from the large speakers MegaComp had brought in. I followed Craig back around the edge of the stage. Nearly all the seats were taken now and people still flowed in. Craig stopped a few rows back, watching from the side of the room just far enough beyond the stage that he could see all of it. I continued on until I was halfway back. Scott had gone around the other side of the stage and now stood opposite Craig, about the same short distance from the dais.

Several people gathered near the steps to the platform on Scott's side, Thomas Hovey among them. I recognized one of the men with him from earlier. Size and a certain vigorous alertness about his stance screamed bodyguard. I looked around for the assistant, the man who'd been directing the set-up, but just then the lights went out, pitching the room into momentary blackness.

Show time.

When the spotlight snapped on, focused on the stage, it circled the area a couple of times before finding Thomas Hovey, still dressed informally in black jeans and a green polo shirt, standing in a far corner. As the light burst over him, music swelled further, a pantheon of colored lights danced across the black curtains and stage, and the huge screen behind him lit up with kaleidoscopic images of blazing fireworks, flowers unfurling, and showers of glittering sparkles.

Taking my gaze off the stage, I noted people still moving around, trying to find seats, but I didn't see anyone who appeared bent on trouble. Not that I'd necessarily recognize trouble until it was already well underway.

The music sank to a lilting whisper and all the extra lights went out, leaving only a single spotlight centered on Hovey. If I thought he'd glowed with charisma earlier, the man moved in a cloud of it now, more than just the radiance from the single light. Something shone from within him as well. Thomas Hovey thanked everyone for coming and promised he had something totally new and crazily exciting to show them all.

Cheers and loud applause came from certain corners of the audience. Not so much from the members of the press, typing away madly on laptops or recording with handheld video cameras or smaller voice recorders, but from others clustered in small groups throughout the auditorium. Ringers? Hovey made some kind of geek joke that I didn't get at all, but laughter rolled around the room, led by particularly loud bursts from the same groups that applauded wildly seconds before. Definitely ringers.

The room got very quiet, though, when Hovey said, "And now the moment I've been waiting for for months. I finally get to present to you…the eTab 400."

The screen lit up with a picture of a gizmo that reminded me of a smartphone's big brother. I'd seen other tablets, but this one had an odd, funky shape, with curves, and some button controls along the side.

Movement in the corner of my vision drew my attention away from the stage. A figure moved down the center aisle, silently, almost stealthily, picking his way through the thicket of bodies leaning out, holding up the cameras. I sucked in a sharp breath and my insides twisted. I looked up to see if either Scott or Craig had noticed. Both were zeroed in on the shape.

He crept forward a few more steps before he stopped, about thirty feet from the stage, crouching amidst the photographers who knelt in the aisle for a clearer shot. He raised his arms and I realized that he, too, had a camera pointed at the stage.

I let out the breath I'd been holding as the man silently snapped his pictures while Thomas Hovey rambled, demonstrating with images on the huge screen how "amazingly awesome" this new device was. He wound down by listing a dizzying array of technical terms and numbers. I heard a collective gasp from the audience, so maybe the new widget was a groundbreaker. Finally Hovey thanked everyone for coming, the lights came up, and people in the front rows dived for the door, shoving past anyone who got in their way.

I stepped back and let the first wave race by me, before I joined the crowd heading out of the room.

My stomach still hadn't completely untwisted itself, but I couldn't decide if I was relieved or disappointed. Maybe neither. As I reached the exhibition floor I realized I was still keyed up, still uneasy and nervous.

There was one message on my phone, from Janelle, asking me to check in at a booth near the far side. They'd had some trouble with the electrical connection there and she wanted me to be sure it had been fixed.

I was halfway across the floor when the phone buzzed again. I ducked into a corner of a booth, out of the mainstream of traffic when I saw the caller was Chase Markham.

"Hello, Chase?"

His "hello" in response sounded impatient. "You wanted to talk to me?"

"Yes, I need to—"

"Wait. Hold on a sec."

I heard muttering on the other end and made out the words "early" and then "What are you—?" but they were cut off abruptly by a crash that sounded like something large, heavy, and metallic hitting against something else, maybe a hard floor. Then another noise so loud it had to be the phone itself being dropped. Chase's voice still came through, but muffled and distant when he said, "Hey, what're you doing? Wait! What? No. No!" A brief pause, then more scuffling, and the same voice said, "Stop! Why? Help!" That was almost a scream, then another yell, cut off.

A gurgling sound followed. Heavy breathing and another, even more horrible gurgling. More shuffling and scraping, a muffled thud. And then silence. A dreadful eerie silence that was the worst sound of all.

"Hello?" I said, hoping, hoping, *hoping* someone would answer. "Chase?" My hands were shaking.

Nothing. No sound.

I almost screamed, "Chase? Is someone there? Anyone? Please, God, answer."

No one did. It was a terrible silence.

My hand shook, so slick with sweat I almost dropped my own phone. My heart pounded and ears buzzed. What to do? I didn't want to hang up on that call, but I had to do something, get someone. My brain felt mushy, like it didn't want to deal with any of this. I pushed the speed dial for Scott's phone.

He answered on the first buzz. "Scott, I…" The lump in my throat made it hard to talk. "I had a call. I think I heard…" I tried to swallow again to get past the obstruction. "It might have been murder."

"What? Heather? What's going on? Are you all right?"

"No. I'm not."

"Where are you?"

"Eight hundred."

"Stay where you are," he said. "I'll be there in two minutes."

That was just enough time for me to dial 911 and report the phone call. I don't think the operator was too impressed by my story, but he was professional and courteous. "I'll have someone out there in a few minutes," he promised. "Do you think you're in any danger?"

I told him no, but someone else might be. He asked me to stay on the line, but I had another call I needed to make, so I told him I was fine, begged him to have the responding officers hurry, and ended the call. I contacted Janelle next.

"Scott just called me," she said without preamble. "I'm on my way down. He said you were upset about a phone call you got."

"Janelle, this sounds crazy, and maybe it is. I think I just heard a man being attacked. Maybe worse. Oh, God. We have to figure out how to find him. Quickly."

"Did you try calling him back?"

"No." I breathed out a long gust of air. "I'll try it now."

"I'll be there in three minutes." She ended the call.

I found the call from Chase Markham in my incoming

list, and pressed the call-back button. It went right into voice mail. Was his line still open from the earlier call?

Scott showed up, gave me a single, hard glance, and pulled me into his arms. He felt solid, warm, strong, reliable…wonderful. I let that strength sink into me for a moment, then stepped back. He didn't try to stop me.

"What's going on?" he asked.

"I think I just overheard an assault. Maybe worse."

He stilled for a moment, frozen by shock, then blinked and said, "Tell me."

But Janelle appeared at that moment, and another thought occurred. "I called the police. We need to let the guys up front know to let them onto the floor."

Scott's lips crooked in a grin that was more ironic than amused. "Don't expect any 'them.' More likely to be a 'him' or a 'her.' I'll take care of it." He pulled out his phone and gave the message to Craig. It would get passed on. "Now," he said, glancing at Janelle, then back at me. "Tell us what happened."

I thought I managed to be pretty coherent as I told them both about the call and tried to reproduce the noises I'd heard through the phone line.

Their expressions grew increasingly grim. "I tried calling back," I said, "but I got voice mail." And then my brain did finally come through with something useful. "Come on." I didn't turn to see if they followed. The RTX booth was six aisles over. All I could think of was the possibility that Chase Markham was still alive but in desperate need of immediate help, maybe in danger, or maybe badly injured. I couldn't let myself consider any other possibilities. It took too long to get there, but finally I tore into the booth, looking around for a familiar face. I finally saw Sandy and breathed out a sigh of relief.

"Hi, it's Heather, right?" Her smile faded as she took in my expression and glanced at the other people who must've followed me. "Is there a problem?"

"Where's Chase?"

She looked blank. "I don't know. I haven't seen him since this morning."

"Is he in the back? Can I look?" I didn't wait for permission but headed over to the curtain and yanked it back. The space was empty. I walked around until I could see into the narrow space behind the back wall of the booth. Nothing there. I turned around to face Chase's befuddled-looking co-worker.

"What's the matter?" She clutched a clipboard to her chest like armor. "What's he done now? Is something wrong?"

"Maybe. Have you talked to him? Do you have any idea where he is?"

She looked around, staring briefly at Scott and Janelle. "No idea," she said. "Off talking to some of his geek-tech friends, probably. Or… I don't know."

"Who else is here?" My question came out as more of a demand.

"In the booth? Right now? It's just me. Drake is here, too, but I haven't seen him for more than an hour. Drake Galloway. He's the company president."

"You don't know where he is, either?"

"All I know is that he was planning to meet with a couple of guys to talk about some marketing partnerships."

"Chase didn't tell you where he was going?"

"No." Her lips pressed together in a tight line.

I thought of another possibility. "Someone said Chase

Markham had three cell phones. Do you have the numbers for all of them?"

She pulled out her phone. "I know I have one. Maybe two. The third one didn't have a number. It was just a toy. Has something happened to Chase?"

"I don't know. Maybe." I could barely contain myself while she fumbled with the phone, looking for numbers. I wanted to scream at her to hurry up. My stomach twisted in rapid convulsions while my pulse thundered a beat I felt all over.

"Here's the first one." She rattled off the number I already had.

"And the other?"

It took her another long few seconds to find it. Finally she gave me a second number. I pressed the keys as she read it off, then waited, walking in small circles around the booth because I couldn't stand still. It chirped repeatedly until the annoying voice mail message cut in.

"Damn, damn. Shit!" I shook the phone.

Scott looked surprised, probably more at my language than the outcome of the call. "No answer?"

"No. What now?"

Scott's phone buzzed to let us know the police officer had arrived. By now the clipboard Sandy held was shaking and she blinked back tears. "What's going on? What's happened?"

"I'll tell you as soon as we know something," I promised. "Call me right away if you see or talk to Chase. Right away!"

Scott and I left to meet the cop. I hoped he had an idea. Maybe he could trace the call from Markham?

Apparently not. "We could probably trace it to this

building," the cop said, "but not to a specific spot. You're sure he was here when he made the call to you?"

I thought back to the call and all the sounds I'd heard. One in particular I'd heard way in the background suddenly stood out. "He was when he called me." I raised my head and nodded toward the roof behind me. "Hear that metal on metal hammering? I heard it very faintly in the background. I didn't really notice it right then, but it was there. What can we do?"

"Nothing to do but search."

Craig had joined us by then, along with two other security guys. "Let me call in the maintenance people to help," he suggested. "Each one of us can take an aisle, check out any places in the booths where someone could hide. There aren't really that many, so with enough of us, we can cover it pretty quickly." He looked at the police officer. "Would you stay here and coordinate? The rest of us know the lay of the land better."

The cop nodded and added that he'd try to call in a couple more people to help. He and Craig assigned each of us an aisle, and I tore off as soon as he told me to cover thirteen-hundred, on the edge of where the bigger booths were.

The area closest to the door belonged to a telephone services vendor and spanned the aisle. No one even commented when I checked under the tables and behind the screen made by their backdrop.

The next booth sold accounting software. I had to identify myself as Center personnel before the man in charge would let me look behind the backdrop.

Beyond that a group of smaller one- and two-block booths offered few potential hiding places, but required nothing more than a quick look.

My heart refused to stop pounding out its urgent, hard beat of *hurry, hurry, hurry.* I think I knew even then how stupid that was, but a more visceral part of me couldn't handle waiting for the inevitable.

The next booth was larger and still in the construction process. It seemed to belong to some kind of computer equipment manufacturer. I had to maneuver my way around boxes with pictures of laptops and tablets to get to the enclosed area a pair of guys were hammering together.

Not likely someone had left a victim nearby without them seeing it, but not impossible either, so I poked into every cranny. Nothing.

I was beyond the center cross aisle now, with nothing to show for it. A glance at my phone showed no missed calls or messages. A few more smaller booths came next and I checked those quickly.

Just one booth remained on this side of the aisle, some kind of security systems firm. The company name on the banner was SteadySafe. It was one of the bigger booths that encompassed twelve blocks on our grid. It faced both this aisle and the one on the other side of it, which meant someone else would be looking at it, too. Still…

Only one person was on duty in the area, a very young man with a head of wildly curly strawberry blond hair. He sat by a small desk in the corner, reading a book. He set it down as I approached and stood up.

I lifted my badge and babbled at him. "Center personnel. We're looking for someone who may be hiding. Need to search your booth." He gave me a startled stare and backed up a step. I doubted he could even understand most of my verbal barrage, but he didn't interfere when I rushed into the area behind a set of cloth panels hung from a metal frame.

I stopped just inside. On my right, stacks of boxes formed neat towers to about shoulder height. On the left… My eyes refused to process what was on my left. Behind me, the young blond who'd followed me into the center of the booth made odd gasping and choking noises before he let loose a couple of nasty curse words and added, "What the hell? Who's that? How'd he—? Who is he? What's he—? Christ! Is he…breathing?"

FOUR

Monday

I WENT ON auto-pilot for a bit, turning off the emotions, thinking without being aware of thinking—or much of anything at all.

The guy who'd come in behind me went over to the body sprawled on the floor amidst the chaos of tumbled boxes, tipped-over chair, and assorted debris on the floor. He put a hand on the guy's throat, searching for breath or a pulse. When he shook his head, I told him, "Don't touch. Don't touch anything else. Get back here."

I pulled out my phone and pressed the speed dial button for Craig. "Thirteen hundred, SteadySafe Systems. All the way in the back. Bring the cop."

While I waited for them, I stayed in the area to be sure the other guy didn't touch anything. He looked even more shell-shocked than I felt, his face pasty white, but he cursed steadily and rather creatively in low mutters.

The body rested beside the toppled chair. I was quite sure it was a body and not a man any longer. I couldn't bear to look at his face, too clearly visible since he lay on his back, so I took a moment to study the area around it. The floor was a mess, suggesting there had been a struggle, which went along with the noises I'd heard on the phone. There was a desk on this side of the space, but it looked as though all the papers on it had been swept off onto the floor. The stack of boxes nearby had been toppled. And speaking of phones, a smartphone with a smashed screen lay on the carpet near the body. A pair of glasses with one earpiece shooting off at a strange angle was partly on top of it.

Something seemed wrong about the whole thing. It just wasn't clear what. Something knocked at my brain, though, trying to break through the haze of shock and dismay.

Before I could sort it out, voices sounded outside the booth. Craig Vincelli and the police officer had reached the carpeted area by the time I drew back one of the canvas flaps. Scott, Janelle, and two of the maintenance guys weren't far behind.

"He had a cord wrapped around his neck," I told Detective Peter Gilmont of the M.P.D.C., a little while later. "A phone cord, I think. And I could tell by the way he looked that he…that it was too late to do anything."

"How did he look?"

"His skin was kind of bluish, with red blotches. His expression…" I swallowed hard and had to wait a moment for the nausea to calm down. "Sorry. His expression was fixed in this grimace. It was awful. And he was too still. The kind of stillness no one ever is when they're alive." I drew another shaky breath. "Sorry, I'm not dealing with this too well."

"You're doing fine," Gilmont said. "You didn't move the body or touch anything?"

"I know better. The guy who was there in the booth checked him for a pulse, but I told him not to touch anything else."

"I guess you do know. Second time in as many months. You have a talent for finding murder victims."

"God, please don't remind me." I shivered, reluctantly recalling the body I'd found in the trash bin just a few weeks ago. You don't get used to this kind of thing. At least I had no plans to. And that weekend had been a nightmare. "This was murder?"

Gilmont gave me an odd look. "He didn't wrap that cord around his own neck."

"No. Of course not." I drew a deep breath, trying for control, when I really wanted to break down in a fit of hysterical crying. Later.

Maybe the control wasn't as good as I hoped. An alarmed frown flashed across Detective Gilmont's face. "Heather? Are you all right?"

I pulled myself together. "Yes. I think so."

A clatter of footsteps sounded in the hallway just outside the conference room and a moment later the door opened. Scott stuck his head in. "Heather, are you okay?"

"Heard of knocking, Sergeant Brandon?" Gilmont asked. "We're having a private conversation."

Scott's eyebrows rose and he sent a hard stare toward Gilmont. "It's not 'Sergeant' anymore. Questioning a suspect?"

"Interviewing a witness." It was practically a counterpunch, he said it so hard. "You're not invited."

"Heather looks all in. Janelle sent me to check on her." He looked at me and added, "She thought you might need these. Both of you." He held out a cardboard tray with a pair of cups. Curls of steam rising from them carried the marvelous aroma of fresh-brewed coffee.

"Oh, yes, please." I took one from him with probably unseemly enthusiasm, but it was so exactly what I needed. I thanked him. Scott and Gilmont traded stares that I couldn't interpret while Scott handed over the other coffee. He gave me one more look and an attempt at a reassuring smile before he withdrew and closed the door again.

Gilmont turned the hard look back on me. "Something between you and Brandon?"

"Interest," I answered. "Is there a law against it?"

He tipped his head in a motion that wasn't quite a negative or positive. More thoughtful and dubious. "I have to wonder if it's a good idea, but it doesn't matter what I think, especially not to you. Or him."

I wished I knew what was going on between Scott and Detective Gilmont. It must've gone back to Scott's days on the police force, and possibly to the incident that led to Scott's leaving it.

Gilmont didn't give me time to dwell on it. "Back to the murder victim. Tell me again what you saw when you went into the back of the booth. Every detail you remember." He waited with pen poised above notebook.

I tried to visualize the scene in my mind again, forcing myself to endure the image. "He was on the floor, mostly on his back. There was a metal folding chair on its side right next to him. Like he might have been in the chair, but partly stood up when he was attacked and knocked the chair over when he struggled.

"There were other things all over the floor. Papers from the desk, his broken cell phone, glasses, some of the boxes that had been stacked."

"Anything else make you think there was a struggle?" Gilmont asked.

"His clothes. He was still wearing the same clothes

he had on when I saw him argue with Hovey, but they were rumpled and his shirt was torn."

"His hands?"

"At his neck. Trying to…" I couldn't force the words past the lump in my throat.

"Trying to get free of the cord choking him," Gilmont finished for me.

"Is that how he died? Choking?"

"We won't know officially until we get the autopsy results, but it looks like a good bet. Anything else interesting you noticed?"

What was he after? I thought again. "His cell phone was on the floor. One of them, anyway. I've heard he had more than one, though."

"Really?"

For the first time I'd told him something he didn't know. "Did you find any others at the scene?"

"Just that one."

"I think they said he had three."

"Who's 'they'?" Gilmont asked.

"The people at Gryphon-Loyall. Several of them had worked with him. And Sandy at RTX."

Gilmont scribbled notes in his little book. "What else do you know about the victim?"

"Nothing. Never actually met him. I told you about the fight this morning with Thomas Hovey and the phone call I got from him. That's all the contact I've ever had with him."

The detective closed his pad. "We're going to have to tape off the booth where he was found and the booths next to it and on either side until we're finished processing the crime scene. It might be a day or two."

"Ohmigod, you're kidding! People will pitch fits."

"That's why I'm warning you. We'll have to keep everyone out for now."

"Oh, cripes. This is *so not* going to be popular." How were we going to explain this to those displaced exhibitors? What could we do for them?

"I know it's not, and I'm sorry, but this is a *murder* we're talking about. Keep your priorities straight."

"Oh. Yeah."

Gilmont paused, thinking a moment. He was probably in his early to mid-forties, still a good-looking man, though his dark hair had silver streaks, and deep grooves carved the skin around his eyes and mouth. He drew a breath and let it out on a sigh. "That's it for now. But will you do me a favor? Keep me apprised of whatever you learn that might be relevant."

I blinked at him. "Last time you didn't want to hear anything I said."

"I like to think I'm man enough to admit my mistakes. And I made a big one when I didn't listen to you the last time. I'm listening this time. I'm even enlisting your help. I might as well. You'll know more about the whole situation by this time tomorrow than I will anyway."

I really had no idea how to respond to that, except to say, "Okay."

I checked my phone as I left the small conference room. There were three messages from Janelle. They all said, "Call me as soon as you can."

The exhibitors whose booths were being sealed off had already gotten the word and brought their complaints to her. She was working on a stopgap solution. "We're going to set up temporary spaces for them in the front," she told me when I got through to her. "Jo's gone to get some emergency signage made up. Maintenance is set-

ting up spare tables now. The cops are letting the exhibitors get some of their merchandise from the booths after
they check them. Mark, Sam, Scott, Craig and a couple
of the temps are moving whatever they can to the new
spaces. I know it's late, but we need to get this set up tonight so they can be ready to open tomorrow."

I checked the time while she was talking and was
stunned to see it was nearly seven. Still, the idea of working late had a certain appeal. Less time to think. Better
to wear myself out with work in hopes I'd sleep without
seeing Chase Markham's body in my dreams. I turned
cold and started to shake as the image crept into my
awareness. *Couldn't afford this right now.* I shook myself out of it and went to the show floor to find Janelle.

Aside from the squeak of rolling wheels somewhere
off to my right, and the more distant sound of traffic
outside, the space had gone eerily quiet now compared
with the cacophony of earlier. Most of the debris had
been cleared from aisles and booths, which stood pris-
tine and ready for commerce the next day. The sound of
voices drifted from off to my right, leading my gaze to
where Janelle spoke with a couple of men I didn't recognize. Behind her Sam and Tim were setting up tables
for the temporary booths. They had moved aside a couple of the *pro bono* charity tables from along the front
wall to make room.

I joined them just as another man I didn't recognize
brought a dolly full of cartons to the site. When he asked,
"Which one is ours?" Janelle pointed to a table to our
right. She moved and I spotted the spread of open boxes
on the table behind her, just as the aroma hit me. Pizza!
My stomach rumbled an urgent request for closer acquaintance.

Janelle saw the direction of my gaze and got out of the way. I glommed onto those slices of sausage-and-pepperoni-enhanced nirvana like they were water in the desert. Three of them disappeared before a curl of guilt found room to creep in. A man had died just a few hours ago and here I was stuffing my face. But I was still alive, and I needed strength. Strength to go on, to cope with the aftermath, to do what I could to find out who'd killed him.

Ohmigod, had I really just thought that? Good thing I hadn't said it out loud. Janelle would have my head and Scott would help her. Last time I'd identified a killer it had been damned near fatal for both me and him. Not to mention I'd come within a hair's breadth of losing my job. I had to try to mind my own business this time.

I grabbed a soda from a cooler beside the pizza boxes, popped the top, and guzzled.

Right. There was no "try." Just "do" or "do not." It had better be "do not" this time. After all, it was the cops' job, not mine. Detective Gilmont had asked me to pass on anything I learned to him and promised he'd pay closer attention this time. I could leave it to him. And give him a hand with a few facts he might find harder to learn than I would. That was it. No more.

I hoped the resolution wouldn't be challenged too hard before the show ended on Sunday.

Janelle finished her conversation and came over as I disposed of the drink can and napkins. "Holding up?" she asked.

"So far. Thanks for sending the coffee care package earlier. It was life-saving."

"Figured you'd need it. Good thing you've fueled up again. We've got to get these guys set up and ready for business first thing in the morning." She showed me the plan for the temporary booths, which were only supposed to stay there until the police released the exhibitors' spaces on the floor. For the next couple of hours I helped move merchandise and set up displays on the steel shelving the maintenance guys who'd stayed were putting together as fast as they could.

Scott came and went, along with a couple of the other security guys, hauling things from the booths as police released stuff to them. The exhibitors wired things together, tested their set-ups, placed merchandise for better display, and made us move things around until they reluctantly agreed it would do as an emergency measure.

It was almost ten by the time everything was ready for the next day. Scott offered to drive me home. I normally take the Metro, but at this hour I'd probably have to wait a while for a train. We made the trip mostly in silence, but a few blocks from my building, he said, "You need to talk about it, you know."

My stomach lurched and did a flip-flop. "I do?"

"It'll help with the trauma."

"Old cop trick?" I asked.

"New psychologist trick, actually. Critical stress debriefing. We're 'strongly encouraged' to participate in one after bad things happen on the job. Bad accident scenes, multiple homicides, especially if they're really gruesome or involve children, fires, anything that might cause post-traumatic stress."

"What's a critical stress debriefing? Have you ever done it?"

He paused a moment before answering, maybe because he'd just spotted an empty space next to the sidewalk in front of my building and had to concentrate on parallel parking. Or maybe not. He drew a long breath once he'd turned off the engine before he said, "I've done it. I was just four months out of training when I was first responder to a really bad accident on the beltway. Six people killed, including two small kids. I found one of the kids who'd been thrown out of the car. It's not something I like to remember."

"What do you do in the debriefing?"

"Mostly sit around and talk about it. What we saw, how we felt."

"Hard to imagine a bunch of cops sitting around talking about their emotions. But it helps?"

"Surprisingly, yes."

"Okay." A warm, late May day had cooled down to a pleasant evening temperature, so we had the windows open to let the gentle breeze blow through. I reached for the door handle, ready to invite him to come in with me, then decided I preferred the shadows out here for telling the story. A streetlight half a block down offered enough light to see by, though it made it harder to discern Scott's expression as I began to tell him about the day.

He'd been there for some of it, but he wasn't at the two most critical moments—when I'd gotten the phone call from Chase Markham and when I found his body. Scott had heard most of the facts, one way or another, but not the awful details.

He asked questions occasionally, but mostly let me talk. What had happened and how I felt about it.

I should have seen it coming. It got harder and harder to speak, and the lump in my throat kept growing as I filled him in. When I got to the point where I actually found the body, I couldn't make the words come out anymore. The tears started right about then, and I reached blindly for my purse, searching for a tissue. Scott handed me his handkerchief and drew me toward him, letting me rest my head against his shoulder and soak his shirt.

I have no idea how long we sat there, but it felt like I cried on him for a long time before I finally straightened, shook myself, and drew a long, shuddering breath. I mopped up with his handkerchief and found enough voice to say, "I'm sorry. I hope I didn't ruin your shirt."

"I'm not sorry. You needed to do that."

I looked at him, trying to read his expression in the shadows. "Most men hate it when women cry on them."

"You needed it. You're too controlled." He put a finger on my lips when I opened my mouth to protest. "I know it's generally a good thing, and it's what makes you good at your job. But you've heard of too much of a good thing? Definitely applies in this case. You needed to let out some of the emotion."

"Is that part of the debriefing?" I asked.

He sighed. "Sometimes. It's pretty much why *we* need it, too. Cops are trained to fierce self-control, which means we have a hard time dealing with the emotion of trauma. Most of us just punch the wall or throw a chair. Whatever it takes. We try not to pummel each other too much."

"Scott—"

He stopped me with his mouth on mine this time. The kiss was more sweet than hot, but it was starting to warm up nicely when he broke it off. "It's late and you need your sleep. Tomorrow isn't going to be easy."

FIVE

Tuesday

I ACTUALLY DID sleep solidly, dreamlessly, until five the next morning. I didn't really have to get up for another hour, but if I'd let myself doze there's no telling what images might have crept in, so instead I got up, showered, dressed, and headed to the Metro stop. Janelle would want to get started as soon as possible anyway. Damage control loomed large for the day.

Fortunately the coffee shop I passed on my way to the station opened at six on weekdays, and I was able to fortify myself with a triple-shot latte.

I got to the Market Center at a couple of minutes past seven o'clock. Janelle wasn't there, so I settled in to weed through the clutter of my snail mail inbox. I didn't get far before she showed up.

"I figured you'd be here early," she said, stopping at my desk. "Did you get any sleep at all?"

"Actually I did. Scott put me through a critical stress debriefing last night."

"A what?"

I explained it to her. At the end, her brows went up and she said, "Good work. You needed it."

"Evidently. That's what he said, too."

"Smart guy." She shot me a quick glance I couldn't decipher before she waved a hand and said, "We've got work to do now. Jo sent me a draft of a statement last night. I've reworked it a bit and it's ready to print. You know the drill, unfortunately."

I was already on the way to turn on the machine and load paper. I went through a few more flyers and notices while the printer spat out three hundred copies of the statement, then Janelle and I took them down to the show floor to distribute before the doors opened.

Before I finished, exhibitors were arriving at their booths, setting out things that had been locked up, putting out sell sheets, unfolding displays and dishing up giveaways. I eyed those to distract myself from remembering yesterday while I handed out the rest of the statements. The bowls of hard candy didn't tempt me, though some good dark chocolate would have, but the pens were harder to resist.

I have a thing for interesting pens. My desk drawer contains a nice assortment of unusual and different ones, as does my pencil holder at home, the niche by the phone, the drawer in my bedside table, and the work area in the kitchen. One of these days I'm going to find a display case to show off the most striking ones.

Most of what I saw that morning were cheap stick pens, however. Disappointing.

Once I finished handing out the copies, my first stop had to be the new booths up front, to be sure they were all okay and not needing anything.

I'd planned to spend just a couple of minutes there, but I should have known better. At the first stop, the people manning the makeshift booth had a problem with one of the tables we'd provided. The female half of the pair demonstrated how it wobbled and threatened to collapse.

A call down to maintenance produced a promise to bring up a replacement as soon as possible.

I would have left at that point and gone on, but the man and woman sitting there had no prospects right then and they were curious about what had happened. Since their regular booth had been roped off as part of a crime scene and a detective had questioned them about what they'd seen and heard the previous day, they knew something was up. The rumor mill filled in many of the blanks, with mostly accurate information. Naturally, they had questions themselves, and since I was a representative of the Center, they assumed I would know the answers.

"Was a man really murdered in the booth next to ours?" the male half of the pair asked once I'd gotten off the call to maintenance.

I paused a moment, wondering if he'd go on, but he wanted confirmation first. "A body was found there," I answered, wondering how much I should say. "And it appeared there had been a struggle. I think we have to assume it was murder. The police are treating it as one."

The man nodded. "You know that's part of what I don't get. How could it happen and we didn't hear a thing? I mean our booth is right next to theirs."

"You were there all afternoon?"

"Yes—"

"Wait," the woman interrupted. "We did go to see Tom Hovey's presentation at three. But we were only gone around half an hour."

"Oh, right, we did," the male half agreed. "I suppose it could've happened then."

I didn't tell them that I knew it hadn't happened during the presentation, but shortly afterward. "You came straight back after it was over?" I asked.

"Not exactly straight back," she said. "We met some people from Vibramatics and had to talk to them for a while. They're one of our bigger clients."

"We didn't talk long, though," the man added.

"Maybe long enough." I covertly glanced at my phone to check the time. "You never heard anything odd from your neighbors' booths?"

"Yesterday it was so noisy in here, we could barely hear each other when we were more than three feet apart," the man answered.

"True. It gave me a grand-daddy of a headache."

"Not that it's exactly quiet in here now," he added. The doors had opened to attendees and the usual chaotic symphony of voices, rolling bags, and hundreds of people moving around signified life—and commerce—going on, despite death's invasion yesterday. "But better," he continued. "Still, I heard the victim was Chase Markham."

"You knew him?"

"More like I knew *of* him." The man glanced around as though checking for eavesdroppers. "I'd recognize him on the street. And of course we heard about the shouting match he had with Hovey yesterday…" The word drifted off as the implications sank in. "You don't suppose…" He shook his head. "Nah. Hovey might squash him like a mosquito, but only in the more figurative sense."

"I got the impression Chase might have plenty of other enemies," I offered.

"Markham? Yeah, I'd think so. From what I've heard he was brilliant, but a pain in the rear end."

"Do the police have any idea who might've done it?" the woman asked.

"If they do, they haven't shared it with us," I replied as Mark and another of the maintenance guys showed up with a replacement table, freeing me to move on.

The next two tables belonged to SteadySafe, the company whose meeting area had been the scene of the murder. Only two people manned it at the moment, and one of them was doing a demo that involved using the video screen it had taken Sam, Howie and one of their other guys almost an hour to set up the previous evening. Neither of the two in the booth was the young blond who'd been with me yesterday when I found the body.

The man doing the demo was in his late thirties and so lean he looked like he might disappear if viewed from the side. His dark, curly hair was clipped short on the side but stood up more at the top and already looked like he'd been running his fingers through it. He all but vibrated with excitement and enthusiasm as he talked to the customers.

The other man was fortyish, attractive and orientallooking; his name tag said he was Dean Lee, Account Coordinator. His eyes lit when I walked up and the interest didn't fade—as it often does—when I identified myself as Center personnel. An awful lot of sales representatives only want to talk to potential customers.

Lee shrugged when I explained that I was checking to be sure everything was satisfactory. "Not perfect. Not even really good," he admitted. "But we do realize you've done the best you can."

"We've tried. I'm sorry about the circumstances."

"Not much you could've done about that. I just can't

imagine why someone would choose our booth to do such a thing."

"Did you know the victim?" I asked. "Was there a reason he might've come to your booth?"

Lee looked down the length of the table to his partner, still showing off the finer points of their security system, before he turned back and answered. "Not that I know of. Other than Shawn, we barely knew him. Shawn—" his gaze cut to the other man again "—worked with him for a few months. They talked, but I don't think they were close friends or anything." He sighed and looked back at me, lips narrowed in a worried frown.

"I guess the police have already asked you all about this."

"I talked to them for a little while yesterday. Shawn had a much longer interview."

We both glanced over at Shawn again, who didn't seem any the worse for wear. He still radiated enthusiasm as he demonstrated how their security system could not only send alerts to a smart phone, but also show video from hidden cameras.

"Do you know if he actually talked to Markham yesterday morning?"

Lee chewed his lip for a moment as he considered. "I think he said he'd seen him, but not that they talked."

"He seems pretty much in form this morning," I said.

Dean Lee gave me a wry grin. "Whenever he's with a client, he turns on. He's different when they're not there. We call him Mr. Schizophrenic." He laughed at my expression. "Hey, no, it's a compliment. He's good!"

"If you say so. How's that young man that was here in the booth when we found the body?"

"Young—Oh, you must mean the temp, Joel something or other. He spent a lot of time with the cops yesterday, too. I think he's supposed to come back this afternoon to spell us again, but I don't know if Frank will want him."

"Why not?"

"He was supposed to be watching the booth while the rest of us were away, but apparently he wasn't paying as much attention as he should've been. I don't know the details of what happened, but I gather Chase was strangled and he struggled some. That can't have been quiet. So why didn't Joel hear it?"

"Good question," I admitted. "It was pretty noisy in here yesterday."

"Why didn't he even know they were there? How did he not see them go in?"

"Good point." And something I'd like to know, too.

Dean just raised a hand, palm up, and gave me another wry smile. I took it as a hint. I handed him one of my cards. "Call me if you have any problems or need anything."

"Will do," he promised. His expression changed in a way that made me cringe every time I saw it. "Hey. You ever have time to take a break and go for coffee or lunch?"

It wasn't the first time I'd been asked that, so I had a stock response. "I do appreciate the offer, but I can't while a show's going on. I stay on the run pretty much all the time during a conference or exhibition. But if you're around when it's over, you can give me a buzz and see what my schedule looks like." It was actually mostly true, and not many guys argued. Since most exhibitors came from other parts of the country or even other parts of the world for the show, it usually got me off the hook. I'd only had one or two actually call back.

He sighed. "We're here from San Francisco and heading out on Sunday, but if I'm in the area again I'll give you a buzz."

I nodded and smiled as I turned toward the last two of the four temporary booths. Two of the three people in one group were demonstrating their brand of tablet computers to potential buyers and the woman at the last booth talked to someone who wore a press badge. I'd have to catch them later, but it didn't look like they were suffering.

I checked the messages on my phone and found two from Janelle asking me to check out some minor problems. The first one really was minor—an exhibitor needed a new bracket to replace a broken one that had been holding a corner of their display shelf. Another call to maintenance took care of that.

The second stop was at a smaller booth near the lower end of the hall. I guessed they sold some kind of software for mobile phones, since their backdrop showed large images of a variety of phones superimposed over invoices and receipts, with the phone screens displaying rows of figures or pie charts. Only one person was in the booth, an expensively dressed woman in her mid-thirties who introduced herself as Vanessa Connelly. She wore heavy makeup and not a strand of hair twitched when she moved.

"I'm almost embarrassed to bring this up," she said after I'd introduced and identified myself. "I'm not sure if I'm losing my mind, losing my grip, or something else is happening."

"What's going on?"

She glanced around, looking guilty. "I suppose it's possible that I mislaid it or even forgot to bring it, but I don't really think so. I'm pretty sure I saw it earlier. I just can't figure out how, though…" She saw my confusion. "Sorry. A couple of things have gone missing from the booth. Well, really just one thing."

"What?"

"We do a mobile app that lets business people track their expenses by scanning a receipt into their phone or tablet. So of course, I brought a variety of phones and tablets to demonstrate it on. When I was setting up this morning, I took them all out of the shipping boxes and had them ready to load into the display cases. Several of them were sitting on top of the boxes while I got them hooked up and made sure they were charged and working. Then I turned to talk to someone, and when I turned back, the MegaComp GT6 wasn't there."

"It disappeared that quickly?"

A bit of color bloomed in her cheeks. "It couldn't have been more than a couple of minutes. And it wasn't like I'd left the booth unattended or anything."

"No. I was just surprised. This was before or after we opened this morning?"

"After. I overslept a bit, so I was late setting up. But not by much. It was probably around nine-fifteen or nine-thirty." She swept the area around with her gaze and I followed it. There weren't many attendees in this area yet. Only two of the exhibitors in the vicinity were engaged. A couple of them talked to each other across the smaller booths, while others watched us or eyed the aisles waiting for business.

I had to ask and hoped my reluctance wasn't too obvious, "Do you want us to notify the police?"

"No!" Her voice squeaked and she took a moment to control it. "No, please. That wouldn't be good. And I suppose it is still possible I mislaid it somewhere and just forgot." She didn't sound terribly convinced of it and neither was I, but it was her decision.

"I'm not sure how much we can do," I admitted, "but I'll certainly talk to our security people about it and see if they have any suggestions. They may want to come and talk to you. In the meantime, why don't you tell me exactly what happened." I pulled out a pen and pad to take notes.

"I've pretty much told you. I was putting out the demo machines. I'd taken them out of the boxes and put them on the top of the display cases, but hadn't locked them in, when Sally—" she nodded toward the booth on her left "—asked me a question. I turned, we talked for a minute or two, and when I turned back, it was gone. I don't remember seeing anyone come by or anything, but they must've…" Vanessa sighed. "I don't know what to do. I mean, I'm responsible for this stuff. This is going to be so hard to explain."

I wished I had some kind of comfort for her. "You've locked them all in the displays now?"

"Yeah. But, you know, barn door, horse gone," she said.

"I'm sorry. I'll talk to our security people about it. We do have video surveillance, and we'll review it. That's all I can do for now. Have you asked your neighbors if they saw anyone or anything odd?"

"I asked Dan right there," she said, pointing to the booth on her right, "but he didn't see anyone. Of course, he wasn't looking this way every minute. I mentioned to a couple of others that a tablet had gone missing from my booth, but no one saw anything helpful."

"What about the person you were talking to? Sally? Surely she would have seen it if anyone came up behind you?"

"I asked her. She said she didn't see anything. You know, because of where we are, at the side, we get a lot of traffic early. When people first come in, a lot of them tend to turn to go to one end or the other. Like when they go to the grocery store. You know, start at the far aisle and work your way back. We had quite a few people right then."

I tried to think if there was anything else I could suggest. A quick glance showed she had locked the other gadgets into their display cases. In truth, I wasn't sure whether I really believed the missing merchandise had been stolen by someone else, but I couldn't let on to any doubts. My phone buzzed, sparing me the need to come up with too many more platitudes. "I'll make a few inquiries for you," I promised.

I answered my phone as I walked away.

"Heather?" Janelle sounded oddly hesitant. "Meet me at the MegaComp booth in ten minutes. We have some ruffled feathers to soothe."

SIX

Tuesday

I'VE SEEN SOME elaborate booths in my time here at the Center, but the MegaComp castle was easily the biggest and most complex of them all. It encompassed the back half of two entire aisles. Though most of the space was open to allow customers to move in and out freely, it had an enclosed area at the back that served as a small theater, where they showed product demo videos every fifteen minutes. To lure people in, they offered a tee shirt to anyone who sat through an entire showing. The shirt had the MegaComp logo emblazoned on front and back. It seemed sort of ironic to me that people would sit through the company's promo to get a shirt that would turn them into a walking advertisement for the same. Brilliant marketing, though.

What really gave it the castle ambiance were the cylindrical-shaped, turret-topped towers built around the entire area. There were three to a side, spaced about ten feet apart, and each provided a small private meeting area, reached by a short staircase on the inside. They had pointed cone-shaped roofs. With the high square structure of the theater at the back forming the main keep, those towers really sold the whole castle appearance. No question who ruled in this domain, either.

Thomas Hovey wasn't all that imposing up close. If

you'd passed him on the street and didn't recognize his face, you'd never guess he was one of the world's richest men. Even here, where most people dressed to the nines, he wore black jeans, his usual open-necked green polo shirt, and loafers. Only someone who was very rich, very successful, and very arrogant would dare to dress that way at a trade show. Everything I'd heard suggested Hovey fit the description on all counts.

I'd read an article in a news magazine about him not too long ago. It complimented his genius at anticipating products the public would adore, but it didn't gloss over his faults. Autocratic, arrogant, and control freak had all come up in the story. In fact, he sounded like a tyrant, a man who insisted on having his finger on every phase of the technology development to ensure it met his standards of perfection. It should be interesting to see the genius in action.

On arriving at the MegaComp booth, Janelle and I had been ushered into one of three small, enclosed cubicles at the back, behind the theater area. The space was empty when we arrived, but moments later Hovey and his entourage paraded in. The man himself came in first and introduced himself tersely, as though he knew it was a formality and of course we already knew who he was. He deigned to shake hands with us, though he didn't bother to make eye contact for more than the briefest of seconds as Janelle and I each said our names and positions on the Center staff.

Hovey's hair was cut neatly but not in a way that screamed money, though the rinse that kept his silver hair glowing hadn't come from a drugstore bottle. The wire-rimmed glasses made him look more geek than genius. But then one didn't negate the other. Only the sharp, dark-brown eyes behind the lenses gave away something of his force of personality, with their narrow, hard glance.

Having several men in dark suits stay near him all the time belied any suggestion of just another guy in the tech industry. He didn't introduce the others, but I took a moment to study his companions more closely. One that I'd seen the previous day stood beside him again. I pegged him as the personal assistant.

A second was new, but cut from the same body-builder mold as the one he'd replaced—a large, tall, solid-looking man. His neck was so short and so thick you could hardly tell where his shoulders stopped and his head began. I was willing to bet his jacket hid a holstered gun, even though concealed weapons were prohibited in the center. The ban was virtually impossible to enforce. In fact, the guy probably had multiple weapons on him, including huge hands that would likely qualify as deadly weapons. His expression was neutral but alert. Eyes flicked left, right, up and around, constantly.

Hovey took one of the two chairs in the small area and waved Janelle to the other. While she was sitting and I stood there feeling uncomfortable, he pulled out a fancy smart phone, pushed a couple of buttons and read the display. He didn't react to what he saw, but slipped it back into his pocket. Then he turned his laser gaze on Janelle.

"Mr. Hovey," she said, "I want to—"

"Tom. Everyone calls me Tom." And that was decidedly an order.

"Tom. As I was saying, I want to apologize to you on behalf of the Market Center. We very much regret the inconvenience and sadness yesterday's events have caused to many of our exhibitors, including yourself."

He stared at her for a moment with no particular expression on his face. "Not much you could do about it, I suppose. Things happen."

Another man poked his nose into the room, started to back out when he saw all of us, but stopped when Hovey called, "Jim. Come join us. Since you were there yesterday during the argument, you might as well be here for this too."

He introduced us to Jim Driscoll, chief technology officer for MegaComp. Interesting that this man rated an introduction where the others didn't. I recognized Driscoll as another of the group who'd been with Hovey during the argument, though I'd barely noticed him at the time. I remembered him from later, when he'd supervised the setup for the announcement. He was a large man, tall and broad-shouldered, but not heavy. He certainly wasn't the nerdy type I associated with technology honchos. He looked the sort who'd got through college on an athletic scholarship, and then kept himself in shape since. He was probably mid to late forties.

Hovey turned to Janelle. "Ms.—"

"Addison."

"Jim, Ms. Addison has just been apologizing for all the fuss and inconvenience that annoying young man who accosted us yesterday has caused."

"Markham?" Driscoll said. "The kid's a lunatic. Not saying that he deserved to be murdered, of course."

"No, of course not," Janelle said. "And it's a tragedy for his family and anyone who loved him, but I do realize it's created circumstances that have been difficult for many people." She spoke to Hovey directly when she said, "I know you spent some time with the police yesterday evening and it must've been an inconvenience.

I hope it hasn't impacted yourself or your business too badly."

He waved it off, but his gaze sharpened and the next words weren't at all casual. "I'm co-operating with the police to the best of my ability. We all are. I'm aware that after that very public confrontation with Markham yesterday, I have to be a suspect. Fortunately, I can prove I wasn't anywhere near him during the time he must have been killed." He looked around at his associates as he added, "I'm sure the police have already checked with some of the many people who were with me or saw me from the time of the announcement yesterday until the time I finished with the press afterward and…"

He paused briefly when another man pushed back the drape that formed a door to the cubicle and poked his head in. The newcomer stepped back sharply at Hovey's glare, muttered, "Pardon," and "Later," before he disappeared again.

"…and came back here." Hovey picked up the sentence. "I'll do everything I can to help them find the killer, if only to assure people that I had nothing to do with it."

"I doubt anyone would believe you did," Janelle said.

"Oh, they would." The tone was icy. "No matter what the facts. Plenty of people would love to see me dragged off in handcuffs." Hovey was deadly serious and a bit scary for it. "That idiot made sure they'd have plenty of reason to think I was involved."

I felt my hackles rising, but kept still and silent. *That idiot* was dead. Murdered. No matter how much of a fool he'd been, he hadn't deserved to die for it. I had to bite my lip to keep from saying something I'd regret. Janelle could handle this one.

She studied his face for a moment. "I can see how that might be. But if you need any assistance, please let me know. The Center will do everything it can to try to minimize inconvenience and negative exposure for any and all of our exhibitors and attendees."

"I'm sure you will. Now, if you'll excuse me…" Hovey picked up his phone again and glanced at it, a clear and rude dismissal.

Of the other three present, only Driscoll came over to say, "Thanks for coming. I know Tom didn't mean to sound callous. He's very focused and this is difficult for everyone."

Janelle and I thanked him and left.

I waited until we were well out of earshot of the Mega-Comp booth, glanced around to make sure no one would overhear me, and said, "You think His Majesty is sufficiently appeased?"

Janelle grinned. "I hope so. I thought we did the bowing and scraping rather well, don't you?"

"Too well. What an arrogant twit. A brilliant one by all accounts, but still."

"He's an exhibitor," Janelle reminded me. "The biggest and most important one here."

"Message received and noted. I don't have to like him, but I will be polite and professional."

"Not that I don't agree with you. But…" She sighed. "I hate to do this to you, but we have one more stop to make, and it's not going to be fun."

"RTX?" I asked.

"Yes."

"Not fun. But necessary, I suppose." We turned and headed toward their booth.

"You checked on the temp booths this morning?" Janelle asked.

"Went by there. One had a problem with their table. Maintenance took care of it and the exhibitors pumped me for info while we waited. One guy at the SteadySafe booth tried to hit on me while another was doing a demo of their security solutions. The people at the third booth were already busy talking to customers and the woman at the fourth was being interviewed by someone with a press tag. I'm betting we can guess what that was about."

"Mostly under control, then."

"For the moment. What about the tech guys looking for the interference?"

"Said they'd come by and check it out later today."

"Not holding my breath. Oh, and there's another thing." I started to tell her about Vanessa Connelly and the missing gadget, but we got to the RTX booth before I could completely fill her in.

Sandy was restacking boxes in front of a large banner display. I hadn't paid much attention on my previous visits, but it appeared that in addition to the pagers, the company sold high-end smart phones and tablets that—if their long checklist of abilities was true—did practically everything but wash your dishes. They apparently *could* make sure your refrigerator was stocked, and notify you when you were low on milk or cheese. They would even send an alarm if you left the stove on for too long. I could use one of those, except that I didn't actually turn my stove on all that often.

Sandy looked up and put on her professional smile as we approached, until she recognized me. Her expression faltered into a more sincere solemnity as I introduced her to Janelle. I had to glance at her name tag to get her last name: Pangborn.

"Is your boss around?" I asked. "I'm not sure of his name?"

"Drake Galloway. He went up the aisle to talk to the guys at *TechToday* magazine. Is there something I can help you with?"

"We just wanted to express our condolences on the death of Chase Markham. I'm sure it was a terrible shock to you and a tragedy for the company," Janelle said.

I couldn't tell what Sandy was thinking, but if she was grief-stricken, she hid it well. Her skin did look paler than yesterday and her eyes showed hints of red around the edges, but her expression appeared composed. Still, the box she'd been about to put on the stack shook in her hands. She hesitated a moment before she answered. "Whatever I thought of him, he didn't deserve…that. Nobody does." She stopped and her face twisted in real pain, then tightened even more and she drew in a long breath before adding, "It might have been more than just a tragedy. I'm afraid it might be a real disaster for the company."

I wasn't quite sure what to say to that. "I'm sorry. I've heard Chase was a brilliant engineer. I can see where it could be a devastating loss. I hope you'll manage to survive it."

Sandy's tightly controlled expression might have hidden just about anything.

"You're planning to continue with the show?" I asked.

"We have to. The company's future is riding on it. We've just introduced the SKC smart phone and tablets with the new Paris operating system. Drake's pretty much bet the company on it." She looked up and her expression changed again. "Wait, here's Drake, now."

We turned to follow her line of sight to a tall, slender man whose hairline had receded almost beyond the horizon. Glasses and a neatly trimmed, short black beard helped compensate for the very high forehead. He walked toward us with heavy, grim determination, and his expression matched his gait. I couldn't tell if that was grief or anger that radiated from him, but he was definitely *not* a happy exhibitor.

Then he looked up, saw us standing with Sandy, and the professional salesman persona pushed past the private emotions. His final approach featured a plastered-on smile, an extended hand, and a hearty, "Hi, I'm Drake Galloway."

The white, white smile faded when we introduced ourselves. Still he shook hands and said, "Ladies. What can I do for you?"

Janelle said, "Actually, we came to see what we could do for you. All of us at the Center are shocked and saddened by Chase Markham's death, but you've known him for much longer than we have."

"In truth, I've only known him for about a year. He's only worked for us for six months, since we bought out SiloSystems. Still, it's a shock. I feel like I'm in one of those nightmares. You know the ones, where you run and run but you never get anywhere, and then you want to wake up but you can't?"

Janelle and I both knew.

"But I won't be waking up from this one," he continued. "I just can't believe it. Can't believe it happened. Can't believe he's gone."

"Left us in the lurch, too," Sandy put in.

Galloway threw her an unmistakable warning glance.

I figured the door had been opened. I might as well dive through it. "Obviously his death is a tragedy for the company. I hope you can weather it without too big a loss. I understand Markham had the kind of creative genius that'll be hard to replace."

"It's too soon to even think about that." Galloway looked a bit dazed. "Too many things to get through first. I guess the cops have talked to his family by now? Back in Tennessee, I think? Do you think they'll figure out who killed him?"

"Probably," I said. "The cops are pretty good at it."

I did my best to ignore Janelle's arched eyebrow. Galloway just stared absently into the distance. "We'll need to think about some kind of memorial for him. Talk to his family about the funeral. I guess they can't have it right away." He drew a deep breath and let it out on a sigh. "And I suppose we'll have to look around for a new engineer, eventually. The SKC unit still has some issues to resolve. Such a mess for someone new to come in and clean up. But that's to worry about later. In the meantime, we still have work to do here. We thought about packing it up, but Chase wouldn't have wanted that. It's his product and I'm sure he'd want us to sell as many as possible."

I glanced at Sandy and saw something—doubt?—flash briefly across her face. Whatever it was disappeared so quickly I wasn't even entirely sure I'd seen it. I was sure she wouldn't want to talk about it. Not in front of the boss, anyway. A quiet word with her later might be interesting, though.

Meanwhile Janelle was going through her spiel about the Center offering condolences and any help that was in our power to grant. I couldn't read Galloway's expression as he listened and nodded, sort of absently. He wasn't happy, but I thought I saw something other than just grief, if there was any grief at all. I'd swear there was both anger and despair lurking behind his attempt to school his features into passivity. Maybe some fear, too.

He didn't say anything until Janelle had finished, and then he thanked her and assured her that he'd let us know if they needed anything. His tone was sort of hollow and absent. Something had his attention, but it wasn't us.

Galloway and Sandy both nodded as we said good-bye, but Galloway had turned to Sandy to say something very quietly before we'd gone more than a few steps. I really wished I could've heard his words.

"Did that feel decidedly weird to you?" I asked Janelle, once we'd put a few booths between us and RTX.

"I don't know about weird. Certainly sad."

"It was that, but I'm not sure it was sad in the sense of grief for a fallen comrade."

Janelle raised an eyebrow. "You're getting something I didn't. You have some sensitive antennae for the vibes people give off. I'm not sure it's a gift." Then in an abrupt change of tone, she added, "I don't know about you, but I'm starving. Let's go grab a bite at the food court."

The grandiosely named food court was actually a part of the downstairs lobby that had been roped off and provided with about a hundred small tables crammed into a corner. Stands providing the usual fast fare offerings—hot dogs, burgers, pizza, sandwiches, salads, wraps and miscellaneous other treats—surrounded the tables. We grabbed salad for Janelle, turkey wrap for me, and snagged chairs at one of the few vacant tables.

Once we'd torn into our lunch, Janelle said, "So what did you find weird about the emotions at RTX?"

"I'm surprised you didn't sense it, too. Drake was more angry than grief-stricken about Chase Markham. Maybe worried as well. Sandy's emotions were pretty mixed, too. I think she *was* kind of sad about Chase, but there were other things going on."

"The loss of Markham is probably a huge blow to his business," Janelle pointed out. "In his position, I'd be angry too, that the guy made someone so mad he killed him."

"Could be." I wasn't convinced, and I'm not entirely sure why. Something about Drake Galloway felt off to me.

Craig and Scott appeared next to our table, each carrying a lunch tray. Janelle nodded to the single extra chair and Craig sat down. Scott snagged an empty one from a nearby table and pulled it up beside me.

"Hanging in there?" Craig asked, after taking a big bite from the first of his three hot dogs. "How's it going with the exhibitors?"

"As well as can be expected." Janelle forked up a lettuce leaf but didn't lift it to her mouth. "Lots of tension, lots of questions, some uneasiness, but in fact, most people are more excited about having something unusual happen than disturbed that a murder took place."

"Guess that's kind of normal," Craig said. "Doesn't touch them personally, so it's exciting."

Janelle put down the fork and took a drink from her glass of water. "Most of the people here have no idea who Chase Markham was. Except as the guy who had a public row with Thomas Hovey."

"I wonder if that didn't make it a bit easier for people to deal with." I was thinking out loud. "The fact that he had the argument. Gives people a handy, tailor-made explanation for his death. And maybe even kind-of makes people think he brought it on himself?"

Scott had lifted his sandwich but stopped with it half-way to his mouth, his interest piqued.

"I think I see Hovey's point about people believing he's guilty," I continued. "It's easier and more convenient to accept that he did it because of the argument than to live with not knowing who did commit murder and why. Throw in that a lot of people dislike him already because he's a...well, for a lot of reasons."

"Because he's an arrogant twit?" Scott suggested.

"He's an exhibitor," Janelle reminded him.

Scott's mouth crooked. "They're not mutually exclusive. But I only say that privately, among us."

"Well yeah, that," I said. "Of course, most of them don't think he did it himself. That's what minions are for, right? And Hovey appears to have a number of devoted ones, as well as a couple of downright scary bodyguards."

"Interesting insight," Scott said. "How tempting it is to fall into the trap of taking the easy answer." He paused for a moment. "On the other hand, most cops can tell you that the obvious answer is usually the right one."

"Not always, though."

Scott's gaze on me sharpened. "Why do you think Hovey didn't do it or have a 'minion'—I love that word, by the way—take care of the problem for him? From all I hear, he's capable of it."

"Capable, yes. But way too smart. Even to have a minion do it. At least not here. He would know it could be traced back to him. If he was ultimately responsible for it, he'd make sure it was handled in a much more subtle way that could never be connected to him. A car accident back home or some kind of domestic incident."

Scott looked thoughtful. We were finishing up when Janelle's phone buzzed with the distinctive tone that indicated Tina on the line. That probably meant something needed immediate attention. We stayed quiet while she listened and waited while she sighed and wrote a booth number on a piece of paper.

I glanced down at my own phone and was shocked to see it was half past one. Scott and Craig finished while she was still listening. They left, saying they needed to help get a booth ready for the appearance that afternoon of a minor television star I'd never heard of before.

I started to tell her goodbye as well, but Janelle held up a finger. When she concluded by saying, "Someone will be there shortly," I knew the after-lunch email check would be delayed a bit longer.

"Now what?" I asked.

"Couple of things. You take six twenty. Having some kind of electrical or equipment problem. Tina wasn't real clear about what they meant."

Not too surprising. Tina couldn't keep the buttons on the copier straight and was mostly mystified by her own computer. I mentally slapped myself for the nastiness. Tina was a decent receptionist, when she wasn't off gossiping with someone. She handled multiple incoming calls with an aplomb I could only envy, never manage, and she was always polite, even with people who were angry and nasty. She showed more patience than I had sometimes. Of course, she could also ramble away endlessly when trying to summarize the message from an incoming call, without ever quite getting to the point.

"On my way," I told Janelle, and she waved goodbye.

While pressing my way through the thickening
crowds to the six hundred aisle, I wondered about
Thomas Hovey and Scott's mention that the simplest
answer was usually right. Could he have been responsible for Chase Markham's murder? Not that he'd do
it himself, of course, but I felt sure more than one of
his flunkies would be willing and able to take care of
a "problem" for him. It would have to be a heck of a
problem to require a solution that drastic, and no one
seemed to think Markham could've been that much of
a threat to Hovey. Maybe Hovey needed to send some
kind of message?

Apparently Markham had been a threat to somebody.
Or maybe he'd just made someone so furious, they'd
killed him. Everything I'd heard about him suggested
Chase Markham had been good at making enemies.

Before I could follow that thought very far, I got to
six-twenty, purveyors of very small, portable printers
and scanners. I took a moment to watch one of the people in the booth demonstrate how she could send a file
from her smart phone to a printer so small she could
hold it in her hand while it printed. The paper was only
a few inches wide, but the print was clear and crisp and
the photo she sent came out in beautiful color. I was
so intrigued, I almost forgot why I was there, until another man approached, and seeing that I wasn't part of
the group getting the demo, asked if he could help me.

That flipped me back into work mode. Introductions
made and hands shaken, he took me back to a quieter
corner of the booth before he said, "We're having some
intermittent problems with our wireless communications.
It's been happening ever since we set up the display. Yesterday I kept hoping it was the construction stuff and it

would stop once everything was set up and working, but it's still happening. I called our tech guys, and they said it's probably interference from some other equipment in the building. It's annoying and very bad for business, since our products rely on wireless connections. I expected better than this for what we're paying for the space. Is there anything the Center can do about it?"

"We are aware of the problem and already have people working on it," I told him. I didn't have my fingers crossed behind my back, but I'm not sure my tone was entirely convincing.

"Any chance you'll have it fixed before the show ends?" the man asked.

"We're doing our best," I promised. "In fact, checking on the progress of the people looking into it is the next thing I'll do."

"I certainly hope so. Considering how much money we're paying for this, everything should be running smoothly." He went on in that vein for a few minutes and I let him vent. I find people are more amenable to working with you on solutions and tolerating the process if you give them a chance to express their frustrations. In this case—in a lot of cases—they have a right to their anger, even if it isn't something you really have any control over. I looked serious and nodded throughout the harangue, until he wound down. Then I said goodbye and headed for the Gryphon-Loyall booth.

SEVEN

Tuesday

I ALMOST DIDN'T recognize Ted Hanford, the techie geek. He'd donned a tailored suit that showed no hint of crease or wrinkle, complete with white shirt and restrained blue tie. But a closer look at the silk tie made me smile. It had a tiny, all-over pattern of not quite complete circles with a line running vertically through the break in the top of each. Even I recognized the symbol for a power switch.

He grinned when he saw the direction of my stare. "Rocks, doesn't it?" he asked. "Wait till you see some of the others I've got." The smile lit his otherwise ordinary face, making it surprisingly attractive, but it faded quickly. "We heard about Chase Markham. Can't believe it." He shook his head. "I've said more than once that someone was going to strangle him some day, but to think that someone really did… Man, that just doesn't compute."

Larry Barnes, also impeccably dressed in a pinstriped suit and conservative gray tie, came over and joined us. He looked paler than I remembered, and his expression showed more strain than Ted's. He'd worked with Chase and knew him better, so it wasn't surprising the man's death had hit him harder. "Any word on who killed Chase?" He sighed when I told him no and shook his head in a gesture that echoed Ted's. "I can't believe he's dead, even though he could be a pain in the ass and upset a lot of people."

"I know," I agreed. "It's always shocking."

"And you found the body," Ted said. "That must've been rough."

"Not an experience I'm eager to repeat," I admitted. "But that's not why I'm here. I wondered if you had a chance to look for the source of the interference. I've got other exhibitors complaining about it."

Ted looked chagrined. "Man, I just totally blanked on it. Ever since we heard about Chase, that's been all I could think about."

"All any of us could think about," Larry echoed. "Or talk about."

"Not surprising. And we did call in our tech guys, too. But they're slow. If you can spare any time at all, I could really use help finding the source."

"Yeah, we'd better try to nail it down. It's still interfering with our equipment, too. I'll bet there are even more people having problems who just don't realize yet what is." He looked around. "I wonder if it's interfering over the whole place or just some locations."

"A good part of the floor, I think," I answered. "I had a complaint from someone in the six hundred aisle."

"Interesting. But it's sporadic, which is going to make it a lot harder to run down. We have to catch it while it's happening and try to zero in on it."

"Have we got an RF meter here?" Larry asked.

"Yeah, I brought one. Need to calibrate it, which I'll do the next time we notice the interference, then we can search for the source."

"Can you give me a call when you're ready to go searching?" I asked.

"Sure. But it may take a while. Heck, if the interference times are short, it could take several tries before we can home in on it."

"Understood. But the quicker we find it and fix it, the better."

Ted nodded again and changed the subject back to what was uppermost in everyone's minds. "Do you think Hovey did it? Killed Chase? That's the rumor going around, since they had that argument right out there in public."

I shook my head. "Don't have any idea."

"I heard..." He paused and gave me an odd look. "I heard you solved a murder not too long ago yourself." He seemed embarrassed to mention it.

"Yeah, I did. And almost got myself and someone else killed in the process. I learned my lesson."

"Oh. Ouch. I'll bet you did. I'll bet that's a good story, too."

"A sad one." It wasn't something I liked to talk about.

Ted got the message. Larry looked like he wanted to find out more, but a couple of people arrived at the booth and no one else appeared ready to help them. I waved goodbye as Ted and Larry turned their attention to the newcomers.

My phone showed no new messages. I could finally get back upstairs for a few minutes, but first I needed to check on the temp booths again.

I went by there and found them doing quite a brisk business. The people I hadn't spoken with that morning were again busy. I took it for a given that they had no complaints. The people at the other end were also busy with clients. I caught the eye of the man there for a moment, but he just smiled and gave me a thumbs-up.

At the larger center set of tables, Dean Lee was engaged with someone, but the other man, a tall, heavyset guy with thick glasses, was new to me. He looked up and put on his best salesman smile as I approached. "Hi, Frank Merrimon, president of SteadySafe. What kind of security issues do you have?"

"Actually, that's not my department." I introduced myself. His professional smile faded into more serious concern when I told him I'd stopped by to see if they were having any problems with their temporary location.

He readjusted his glasses before he answered. "It's not ideal. We really need a more private space to talk with customers, but I guess it's the best you could do on short notice. I'm assuming we'll get some kind of partial refund for the space rental?"

"You'd need to talk to the director or the show manager about that," I said. "I'll give you their cards. I'm sure they'll work something out with you. My job is to take care of any problems you have right now."

"Any idea when we can get back into our booth?"

"No, but I'll check with the detective in charge."

"That's the best thing you could do for us, although..." He looked around. "This isn't a bad location. We get all the traffic coming in the door." He realized he'd made a strategic mistake and hastily added, "We still need the racks we built for the booth and the private area more."

"Anything else? I hope all your employees are okay after the tragedy of yesterday. I'm sure it was pretty traumatic for them, especially that young man who was at the booth at the time."

Merrimon rolled his eyes. "Imbecile. The kid was a temp. Not paying a bit of attention to what was going on, obviously. Won't be back here again."

"He was the only one there at the time."

"Yeah, we had a sales meeting off-site. He was supposed to be minding the booth."

"It was very hard to hear anything yesterday."

"Noisy or not, he was supposed to be *watching*. That's what we were paying him for. At least two people slipped into the back area without him even noticing? What the heck was he doing?"

"Looked like he was reading to pass the time when I got there," I said.

"*You're* the young woman who found the body?"

"Unfortunately."

Merrimon's jaw tightened, carving deep, angry lines around his nose and mouth. "How did they get into the back of our booth without anyone seeing? And a man was murdered and apparently no one heard it?"

"Actually, someone did hear it," I muttered, not happy that he'd reminded me. Louder, I added, "It was so noisy in here yesterday, I'd be more surprised if anyone in the area *had* heard it. I wonder how they got in there, though. Even if he wasn't watching very closely, your temp should have seen them go in. Unless they managed to get in through the back?"

"It would be a squeeze, but I suppose it could've happened. Doesn't matter though. He was supposed to be checking on the back periodically too."

"Did you know Chase Markham?" I asked.

He looked surprised by the abrupt change, then wary. "Knew of him, mostly. I think I met him once. We approached him about working for us at one point, but decided he wouldn't be a good fit. I heard about his argument with Tom Hovey. Didn't surprise me. He had a brilliant mind, but the output wires from brain to mouth got crossed all too often, and a few things in his head weren't screwed down too tightly. Wouldn't trust him."

That was an interesting new slant on the murder victim. Unfortunately, I had no chance to pursue it. A group of people approached, and Merrimon turned to greet them. I'm pretty sure he looked relieved.

I looked around for the man Dean Lee had identified as Shawn, since he'd known Chase Markham, but he wasn't in the vicinity. Just as well. My phone had beeped to signal new messages a couple of times during my talk with Frank Merrimon.

I took it out to check the messages and was shocked to discover it was nearly four o'clock.

The most important of the messages was from Ted, saying they had an interference signal and he was trying to track it down. I was heading for the Gryphon-Loyall booth to meet him, when the phone buzzed again. Since it was Janelle, I answered and learned that the people at three hundred eight were reporting missing equipment.

I stopped near the sixteen hundred aisle and called Ted.

"Too late," Ted said, before I even identified myself. "Signal's gone again. It's stronger toward the back and far side of the building from us. I'll call you again next time we get it."

I thanked him and hung up. I glanced up the aisle as I passed thirteen hundred. The far end was still roped off with yellow "crime scene" tape. A uniformed officer stood guard, turning back anyone who tried to venture beyond that point, but I didn't see any other activity there. At the eleven hundred aisle the Schwartz-Mann booth was lit up like Christmas with colored lights on strings blinking in patterns and one of the large strobe lights flashing occasionally. Colored lights also winked on and off on the huge wheel in the middle of the booth but it didn't seem to be in use right then.

One quick glance at the people waiting in the booth at three hundred eight told me this wasn't going to be fun. I drew a deep breath and approached the two angry men staring at a stack of boxes. They both looked up as I got near. Because I might've been a potential client they cleared their expressions and welcomed me. The scowls returned with renewed force when I identified myself.

The man who seemed to be in charge didn't even bother to tell me his name. "We asked to talk to whoever's in charge of security," he informed me.

"I know, but they're all tied up right now. If you'll tell me what's wrong, I'll get them on it as soon as I can."

He wasn't happy about it, but I just gave him my sweetest smile and waited.

"Shoplifters!" He almost spat the word. "Who'd think it would happen here? In this place? This crowd?"

"Shoplifters?"

"Someone stole a couple of our tablets. Apparently just waltzed by, picked them up, and walked off with them while no one was looking."

"No one saw what happened?"

The man shook his head.

I debated how to phrase this, but there really wasn't any diplomatic way. "How do you know someone walked off with them? They might have been misplaced in the booth somewhere."

He gave me an impatient frown. "What do you think? We searched. There aren't many places you could hide them here. My people even agreed to open up all their bags and cases as a group. They weren't there."

"How long ago did you find them missing?"

"About an hour ago."

"More than one's missing?" I asked.

"Two." He walked over to a stack of boxes. "Two of these." He handed one to me. "These are top of the line MegaComp tablets. Four G, one hundred twenty-eight gig, two meg downstream speed, twelve-eighty by one thousand screen. We customize them for specific industrial and retail inventory applications. The best and most expensive products we offer."

The last sentence was the only part of his description I understood, but it was clear enough. This was not good. Really not good, if it was related to the possible theft that morning. "Just a minute." I pulled out my phone and punched a speed dial button.

"Craig?" I said when our security chief answered. "I need you in the three-hundred aisle ASAP. We have a problem."

"Whatcha got, Heather?" he asked.

"Merchandise going missing. Two reported incidents today. One hundred and three hundred aisles. Better pull the tapes and get someone to review them quick, then come down here." Honestly, I had no idea how or if that could be done, but we did have video cameras, and at least it sounded like we were trying.

"Done," he said. "I'll be there in ten minutes."

I waited with them until Craig got there and introduced him to the man in charge in the booth, then left them to their discussion. I'd check with Craig later on the result.

I finally made my way upstairs, but it was after five by then. I took a few minutes to go through the messages on my email and the land-line phone on my desk. Technically, I could leave any time after five, but the exhibit hall didn't officially close until six and I rarely left before then when there was a show going on.

I was in the elevator again when my cell buzzed. "We're not seeing much on the tapes," Craig said. "Nothing at all for the first incident. None of the cameras caught anything there. Got a couple of maybes for the second. They can't pin the time down exactly, but we've got a couple of people going into the booth when no one's watching for them and leaving again without talking to anyone. We don't see anyone actually nip anything and there isn't enough to make an identification anyway."

"That's not going to make anyone happy."

"I know. I'll handle telling the guys at three hundred eight," Craig offered.

"Thank you, thank you. But what do we do next? To prevent more thefts?"

Craig paused for several long moments before he said, "Two incidents don't really make a pattern yet."

"No, but the guys at three hundred eight were angry enough to start putting the word out."

"I hear you. I'll do my best to mollify them. I'll tell 'em we're deploying extra security on the floor."

"How do you plan to do that?"

"Not sure yet. I'll figure it out."

I sighed. "Okay. But I better at least warn Janelle. In case they complain to her or something else happens."

"Good idea," Craig said.

I stopped in the lobby and debated whether to wait until I got home or call now. Sooner won out. Janelle was still on the floor when she answered, but hearing that I was in the lobby, she came to join me. She looked as close to frazzled as I've ever seen my boss.

"Rough day?" I asked.

"Not the easiest," she admitted. "Lot of little things going haywire. I suspect you're not going to make it any better."

"Not sure if this is really something we need to worry about or not." I told her about both theft reports.

Once I finished, Janelle thought for a couple of minutes. "Not ready to say this is a trend. The first one might not have been anything more than carelessness or…insider theft." She looked at me. "Your gut on it?"

"No idea."

"Then let's await developments. I'm not sure what else we can do, anyway."

"Here's something else. I'll bet a couple of your complaints were about interference with equipment or communications."

"Since I've never seen any signs that you're psychic or whatever the word is, I assume you've gotten them, too."

I told her about the complaints I'd heard and about what Ted and company were doing to help. "We might want to offer them a discount on the space if they can track it down," I suggested.

"I'm sure we can. And the faster, they can get it fixed, the better. I'll try to light a fire under our tech guys, too, but if your exhibitor can run it down quicker, we'll do something to thank them." She looked at me. "Go on home. You look tired. Tomorrow probably won't be any easier."

I had no doubt she was right on all counts.

EIGHT

Wednesday

I GOT TO the Center around seven-thirty, as usual, but found more activity than I expected on the show floor. A couple of our maintenance guys were already there, along with several of the people I'd seen manning the temp booths. Since they were disassembling equipment at those tables and loading boxes onto carts and dollies, I assumed the police had released the booth spaces back to them.

The move looked to be under control, so I left them to it while I went upstairs to check in and act like I wasn't avoiding the overflowing email inbox on my computer. A quick scan through the messages showed nothing more urgent than an update on the company Internet usage policy. Like I had time to surf the net during the work day. There were a couple of things on the land-line phone I'd need to answer. I scrawled reminders to myself about those on sticky notes and laid them on the desk. There was also a message from Craig about the police releasing the booths so the exhibitors could move back this morning.

Janelle came in just before eight and stopped at my desk. We went over the list of things that needed to be done and tried to anticipate possible problems, including checking on the people moving back to their booths to be sure there weren't any additional issues. "It didn't look like the change was hurting their business any," Janelle said, "but we want them to know we're doing everything possible to ensure their success." She also asked me to follow up with a couple of other booths that had had some minor problems the day before.

"And don't forget NovaCyn's got Lilya appearing in their booth this afternoon. I suspect we'll need all hands on deck for crowd control. Craig had Scott double-checking security and setup prep for it, but it could still be a mess."

A super-model drew super crowds. But… "What's a super-model got to do with computers and cell phones and cloud storage software?"

"'Cloud storage'?" Janelle arched a beautiful shaped eyebrow. "You've been doing your homework."

"It's the hot buzzword right now. I'm seeing it on every other banner. I'm not actually sure what it means, though."

"I'll get excited when they figure out how to move all the junk in my attic up to the clouds for storage," my boss answered.

"Yeah. They aren't really putting information in a literal cloud, are they?"

"Sort of doubt it, but it does make me wonder where that mythical cloud is located." Janelle took a sip of coffee from her mug.

"I'll try to remember to ask someone about it today. What time is the supermodel appearance?"

"Officially at two. Expect crowds to start gathering earlier. NovaCyn's at twenty-three oh eight. Be there by one-thirty. Someone will buzz if you're needed earlier. It's possible."

"Is she performing, talking, or just signing autographs?"

"Just signing autographs today, I think. Tomorrow she's supposed to be helping them to unveil some hot new product."

"That's scheduled for the ballrooms and not on the show floor, right?"

"It is."

I grinned as I said, "That announcement may be better attended than Hovey's. Wonder if it'll give him ideas for his next event."

"I don't see him sharing the spotlight with anyone or anything other than his amazingly great products."

"I suppose not. His products are pretty amazing, though. That's probably why it works. I think it's time I got a new phone, don't you? I've already seen a couple of pretty cool smart phones. And I can think of several ways they could help us."

"Make your case in writing and I'll stick it in the next budget. It's coming right up. Due in three weeks, in fact."

"There's a hidden assumption there," I pointed out.

She looked puzzled. "What?"

"That I'm going to have a few free minutes sometime in the next three weeks. I'm not sure I see that happening."

My cell phone buzzed but I ignored it for the moment. Janelle grinned. "How bad do you want that new toy?"

"Point taken."

I didn't recognize the number showing on the phone, but I did know the voice on the other end. "Heather? It's Sandy from RTX. The booth... It's been trashed."

"What?"

Janelle had started to turn away but that one word got her attention and she stopped.

"It's a mess!" Sandy said. "Everything's scattered all over. Boxes opened. Papers everywhere. You better come talk to Drake before he goes ballistic."

"I'll be right there," I said.

Janelle gave me an inquiring look.

"Sandy from RTX. Chase Markham's employer. According to her, their booth's been trashed." I shut down the email program and got up. "Time to head downstairs." I grabbed the cup of coffee from my desk and drained it before I left.

"I'd better go with you." Janelle went to lock her purse in her desk and joined me at the elevator.

"This can't be a coincidence," I said as we rode down.

"Not likely. But we don't know what we're dealing with yet. Could be just a pile of boxes knocked over."

"Could be. Sandy sounded pretty upset, though."

I saw why when we got to the RTX booth. It was more than just a stack of boxes knocked over. All of them had been taken down, scattered, and the piles left in uneven ridges across the booth. Cartons stood open, their contents scattered. Papers and flyers littered the floor so heavily you couldn't walk across the booth without stepping on bunches of them.

"Call security," Janelle said as Sandy came toward us.

I listened to Sandy say, "It was like this when I got here this morning," as I pressed Craig's number. He was with the police, he explained when I told him the problem, but he'd send Scott over.

Drake Galloway scooped up an armload of sales brochures, straightened them, and dropped them into an empty carton before gathering another bunch. Sandy had started to rebuild one of the stacks of boxes. Galloway saw us, slammed down the pile of papers on a table, and came over. "One of my employees is murdered. And now this! I can't say I'm terribly impressed with your security here!"

"I understand," Janelle said in her smoothest tone. "And you have every reason to be upset. One of our top security people is on his way over here right now."

"Can you tell if anything is missing?" Janelle asked.

Galloway turned to survey the wreckage. "Hard to say. We'll have to do an inventory after we get it sorted out."

"What time did you get here this—" Janelle broke it off when she saw Scott Brandon approaching. "Here's our security guy now."

Scott nodded to each of us and surveyed the damage. "Quite a mess. What happened?"

"We don't know," Janelle said. She introduced him to Sandy and Drake Galloway. They shook hands and then she turned to Sandy. "You said you found it this way when you got here this morning? What time was that?"

"I got here at eight forty and Drake a few minutes later." She pointed to the booth across the aisle from them. "I asked around. Liz over there says it was like this when she got here at eight fifteen. She was the earliest arrival I could find."

Scott glanced around the area. "No other booths are damaged?"

Sandy shook her head. Scott asked when they'd left the night before and was told they'd gone shortly after the show floor closed at six. Then he asked the same question Janelle had asked about whether anything was missing, and got the same answer.

"Can we look in the back?" Scott asked. Galloway agreed, but before we did that, Janelle excused herself.

"I've got a couple of other pressing things to take care of," she told Galloway, "but I'm leaving you with the two smartest people who work here. They'll do whatever is possible to help you out."

"That's a lot to live up to," I muttered. Sandy laughed softly. Scott gave me a small, wry grin but didn't say anything. I followed him into the area curtained off from the rest of the booth. The space was crowded with three of us in it, made even more so by the chaos. Here, too, boxes had been tipped over and contents strewn across the carpet. Bottles of water and cans of soda made untidy heaps and a few escapees had rolled to other corners. The folding table and chair still stood where they'd been, but a mini-fridge that hadn't been there the first time I'd looked into this cubbyhole likely hadn't originally been placed at that odd angle to the wall.

Scott said nothing for a few minutes as he looked around, taking in the mess but not touching anything. Finally he led the way out. His lips tightened as he watched Sandy gathering up boxes and restacking them. He went over to her. "Please don't touch or move anything else."

Her head jerked up. "What?"

He repeated the instruction, and turned to Galloway, telling him the same thing.

"Why?" the man demanded.

"We need to get a crime scene unit here to go over it, check for prints and trace evidence."

Galloway's eyes narrowed and lips tightened. "How long will that take?"

Scott hesitated before answering. "Probably several hours."

The man's hands tightened into fists. A vein bulged in his neck. "You're kidding! No way we can be shut out of the booth for several hours. It's bad enough having an employee murdered and our booth trashed. Now you're telling me we can't even clean it up and do business again for several more hours?" His voice rose to a shout on the last few words.

I stepped in and held up a hand. "Give me a minute." I drew a deep breath, mentally girding my loins for battle. "Scott, may I have a word privately?"

We moved away from the booth, down to the front of the hall. He shook his head. "Look, Heather, I understand we're inconveniencing people, and I don't like doing that any more than you do, but this could be related to a murder investigation. We have to ensure we collect any possible evidence."

"You're thinking like a cop and not like an employee of the Market Center."

He folded his arms across his chest. "Damn it, I am—*was* a cop."

"And you're not now. You're an employee of the Market Center, which means your priorities are different." I hated to say it because I knew it was a sore point with him, but I had my job to do, too. Then I thought of a better way to convince him. "Yes, it's a murder investigation, and I take that very seriously, too. But what are the odds a crime scene unit would find anything useful here? What kinds of things are they likely to find? Even if whoever did this was dumb enough not to wear gloves, how would you know any stray print wasn't from someone who'd just come by and fingered the merchandise over the past few days? And what else are you going to find that couldn't have been left by just about anyone at any time over the past couple of days?"

Arguing with Scott was always a bit intimidating, but even more so when he wore that hard cop expression. Still, he would listen to reason, no matter what his law enforcement training dictated.

His harsh frown lightened as he thought about what I'd said. He glanced back at the booth, ran a hand through his hair, and sighed. When the tense muscles in his shoulders started to release, I knew the argument had carried. "I'm afraid you're right. The place is too public and there's been too much traffic here for any trace evidence to be much use. And even if there had been some useful layers, they've already contaminated the scene pretty thoroughly in the process of cleaning it up."

"Unless any 'trace evidence' came from someone completely outside the Center, there's no way to separate out what would be normal and what wouldn't. And you should know if there was any sign someone from outside had gotten in during the night when the place was closed."

He shook his head in a quick denial. "No, you're right. This was most likely done by someone with legitimate access to the show floor, and at this point there's no good way to establish who it might've been." The underlying irritation said he might know it was true, but he didn't have to be happy about it.

I turned to look back to the booth. Sandy and Drake both stared at me, consternation on Sandy's face and anger on Drake's. "They'd have a conniption if we brought in the cops and locked them out of their booth for even the rest of the morning. And for very small odds that your CSI would find anything useful anyway."

Scott's lips compressed in a frown, but then drew a deep breath and let it out. "At this point it would probably take the rest of the day. Go ahead and tell them we're not going to shut them down."

I nodded toward the booth, and Sandy and Drake both got the message. They turned away and resumed their clean-up efforts.

Scott had gone into thoughtful mode, his expression neutral. "What do you think about the mess? Why?"

I considered what we'd seen. "It looks more like someone was searching for something than just vandalism. There's no real damage other than the mess and maybe some equipment that got broken when it was knocked over. Since the whole place is trashed, the searcher likely didn't find what they were looking for. And, I agree that it probably does relate to Chase Markham's murder. Whatever the unknown person was searching for must be incriminating and probably not too big. Maybe papers of some kind, since he did go through all the boxes of sales sheets and flyers."

Scott stared at the booth. "I think all we can do at this point is help them clean up. And ask a few more questions. Gilmont should know about this, though he'll probably bite my head off next time he sees me for not preserving the scene."

"I'll let him know about it when I talk to him later. I'll tell him it was my decision."

A spark of anger flared in his eyes. "You don't have to cover for me, Heather. I called it and I'll stand by it."

Wow. The offer had been so automatic it hadn't occurred to me he'd be offended by it. "I'm sorry. I guess I'm too used to having to take care of everything and everyone. But I should've known you, of all people, wouldn't need it."

The anger faded, replaced by wry curiosity. "'Of all people?'"

I looked around the area, taking in the booths, the people, the noise, the general chaos. "Some days I feel like I'm just a big babysitter for the crowd. You don't need it. You're an adult yourself. In your own way, you're kind of a babysitter, too, I guess."

"I guess. But you need to recognize that you can't take responsibility for everything. Let others be adults too, which sometimes means refusing to let them avoid uncomfortable issues." Someone bumped him from behind, apologized, and he accepted it without taking his eyes off me. "But this is a talk for another time, and I don't really have the right to tell you how to do your job. Let's go back and finish up with RTX."

Scott had another private talk with Galloway in the back while I pitched in to help with cleaning up the mess. Whatever Scott said apparently mollified the owner of the company. Both men came out looking slightly less angry, and Scott got to work helping Sandy restack boxes. I'd been gathering up papers which I took to the back to place in cartons. Galloway followed me with an armload of flyers. It didn't take very long and Galloway said nothing to me beyond, "Put those in here," as he held out a box for the stack of sell sheets I'd straightened out. I heard Sandy and Scott murmuring but couldn't make out any words. I doubted it would be anything significant since Galloway found reason to pass close to them every few minutes.

Because the clean-up mostly involved picking up clutter, it didn't take all that long to finish. Ten minutes after we returned to the booth, Scott ducked into the back area to say goodbye to me as I was dumping the last batch of papers into a carton. Galloway and Sandy were out front demonstrating something to a client, so Scott gave me a quick kiss in the private area. Then we went out, waved to the others, and proceeded on our separate ways.

My next stop was to check on the temporary booths at the front. They were pretty much gone. Mark, Sam, and a couple of other maintenance guys were removing the last remaining pieces, folding up tables and metal shelving, rolling up cords, and taking the banners down from the wall. I nodded and smiled at them as I went by, but didn't stop.

I hadn't gone more than twenty feet farther on before I was waylaid by a group of exhibitors who recognized me and asked about progress in the investigation into Chase Markham's murder.

I could honestly tell them I didn't know very much. We kept the line of communications open and offered whatever help we could to the authorities, but generally we felt it best to let the police gather evidence and question witnesses. We had increased the level of alertness of our security team, of course. It didn't really satisfy anybody, but most realized there wasn't much more we could do.

I followed up on a couple of complaints from the day before and found that those problems had been resolved satisfactorily. I passed the eleven hundred aisle and went to see what the guys at Schwartz-Mann were up to. Since I hadn't heard the sirens at all, I was giving them credit for heeding my warning.

The string lights were on, or rather were flashing on and off. These were fairly large lights in a multitude of colors, hanging on lines between poles set around the perimeter of the booth. The size and the way they flashed on and off made them much more impressive than those small strings of chaser lights you see at Christmas. As I watched, I realized that they were blinking in interesting patterns. Sometimes all of one color would light, sometimes pairs of colors, then a set of multiple colors would flash. The single strobe in the center of the booth blasted an occasional brighter counterpoint. If there was a pattern to the sequence, I couldn't figure it out, but there was something almost hypnotic about it.

I had to shake myself out of the abstraction to remember why I was there. Most of the booths nearby appeared busy, but I headed for one where an elderly man stood alone, refilling a candy dish. He looked up and smiled at me. The smile remained even when I identified myself as Center personnel.

"Can I help you with something?" He had a slight but charming British accent.

"Actually that's *my* question. I'm just checking around to be sure everything's going okay. Are you having any problems?"

"Oh, no, thank you. You caught me in a quiet moment, but actually traffic's been good. Quite good, in fact. I think the light display over there helps draw people to the aisle. It's rather fascinating, isn't it? You can't help but want to watch it. People come to look and linger to talk to us. It's quite the conversation-starter."

We talked for a few more minutes about the show and his participation, until a potential customer stopped at the booth. I went on to talk to a younger woman at another company who told me practically the same thing, though with considerable more enthusiasm.

"It's great! It brings tons of people up this way and they're happy to stop and chat about how intriguing the lights are. So I'm getting lots of leads and a few even get interested enough to order."

And that seemed to settle the question of whether the display was bothering other exhibitors, so I proceeded back to the thirteen hundred aisle to check with the people who'd just returned to their booths.

It felt odd walking up that aisle again. I hadn't really looked at it closely when I'd searched so frantically two days ago, and I'd been mostly avoiding it since. Now I studied the row of booths, though I can't say what I was searching for. The displays were like all the others in the show, mostly medium-sized ones comprising three or four spaces, selling computers, printers, copiers, phones, tablets, wireless services and other gizmos I couldn't identify. Several of them were software dealers, though generally I couldn't tell exactly what their products were supposed to do. I did see one that had a huge, fuzzy, white puffy thing partially suspended above their backdrop with the words "The answer to all your data storage needs is in the cloud." I made a note to stop in later and ask them where that particular cloud was floating.

A few of the booths represented nationwide service companies—one for setting up networked computers, another a telephone and Internet service provider. I got that mostly from the signage on the booths. A magazine publisher handed out free copies of their latest issue. As I took one, I caught sight of the SteadySafe booth.

A wave of déjà vu washed over me with such fierce power I got dizzy. Panic rushed in behind it. For a moment, I was sure I'd find another body. I could see Chase

Markham lying on the floor so clearly. Dread made me light-headed and nauseated.

I don't think I've ever been so glad to hear my phone buzz. The horrible feeling fled almost as fast as it had come on, but it left me disoriented. My shaking fingers nearly dropped the phone as I pulled it from its case on my belt.

"We've got interference again," Ted said. "We're in the two thousand aisle, heading for nineteen."

NINE

Wednesday

"I'M ON MY WAY."

I breathed a sigh of relief and turned back to the center corridor that cut across the show floor, dividing each aisle in half.

I found him a couple of booths down from the middle in the nineteen hundred aisle. Ted was staring at the screen of a small box, slightly larger than a smart phone, that he held in his right hand. To my surprise, Jennifer accompanied him. She put a hand on his arm to stop him heading away as I approached.

He smiled at me and held up the box. "Got a good strong signal right now," he reported. "Looks to be strongest this way." He nodded toward the lower number aisles, angling slightly toward the back. I sucked in a sharp breath. Many of the larger corporate booths were back in that direction. If one of them was the source, this could get complicated. Jennifer and I both followed him when he turned to the left.

"What are we looking for, exactly?" I asked Ted as he moved slowly along the center aisle, watching the readouts on the box.

"Hard to say. Almost anything that runs on electricity generates electromagnetic noise," he explained. "But most things are shielded well enough to prevent leaking EMR from being a problem. I'm guessing we've got something that's drawing a lot of power and isn't shielded right. Beyond that, it could be anything—from someone's music player to the lights overhead."

Ted laughed when Jennifer and I both looked up. "Not likely," he said. "Just trying to give an idea of the range of possibilities." He nodded to his left again. "It's definitely stronger that way." We stopped at the eighteen hundred aisle.

The entire back half of nineteen, including the right side row of booths on eighteen and the left side row on two thousand, belonged to the enormous MegaComp booth. The front side of eighteen comprised two booths, one of the giant telecoms and a well-known purveyor of gaming software. I wasn't quite sure what gaming software was doing at a business technology show, but we were pretty lenient about allowing whoever had the money and the interest to rent booth space.

Jennifer and I followed Ted as he continued past those and onto the sixteen hundred aisle. I was saying a quiet prayer that we wouldn't trace the signal to anyone who was likely to be awkward about it. He stopped sharply at the intersection of the aisle and the center cross corridor, staring at the box with a puzzled frown, then looked up and around. When he glanced down again, his frown turned into dismay and annoyance. He rattled the box, then shook his head. "Crum-bumalous. Lost it."

"Lost what?"

"The signal. It's stopped again. Blast it. We were getting closer, too."

I shared his frustration, especially given the complaints we'd been getting about the interference. The three of us all looked around, but without the signal we were stuck. This place was full of things that might be creating the problem. I drew a deep breath and let it out on a sigh. "Start here next time?" I suggested.

"Sorry." He checked the machine again. "No luck."

"Nothing you can help. Next time." I started to say goodbye, then blinked and looked more closely at his tie, remembering he'd mentioned having some interesting ones. This one qualified. It was deep green with copper and silver lines all over it. "It looks like you've got some kind of computer thing printed on your tie."

He grinned, showing that charming dimple again. "Circuit board. Isn't it great?"

"It is," I agreed.

"If they're going to make me wear a tie, I at least want it to be an interesting one."

Jennifer spoke up for the first time. "Ted has a whole collection of great geek ties."

His smile got broader. "Got an even better collection of tee shirts, but I don't get to wear them here much." He stopped and lit up as a thought occurred to him. "Hey, I heard you like interesting pens," he said. "We've got a couple you'll love. Stop by the booth sometime and I'll show you."

Interesting pens always snagged my attention. I promised him I would. I had a couple of questions I wanted to ask him, but standing in the middle of the aisle with a throng of people flowing around and past wasn't the time or place.

We parted there and I headed back to the thirteen hundred aisle. I forced myself to head back up that row, despite the reluctance that grabbed hold again and twisted my gut. This was so not like me. I was bold; I was fearless; I had once been fairly stupid and almost got myself and Scott killed. Still, I couldn't let that stop me. I had a job to do. The show goes on, and all that.

I did my best to ignore the rumbles in my gut as I approached the booth beside my target. Theirs had been one we'd had to move for the murder investigation. The man I talked with a couple of days ago chatted up an interested inquirer. The woman whose first name I remembered was Anne saw me and waved me over.

She was smiling, so I didn't expect any problems, but I still had to ask, "Is everything okay? Are you settled back in?"

"Fine," she answered. "Glad to be back here now. But, have you heard anything? About the…you know?" She nodded at the next booth.

"Have they made any progress on the investigation? I don't know. But it is something I need to check on. Can I borrow your booth to make a phone call?"

"Sure," she said, nodding toward the large freestanding display unit that separated their back meeting area from the open part of the booth in front.

I'm not sure what I expected to see back there—a big gaping hole between this booth and the next? A sign saying "A body was dragged through here"? The odds were no one here had anything at all to do with the murder next door. In any case, there were no holes and no signs, just stacks of cartons, a folding table, a pile of flyers someone had knocked over and hastily restacked, and a tangle of cables. The latter reminded me of the murder weapon, but there were probably miles of phone cable in this place.

As I placed the call to Detective Gilmont and waited for him to answer, I studied the cables and realized one of the things that had bothered me about the murder scene. I'd told Gilmont I'd seen a phone cable wrapped around the dead man's neck, but studying these I noticed a difference. These weren't phone cables. The plugs at the ends were different, wider, I thought, and the line itself a bit thicker. The one that had been used to strangle Chase Markham was the same as these. I wondered how common they were and what they were used for.

Before I could pursue the thought, the detective answered. "Gilmont. What can I do for you, Miss McNeil?"

I asked him about the investigation, telling him that I had nervous exhibitors wanting to know.

His pause told me I wasn't going to like the answer before I heard the words. "We're still in the early stages of the investigation," Gilmont said. "We have a few leads, but nothing substantial enough to make an arrest."

"I'm not a newspaper reporter," I told him indignantly.

"I know. But it's the only answer I can give you."

I sighed. "Basically you don't really have much."

"That's not what I said."

"No. It's what you didn't say." I thought about mentioning the cable, then decided it wasn't necessary. The police had it. They'd have someone who knew what it was.

"Do you have any ideas?" he asked. "Has anyone confessed anything to you yet?"

"'Fraid not," I admitted. "It's been pretty chaotic here. But something you should know. Someone vandalized the RTX booth either last night or this morning. The booth was trashed. Boxes of papers dumped out all over the place, stacks knocked over. Nothing seriously damaged, but a big mess."

"And I'm betting it's all been cleaned up now?"

"Right."

"You didn't think to call me about it first?"

"They already had it half cleaned up by the time we got there." It was only a small lie. Maybe it was only a third, but the damage to any investigation had already been done. "We did discuss making them stop, but then decided the possibility you'd find anything useful was outweighed by the amount of grief involved in making them stop and get out of the booth."

"We?"

He already knew the answer but he was going to make me say it. "Scott and I talked it over. He was torn about it but finally agreed that there wasn't much likelihood you could get anything useful."

The pause that followed said louder and clearer than any words how Gilmont felt about that. When he actually spoke, though, he sounded remarkably calm. "There are laws about interfering with a murder investigation, you know."

"The damage was already done when we got there. You could still come out and go over their booth."

He sighed, which was all the concession I would get. "I might just. You could've at least talked to me about it."

"I am. Right now. Because I feel sure it's relevant to the murder investigation."

"All right. Conclusions?"

"It looked more like a fast and thorough search than vandalism. Manufacturer sealed boxes were still sealed. Every other box had been opened and the contents dumped."

"Every box?"

"Every single one that wasn't factory sealed."

"Searcher likely didn't find what he was looking for," Gilmont said.

I agreed and added my theory that it had to be something small, possibly papers.

"That's one possibility," he agreed. "There are others. Lots of things in computers are small these days. Flash drives can hold lots of information in a tiny space."

"Dang, I hadn't thought of that," I admitted. "But it seems like it must've been something Chase deliberately hid before he was killed."

"Which opens up all sorts of interesting possibilities. But it's such a needle in a haystack, it's not likely that's how we're going to solve this," Gilmont said.

"No."

"If you learn anything to the point, let me know," he said.

"I will," I promised.

"And don't do anything foolish, if you do."

"You don't need to remind me."

I hung up, feeling unsettled. The police had no good idea who might've killed Chase Markham, and probably little real evidence. I was betting they found no fingerprints or anything else useful at the murder scene. Not that Gilmont would have mentioned it even if he did, but he would've sounded happier when he stretched the truth and he would've been more upset about not getting to check the RTX booth this morning. They had nothing to match anything else against.

I stepped outside of the curtained area. Anne was still free. I shrugged as she turned to me. "The police aren't saying much. They have some leads but they're not ready to make an arrest yet."

Anne rolled her eyes, recognizing the vaporous words for what they were. "They really don't have much of a clue, then."

"Apparently not," I agreed. "Can I ask you a question?"

"Sure."

I nodded toward the back and she followed me behind the curtain. I picked up one of the cables and held it up. "What are these?"

She looked surprised that I didn't know. "Ethernet cables. They connect networked computers with each other or with a server."

"They're pretty common, then?"

"All over the place." I could see that she was puzzled by my interest but continued. "They carry information between computers. Wireless is gradually replacing them, but Ethernet is still the faster and more secure way for machines to communicate."

I thanked her for the information before I moved on. Was the choice of an Ethernet cable as murder weapon significant or had the killer simply grabbed whatever was closest at hand?

I was pleased to see that Dean Lee was occupied with a customer when I approached the SteadySafe booth. Frank Merrimon was nowhere in sight, but the man I wanted to talk to appeared unoccupied. The tall, thin, curly-haired man plastered on his best salesman's smile and held out a hand when he saw me coming. "Shawn Kelly," he said. "How can I help you?"

The smile dimmed a few watts when I identified myself, but didn't go away entirely.

"You're with the Center," he said. "You're the girl Dean talked to earlier. He said you were pretty." He stopped and looked abashed. "I hope you don't mind. Do you know if there's been any word on who…who…" A flush climbed up the fair skin of his cheeks.

He was kind of cute, but this guy was the least smooth salesman I'd ever met, unlike the man I'd watched earlier. Then I remembered Dean had said he turned on and off. Apparently since I wasn't a potential customer, he was "off" now.

"Who killed Chase Markham?" I suggested. "I talked to the detective in charge a few minutes ago, in fact. They don't really have any suspects at the moment."

Something crawled across Shawn's face at that, but I couldn't tell what it was. Worry, relief, concern? I had no idea. It just looked odd to me. But his expression smoothed out again so fast I had no chance to identify it before he said, "They'd better figure it out quickly. Once the show is over, how likely is it they'll be able to?"

Yeah, that worried me too. "That's a good point. I don't know, but it'll certainly be harder. You were a friend of Chase's, I hear."

He wove his fingers together and cracked his knuckles. "I don't think I'd call him a friend. We worked together for a while at Timmer—on the V-600 tablet. I was in marketing; he was an engineer on the project." He was watching my face and said, "You've never heard of the V-600, have you?"

"No, but—"

"Don't worry. No one else has either. It was a huge flop. Almost an epic flop. Pretty much took Timmer down when it bombed. Almost took down my career with it. And a lot of other people's as well."

"Chase?"

"Not so much. Everyone recognized that his part of it was brilliant. Way too far ahead of its time, however. It used too much of the system resources; drew too much power from the rest of it."

Did I hear a hint of malice in there?

"So it was his piece of the thing that created most of the problems?"

No doubt about it. A flash of alarm crossed his face before he caught it and smoothed out his expression. His response was quick and sharp. "No, no, not really. The whole thing was badly done. Too many disparate development projects; not enough supervision of the whole thing. And the engineers in charge refused to listen to suggestions from anyone. It was probably doomed from the start. People weren't ready for tablets then anyway."

"Are they now?"

He gave me an "are you kidding?" look. "Definitely. They're everywhere now. Ever since MegaComp announced theirs a couple of years ago, it's been the hottest trend in computing."

"Did Chase work for them on that tablet?"

"He wished. He would've loved to, but his reputation for lunacy preceded him. They already had plenty of good engineers who weren't drama queens. Only their founder and chairman is allowed to be that flamboyant."

Decidedly there were hints of malice in *that* tone.

"This was before Chase worked at SiloSystems?" I'd struggled for a moment to come up with the company name but I was proud of myself for remembering it.

"Before. He was fortunate that *his* reputation didn't take much of a hit over the V-600 thing."

"A lot of people were hurt by it though."

He nodded.

"Did—?"

Unfortunately, a customer walked into the booth at that moment and Shawn interrupted my next question to excuse himself, obviously relieved to end our conversation. I was annoyed by it, but the prime directive for our job is that we don't interfere with exhibitors and potential customers.

My stomach rumbled again, reminding me it was lunch-time, so after a quick check at the third and fourth just-moved-back booths, which were still doing a steady business, I went down to the food court to grab a hot dog. I was only three bites into it when the phone buzzed.

"Better get up here now," Janelle said. "It's chaos. NovaCyn. Twenty-three. Toward the back."

I gobbled down the rest of the hot dog in ten seconds. Janelle didn't exaggerate. Not about things like that.

And, heaven help us, she was so *not* kidding about the near approach of chaos. I'd never seen anything like it.

My first impression on returning to the show floor was how deserted the aisles were at the fourteen-hundred row where I entered. Most of the booths had only a despondent-looking sales associate or two covering them and precious few customers in the vicinity. But off to my right I heard a hubbub louder even than normal for the very noisy show floor.

I saw the traffic jam looming ahead as I turned right from the fourteen hundred row into the center aisle and headed toward the higher-numbered rows. By the time I got to twenty-one hundred, I was pushing my way through increasingly thick crowds. I finally gave up trying to get any closer that way, turned around and went back to the two thousand row, skirting the side of the MegaComp booth to the rear of the building. That aisle was almost deserted. At the side of the MegaComp booth, one of the men I'd met the day before, the CTO, Driscoll, was talking quietly to someone turned away from me. Red hair was vaguely familiar, but his back was to me, so I couldn't see his face. Driscoll looked around, saw me, nodded, noted the crowd beginning to back up into this aisle, and drew his companion aside, into one of the tower things, out of sight.

I pushed my way through to the end and then over toward the twenty-two-hundred aisle. The mob extended up that aisle all the way to the back. I stepped away, slipped through an "employees only" door and took the rear service corridor to the next door, which would be at the twenty-four hundred aisle, hoping I could backtrack and get to the booth that way.

No such luck. The twenty-three hundred aisle was blocked, completely and totally, by a crowd that spread two rows down the center aisle on either side and jammed part of the back aisle as well. I checked my watch to be sure, and yes, it was still one-twenty, more than thirty minutes before Lilya's scheduled appearance at two.

TEN

I PUSHED, SHOVED and attempted to squeeze my way through the mob to get to the NovaCyn booth, but it was no-go. I'm not a tiny woman, but I'm not all that large either. Not that it mattered. It would take a bulldozer to get me through this scrum.

I finally stepped back from the crowd and called Janelle, hoping she could hear the phone above the din of the crowd. I was a bit amazed when she answered and not a bit surprised when her first words were, "Yell. I can't hear a damn thing."

I yelled. "I can't get there. I can't shove, push or crawl through this mob."

"Where are you?" she asked.

When I gave her my current location, she said, "Stay there. I'm sending Howie for you."

It took him several minutes to reach me, and the noise surrounding me kept getting louder and louder as more people arrived on the scene.

Howie is one of our security people, a big man, both tall and heavy, but he's in his sixties and I keep wondering how much longer he can continue working here. Still, he managed to make his way through the crowd to me, and then to elbow and shoulder his way back again, with me following so close behind I almost pressed into him. I wasn't a happy follower. Air got scarce and stale, and my skin crawled from the crush of people mobbed on both sides and behind me. We made a slow, tense trip the few hundred feet it took to get to the NovaCyn booth.

By the time we ducked behind the human line of security people manning a velvet barricade around the booth, my head spun from lack of oxygen. Fortunately, fewer people crowded this area than the aisle around it, and I could finally draw a deep breath. I looked around and spotted Janelle talking with Craig and Scott.

They all looked frazzled, which was a bad thing. Very bad. Craig and Janelle have been doing this a long time and neither one of them frazzles easily. After his years as a D.C. cop, almost nothing seems to rattle Scott, but even he looked upset. I didn't recognize the two other men in the bunch with them, so I assume they were NovaCyn people.

As I approached, Scott said, "We've got to move this out of here. Now. While it's still remotely feasible. This could turn into a riot."

I silently voiced my agreement. Silently, because in this gathering, my vote didn't count.

The NovaCyn people were resisting. "The whole point of bringing in Lilya was to draw people to our booth," one of the men protested. "If we move her to the ballroom, it negates all that."

"We'll take as much of your stuff to the ballroom as we can manage," Janelle promised. Then she came up with what I thought was a brilliant suggestion. "In fact, if we move it to the ballroom, we can set it up so that people have to look at your displays while they're waiting in line. You get as many of your people as you can stationed where we put them, get them sales sheets to hand out, and we guarantee everyone will *have* to go past them, listen to them and look at the material before they get to meet Lilya. No way we can do that here, where people are crowded into the aisles in front of other companies' booths. We won't even charge extra for use of the ballroom."

Both of the NovaCyn people present brightened. "Okay, that might work. But how do we manage it in—" he looked at his watch "—thirty minutes?"

"We get to work right now," Scott said. Janelle looked around and started issuing orders. To the NovaCyn people she said, "Get your people together and fill them in. Quick. Gather up as much sales stuff as you can and get it ready to transport, then have your people help ours set up the ropes in the ballroom. First we'll need to get everyone moved out of here so we can get out."

She turned to Craig to ask, "Where is the cause of the fuss right now?"

"On her way. Due to arrive in about ten minutes."

"Are they taking her in the side entry?"

Craig nodded. "Wasn't planned that way, but I've already phoned the driver to give him new instructions."

"Good. Get everyone you can over to the ballroom to set it up. Keep a couple for crowd control in the halls." Craig left. She turned to me. "Heather, make the announcement to the building, then get to the service door, meet the limo, and get her to the ballroom." She looked around and spotted Scott. "Go with her in case there's any trouble," she told him.

I backed as far as I could get from the crowd, turning to face the NovaCyn booth backdrop for privacy as I dialed into the rarely used public address system. It always felt weird to hear my own voice coming out of it. "Ladies and gentlemen," I said into the voice relay, "if I could have your attention, please. The appearance of Lilya, scheduled for two o'clock this afternoon at the NovaCyn booth, has been relocated to Ballroom A at two-fifteen." I repeated the announcement for good measure.

As expected there was a fair amount of grumbling from the crowd, especially those who'd arrived early to get close to the booth, but within moments people had begun to turn away and head for the lobby and the escalators out front.

By then Janelle had gone off with Craig, but Scott was waiting for me. "You okay?" he asked.

"Mostly. This is more chaotic than normal. What about you?"

"Mostly okay. I guess. They told me to prepare for two to three hundred people."

"I've never seen anything like this before. Even when we had a couple of TV stars last year, it wasn't this bad. What is it about this woman?" I asked. *Naïve, much?*

"Beats me. She's a celebrity. She's beautiful and sexy. Why would that attract anyone?" His tone was as sarcastic as the words were snarky.

"I did detect a certain whiff of raging testosterone in the air." But actually there were nearly as many women as men in the crowd.

He gestured to the rapidly emptying aisle. "Shall we go greet the guest of honor?"

We turned to leave the booth, but I noticed that a few of the cannier types around still watched us, and, I was willing to bet, poised to follow. Scott saw it, too. "Let's see if there's a back way out of here," he suggested. We followed a young man into a small storage area behind the main display. From there we pushed aside a fabric curtain at the back and stepped through it.

Not all of the rows had rear alleys like this. The first few rows on either end of the floor were set up with walls to divide the spaces, providing smaller vendors who didn't have their own booths with a way to hang their displays and banners. But for most of the center aisles we'd removed the separators, to allow the exhibitors more flexibility in how they set up their booths. NovaCyn, like many of the larger companies, had bought up multiple spaces that included the right side booths of twenty-three hundred and the corresponding left-side booths of the twenty-four hundred aisle. But between it and the back aisle, there were booths facing either way, with a narrow rear space between them.

We picked our way through the tangle of cords, swathes of fabric, occasional boxes and other pieces of debris that littered the area, squeezing through the twenty feet of confined alley. I led and Scott followed.

We reached the end of the row and I stopped to peer out, checking for potential problems. When I turned to tell Scott the coast appeared to be clear, he put one hand on my shoulder, while the other flicked something from my hair. "Dust," he said quietly.

I felt the tension in him. "What is it?" I asked.

He drew a breath and let it out on a long sigh. "A bit of guilt and frustration. I was supposed to be organizing security for this, but I never anticipated this mess."

"Not your fault. None of us expected it. We've never had a mob like this before. But the one thing you can count on around here is that you can't count on anything going according to plan. A few things will always go off the rails in ways you can't anticipate."

He shrugged and leaned down to kiss me. It was quick, little more than a peck, but still…

He smiled as he drew back and said, "It is what it is. We'd better go if there's no one waiting to follow."

Ignore the dancing butterflies. It's just a kiss. I sighed and leaned out. "Looks clear."

We popped out from between the backs of the booths on either side and scooted along the rear hall to the door to the service area at the back of the building. Mercifully, no one followed us. We headed to our left, finally reaching a space with a utility closet and stairway down. The long corridor behind the ballrooms and conference rooms on the floor below ended in another half flight of stairs down to the service receiving area. A heavy door at the far end opened to the outside, where a small concrete platform baked in the midday heat, and three steps went down to the street.

Perfect timing. The limousine had just turned into the side drive. When it drew even with the concrete steps, Scott went for the door. He reached it just ahead of the driver, who'd jumped out the minute the vehicle stopped and pointedly moved around in front of Scott.

The woman who took the driver's hand for help stepping out of the limo made my jaw drop. We've had celebrities here at the Center before. In fact, it's fairly routine. I've been close to actors, politicians and a few sports stars. Most of them, even the actors, look pretty ordinary close up. Unless they're wearing heavy layers of makeup—and many of them do—the television and movie stars tend to appear more average than you'd expect.

Nothing about this woman was ordinary. Since she was a supermodel, I expected her to be tall and willowy.

She and Scott stood nearly eye to eye when she turned to smile at him, which put her around six feet. Her body had curves, too, slight but in all the right places.

But it was her face that made me gape. It was a work of art. No other way to put it. She wore light makeup, but nature had endowed her with amazing cheekbones, huge blue eyes, a short straight nose and perfect full lips. The dazzling white teeth and lovely blond hair had probably gotten some chemical assistance, but no makeup could add the graceful lines of jaw, cheek and temple. I couldn't even hate her because she looked at me first with a smile of such warmth and sweetness that I wanted to hug her, before she turned that same wattage on Scott.

He returned her smile but didn't say anything, instead waiting for me to step forward as official greeter.

"Welcome to the D.C. Market Center," I told her, holding out my hand.

She took it in her perfectly manicured one and gave it a finely calibrated squeeze—not too hard, not too light. "Thank you."

"I'm sorry about having you come to a side door, but your appearance has caused a near riot in there and we had to do some last minute reorganizing."

She looked a bit dismayed. "I'm so sorry. I never want to create so much fuss."

Her voice was high and a bit nasal, not whiny, really, but grating and slightly unpleasant. *Well, thank goodness. She wasn't entirely perfect.*

"You can't help it," Scott said. "Not your fault." We ushered her into the building and back through the service areas. Workers nearby or passing stopped to look at her as we went by. I doubted most of them even knew who she was, but her looks just had that effect on people.

We finally got her up the stairs and into the ballroom through a rear service door. I glanced in before we entered. As I expected, Janelle, Craig, and the rest of the crew had things under control. People were lined up in ranks separated by velvet cords that snaked back and forth across the room. The table at the far end held several boxes of pens and stacks of pictures waiting for her to sign and give away.

The noise level was close to deafening, and it increased when someone caught sight of Lilya behind us. A couple of awestruck NovaCyn executives stepped forward to greet her. Once they'd said a few words, Janelle and I escorted the model to the seat prepared for her. The people in the front of the line surged forward.

Scott and I joined Janelle in the corner farthest from the action. Her expression worried me. "Under control?" I asked her.

"Here, yes. But we have another problem. It sounds like there's been another robbery on the floor."

"*Another* robbery?" Scott sounded alarmed.

"Didn't Heather fill you in on the robbery reports?" Janelle asked.

"She said some things had been taken from booths, but…wait. Was there any violence involved in those incidents?"

I answered. "No. Things were just taken while no one was looking."

Scott's tension eased. "Good. Technically, it's theft then, not robbery."

"There's a difference?" I asked.

"Legally. It's only robbery if some kind of force or coercion is used in the commission of the crime."

You can take the man out of the police force, but you can't take the cop out of the man.

"Okay," Janelle said. "But this is starting to look really bad for us. Would you go with Heather to talk to them?"

Scott glanced at the crowd, but the line moved forward in an orderly way, so we left by the back door again and returned to the show floor. The report came from a booth in the seven hundred aisle.

I took a deep breath as we made our way across the quieter-than-normal exhibit area. "She's...something, isn't she?"

Scott gave me a sharp look. "Something, yes. Gorgeous. Outrageously beautiful. Dangerous."

"Dangerous?"

"Helen of Troy. Men kill each other over women like her. She caused a near-riot here."

"Oh, but it's not her fault. She can't help it that she looks like that."

He shrugged and gave me a brief, wry smile. "Never said it was her fault. It just is."

I looked at him. Scott's a handsome man from any angle, but his profile was particularly attractive, with its strong jaw and straight nose. Right now it showed signs of strain in pinched lips and narrowed eyes. I suspected he was still angry at himself for not being prepared for the size of the crowd. Distraction was probably the only cure for that, and we had one readily at hand.

"I've been thinking about the disappearing equipment," I said. "I wonder if it's significant that all the thefts so far are on this side of the floor. They're mostly smaller booths with fewer people manning them."

He half nodded, half shrugged. "Possibly." He thought

about it for a moment. "We might be looking at an exhibitor in the area."

"As the thief? That's a scary thought."

"That might be the best possible scenario."

"What would be a worse one? One of our staff?"

"Doubt it. There's no previous pattern of this happening at other shows. The worst would be someone slipping in; that could be hard to catch. And if it's a legit attendee that could be a nightmare to track down."

"Would more cameras help?"

"Can't hurt, but may not help all that much." Scott can be maddeningly enigmatic at times. The cop thing again, I suppose.

"How are we going to do this, then?"

"Good question. I need to consult with Craig about it."

The company at booth seven hundred eight showed some kind of graphics-heavy software on a group of tablet computers in a variety of sizes. Two people were working the area. A woman was talking to a pair of customers, so I approached the other man. I introduced myself and Scott to him. He identified himself as the sales manager for the company.

"We were told you've had a theft from your booth," I said.

"Got to assume that's what happened," he answered. "Inventoried all our display models this morning and everything was there. But I went to demo on the MC HiTell 2600 this afternoon and realized it wasn't on the display shelf where it should've been. Shelly didn't have it either." He nodded to the woman talking to the customers.

"You didn't see anyone take it?" Scott asked.

"No."

"Did you see anyone other than yourselves pick it up or handle it?"

The man shook his head. "Didn't even see anyone looking at it particularly."

"Was there any time that the booth was left unattended?"

The man hesitated, and I wasn't sure if he was thinking back over it or trying to decide how to frame the answer. Finally he said, "Not that I can recall." I was pretty sure that wasn't exactly true, but there was no point in calling him on it right then.

"When was the last time you noticed it was there?" Scott asked.

"Probably a little after noon. I used it to demo our product to a group using several HiTell branded products, and I'm sure I put it back on the display shelf when I finished. After that things got busy and I wasn't paying close attention."

"What do you mean by 'branded'?" Scott asked.

"It's actually a MegaComp-manufactured machine, but HiTell makes some modifications of its own and resells them."

"Ah. I see." Scott asked a bunch more questions, trying to narrow down the time frame for the disappearance and what he and Shelly, the only representatives at the booth, had been doing for the afternoon.

We didn't really learn very much, though Scott managed to squeeze the time window down to about an hour from one-thirty to two-thirty. He got a description of the stolen device, then promised we'd do everything we could to find out what had happened and return their missing tablet.

"Ideas?" I asked Scott as we walked away.

"Are you busy right now?"

I glanced at my phone. For once there were no messages waiting. "Not at the moment."

"Let's go check some video."

I went with him upstairs to the security area, past the reception desk and down the hall that led to Craig's office. Across from it, Scott led the way into the room where a bank of monitors showed feeds from the security cameras. He sat down at a desk and turned on one that wasn't showing a picture right then, a flat panel screen the size of a smaller television or large computer monitor, so that we could both see it.

He typed in a couple of commands on the keyboard and chose from a dropdown menu, and a file. "Bit of luck. This camera was focused right on the seven hundred aisle, and since they're close enough to the front, the video should be fairly clear." When the video opened, he fast-forwarded through it, until he said, "This should be close to the right time."

He left the screen frozen for a moment as he located the booth, then ran the film at double speed, watching people come and go in the area. We watched the grainy video as the salesman demonstrated software on a tablet and then replaced it on a shelf of the display unit.

"No locks or fastening to the shelf. Not smart," Scott said. A few more people came and went in the booth, but the tablet sat on the display undisturbed. He fast-forwarded and stopped it a couple of times before we saw a shot that showed the shelf clearly empty.

I leaned in to peer more closely. "It's not there now."

Scott backed the video up rapidly, then edged it forward in increments. People went into the booth, talked to one or the other of the salespeople, and departed. Sometimes they came individually, sometimes in groups.

Several times a small crowd, large enough to engulf the booth and hide all the display shelves, gathered in the area.

After the first of those, when the people dispersed, and we could see the display again, the tablet was still there. Same with the second and third times. I kept watching as the female salesperson stepped away from the booth, taking a break, I supposed.

Moments later a group of three people approached. I thought they were all men, but couldn't be entirely sure. The image's resolution was too low for a really clear view.

Two of the three engaged the remaining salesman in the booth, maneuvering him so that his back was to the display shelf. The third one seemed to hang back, looking around. He blocked the camera's view of the tablet on display. After a few minutes, he moved away, while the salesman still spoke to the other two. I looked closer. "It's gone. He must've taken it with him."

Scott nodded and stepped the video back so we could watch it again. He stopped it after the man walked away and zoomed in on the frame, focusing on the shelf, until we could verify that the tablet was gone. Then he stepped it back, frame by frame.

Unfortunately, the man's back stayed toward the camera and his body mostly blocked our view of the display as well as whatever he was doing while standing there, looking at it. When the man walked away, he turned only enough that the camera got a quick, blurry glimpse of profile.

Scott backed up the video to the point of the men arriving. I'd thought at first all three came together, but on slower viewing, the first two walked into the scene and engaged the salesman, and the third one arrived moments later.

I looked at Scott. "Is this a group effort or someone piggy-backing on what others are doing?"

He shrugged. "Not clear. I wish we had better views of the other incidents."

"I wish we had a better view of the thief's face."

"That would be helpful," Scott admitted. He went back and forth on the video a couple more times, and finally stopped on the frame that offered the best view of the likely thief's face. He blew it up as much as possible, and used some other feature of the software to enhance the image. It still didn't show much—a snippet of nose, a fuzzy slice of cheek and jawbone, the corner of an eyebrow, and possibly a hint of short, dark hair. Scott hit a button to print the image out.

"What next?" I asked him. "I don't see that helping us much."

"No," he admitted. "I'd like to go back and talk to the people at the other booths who've reported thefts. From what you said, it didn't sound like this was a group operation, but it's hard to be sure. I'd like to know. It changes the dynamics considerably."

My phone buzzed again. It had done so a couple of times while we were looking at tape, but I didn't recognize the number so I'd ignored it. Whoever it was didn't want to talk to my voice mail.

"I'd better take this," I told him. "I'll be right back."

He went back to stepping through the video as I left the little room to answer the call in the hallway.

"Miss McNeil?" a young man's voice asked, but went on without waiting for a response. "This is Joel Halloway. You probably don't remember me, but I was working at the booth where you found that man's body?"

Since he framed it as a question and did wait for an answer this time, I said, "I remember. In fact, I've been hoping to talk to you."

"Good. I need to talk to you too. Can we meet tomorrow sometime?"

"Sure. I can meet you in the food court in the lobby for lunch."

He paused. "Lunch is fine, but I'd rather not do it there. Is there someplace nearby we can go?"

Despite a few misgivings, I arranged to meet him the next day at a café two blocks from the center. I would've preferred some place closer, but he was pretty adamant that he didn't want to be too close, so I agreed before I ended the call.

When I went back into the video room, Scott was pulling a flash drive out of the port.

"I've made a copy of the relevant piece of video," he said. "I want to run it by someone I know who's more of an expert on this."

Probably someone from his days as a police officer. I told him about Joel Halloway's request.

"Any idea why he wants to talk to you?" Scott turned off the machine he'd used to view the recorded video, leaving a couple of other monitors in the room showing near-deserted aisles on the show floor.

"Probably just wants to complain about the way SteadySafe treated him. I'm willing to listen only because I'm wondering how a man was murdered in the booth he was minding without his noticing anything."

Scott stood up and turned to face me. "Heather…" I heard the warning in his tone.

"Not just curiosity," I said quickly. "Potential liability issues, too."

He gave me a narrow frown that made his gray-green

eyes go icy cold. Scott can manage to look seriously hard and tough without even trying to. That side of him can be pretty intimidating.

"Honestly, I'm not playing Nancy Drew. I'm doing my job."

His expression didn't exactly soften, but some of the ice melted. "I can't help wondering why he wants to meet you off-site and won't say why."

"I am, too," I admitted. "I'm guessing he just doesn't want to run into any of the guys from SteadySafe. I don't suppose I'd want to either, in his position. But it's a public place and I promise to scream and run away at the first sign of a threat."

He stared at me a moment longer before his frown faded into a wry grin. "You are who you are," he said, his tone oddly ironic. "I'm hungry. Want to get something to eat?"

That grin, coming after the harshness, and the concern behind it were doing dangerous things to my hormones. I was definitely hungry and food was only part of it.

I checked my phone. It was five to six and there were no emergency messages. "Only if we split the tab," I said.

Something flickered across his face and was gone so fast I had no chance to read it. He shrugged. "All right. Chinese?"

"Sounds good to me."

It was good, too. We took our time, relaxing with a couple of glasses of wine before he drove me home. We lingered over the goodnights, too, and that was even better than dinner. For a while I forgot to worry about all the problems at work and wonder what Joel Halloway wanted to discuss.

ELEVEN

Thursday

THE NEXT MORNING I spent an hour or so going through email, messages on the land-line phone, and all the papers in my inbox. I made some progress on the paperwork, but I barely made a dent in the email box.

Janelle came in and we spent the next half hour discussing the rest of the supermodel event, which went well after we left, and the theft and what Scott and I had discovered.

"We need to get something out to warn people," I suggested to her. "They need to be careful about locking down valuable equipment."

"Carefully worded," Janelle said. "People are already on edge. We don't want to cause panic."

"True. That's your specialty. Careful wording, I mean. Not panic." I looked at her expression. "Okay. Time for me to get out of here and get back to work."

Janelle looked down at her desk. "I'll have a notice ready to distribute in an hour. By the way, the tech people came by yesterday, took some measurements, and said they couldn't find any problem with the wireless communications in the building. I'm about to have a further talk with them. In the meantime…"

She handed me a couple of slips of paper. I took them and glanced through, hoping there were no complaints about missing equipment. One of them was in a way, but fortunately not *that* way. A missing pair of glasses at twenty-two oh three. "Heading downstairs," I said. "Buzz me when it's ready."

She nodded absently.

First thing I did was stop at the lost and found cabinet in the security office and dig around. A hoodie, a sweater, another jacket, an empty wallet, a pair of nice leather gloves, one tennis shoe—huh?—several empty phone cases and a couple of chargers, a bracelet and assorted singleton earrings, one nice silver pen—kind of hoped that one went unclaimed—and various cheap trinkets. No glasses.

I headed downstairs to talk to the person who'd reported them missing. He was on the same aisle as the Gryphon-Loyall booth. I needed to stop in and talk to them after I finished with the straying glasses issue. I called the registration desk and maintenance on my way downstairs but no pair of stray glasses had been found or turned in. My phone buzzed as I made my way to the twenty two hundred aisle. Sam, one of the maintenance men, had found a pair of glasses the previous evening, but he'd stuck them in his pocket and forgotten about them. He agreed to meet me at the booth.

The company sold software for doing forms and surveys for websites, according to the banner. Two men, both on the far side of fifty, sat behind the long table that formed the front of their double-space booth. Both wore glasses, so either the missing ones belonged to someone else or one of them wore a back-up pair.

They looked up at me as I approached. One immediately launched into his sales lead-up. "You work with websites at all? If so, you'll love how fast and easy our page and form generators are and how they'll simplify your..." He trailed off as I shook my head and looked almost mournful when I identified myself as Center staff.

"We had a report of a lost pair of glasses," I said.

The other man suddenly looked more interested. "Have you found them?"

"Maybe."

I saw Sam approaching and waited until he got there. He held out a pair of the glasses. The interested man smiled broadly as he accepted them, took off the pair he wore, and put on the ones Sam gave him.

His smile broadened. "Yes, these are mine. Thank you!" He beamed at Sam and me. "This is wonderful. I was afraid I wouldn't get them back at all, and those others just aren't as good. I can't thank you enough." He reached under the table. "I'm sure you're not allowed to accept rewards, but how about one of our pens?" He held one out to each of us.

Sam, who knows my weakness, laughed. "Heather likes pens. A lot."

It was a pretty awesome pen, I had to admit. Standard imprinted ballpoint pen bottom, but the top was clear and filled with some kind of viscous liquid with globs of varying shades of blue floating in it. When the tip pressed against paper, it lit up, making the blue bubbles appear to be floating in a sea of light. "This is great. Thank you," I told him. Sam thanked them, too, and left.

"You're welcome. The least we can do." When I started to walk away, the first man stopped me. "Wait, please, Miss. Since you work here, can I ask you something? That young man, who was...killed. Have they figured out who did it?" He gave a sharp nod. "It's not just idle curiosity, you understand. Well, maybe it is, but we sort of knew him. I mean we'd seen him going up and down the aisle here a couple of times. Once he even stopped right there." He nodded toward the Gryphon-Loyall booth, diagonally across from his booth. "And he had a long, rather heated talk with one of the people working there. Not either of those." Keeping his hand flat on the table, he pointed toward Ted, who was demonstrating something on a laptop to a potential client, and an even younger man setting out a new bunch of flyers. "I don't see him right now. The one with the red hair."

I grappled for a moment before I came up with the name: Larry Barnes.

The other man in the booth followed up with, "It just seems too strange. Murder, I mean. That's something that happens to other people, in other places. Not to someone you know."

"Yeah. You see it on TV. Not in real life," the first man agreed. "But I hear it happened."

"It did," I said. "And it's pretty ghastly." As much to distract myself from following that thought as anything else, I said, "I gather Chase Markham was a rather volatile sort. He seems to have argued with a lot of people."

The man who'd lost the glasses blinked and rubbed at his temples. "This wasn't really an argument that I could tell, though that young man looked a bit upset about it."

Interesting but not my business, I reminded myself. I reassured the two men that the police were doing everything they could to find out who was responsible, then excused myself and tucked my new pen into a pocket.

My plan to go directly across the aisle to the Gryphon-Loyall booth was thwarted when I got a call from Tina with a couple of requests from other exhibitors. I directed one young woman to a local nail salon to deal with a manicure emergency, and intervened in a dispute between an exhibitor and a caterer. The first was easy. The second taxed my patience and diplomacy, but I think I managed a resolution that left them each equally irritated, resentful, and resigned.

My phone buzzed while I was still smoothing ruffled feathers, but I ignored it until we were done and some level of equanimity restored. Janelle left a message that the release about guarding property carefully was ready to distribute. I went up, got a stack of paper, and spent the next half hour helping to pass them out and trying my best not to get suckered into conversation.

With that done, I made my way back to the Gryphon-Loyall booth, with a couple of missions in mind. I wanted to check with Ted on his progress in locating the interference, and see if I could find out more from Larry about his discussion—argument?—with Chase. Neither Ted nor Larry was anywhere in sight, however. Instead I found a worried-looking Jennifer pacing one side of the booth. Since the young woman had almost sparkled with warmth and good humor every other time I'd seen her, the change was alarming. "What's wrong?" I asked when she gave me a strained smile.

She tried for her normal bright smile as she said, "Nothing, really. I'm just..." A sigh slipped out. "I don't know." The faux smile faded back into worry, but she drew a breath and looked around, checking for other potential customers, before she answered. "Oh, hell. It's Ted."

"What about Ted? Is he in trouble?"

"I don't know. Maybe. He's gone to talk to the police."

"I'm not surprised. I'm sure they're talking to everyone who knew Chase."

Jennifer shook her head. "It's more than that. He talked to them once before when they went around interviewing everyone. This is something worse. I'm pretty sure they suspect him of killing Chase."

"What? Why?"

"Chase and Ted had an argument on Monday. Ted might've even…made some threats."

"Like he might harm Chase?"

"Yes. I'm pretty sure…yes."

"Do you know what they were arguing about?"

Her fingers clenched tightly on the clipboard she carried. "Me, I think."

"You? Why?" Then I remembered. "You said Chase had harassed you before. Was Ted warning him off?"

Her voice cracked when she said, "I think so."

"It's a motive, but they must have more than that if they're seriously questioning him about it."

"I don't know what it is. But apparently it was a pretty loud exchange with Chase. And a lot of people saw it. Or heard it."

So why hadn't I heard about it before? And who did I think that I was? Miss-Needs-to-Know-Everything? "Chase was doing a lot of that on Monday. Was this before or after his blowup with Tom Hovey?"

"I'm not sure. Before, I think."

"And it was about you? Did Chase try to hit on you?"

She sighed. "He stopped me in the aisle near his company's booth early Monday morning. Said he had to talk to me. Right away. I told him we really didn't have anything to talk about. When I started to walk away, he grabbed my arm and tried to pull me aside. I got away from him and almost ran." She stopped for a shaky breath. "The thing is, we have a history. I made the mistake of dating him a couple of times. He pushed me a bit too far. After that he refused to accept it when I told him it was over. He had this delusion that I was just playing hard to get."

"You told Ted that Chase had grabbed you?"

"I wish I hadn't said anything." She held the clipboard close against her chest. "Of course, I don't think it was the only thing they were arguing about. Ted said it wasn't. In fact, he said it wasn't even the main thing. I'm not sure it's true, though. He might've been saying it to make me feel better."

"Seems to me it's more likely it's true," I said. "Ted had some sort of history with Chase, too. Other than you. Chase had a real talent for turning friends into enemies."

She gave me a lopsided, sad attempt at a grin. "True, that. Still, none of us would've done anything so extreme. Ted has a temper, but he wouldn't hurt anyone. Ever. I know people say that, and someone will do something crazy and you find out you didn't really know them at all, but with Ted I'm pretty sure it's true. He just wouldn't."

"I understand Larry had an argument with him, too, right here at the booth."

"That wasn't exactly an argument. Chase wanted Larry to do something for him, give him some kind of recommendation, I think, and Larry was like, 'What? Are you nuts? Why would I do that?' Chase wasn't happy about it, of course, but eventually he went away. That's what Larry said, anyway." She looked at me and shook her head. "He wouldn't kill Chase either. Not over something as stupid as that. Not over anything! Neither would Ted. There's just no way."

I wasn't as sure, but there wasn't any point in saying that to Jennifer. I didn't know Ted or Larry as well as she did, but I also knew—all too well—that people could do things you'd never guess when pushed hard enough. I did tell her it was too early to make any assumptions.

I was about to go when I remembered the main reason I'd come in the first place.

"Did the interference happen again yesterday afternoon?" I asked. "I didn't get a call from Ted, but I was tied up with other things."

"Yes, it did. Several times, but they were all too brief for Ted to get very far in chasing it."

I told her I needed to go, but something else occurred to me. "Did you all go to MegaComp's big announcement on Monday?"

"Ted and I did," she said. "But we went separately since I had to stop and say hello to one of our partners first. Larry manned the booth for us."

"Did Ted save you a seat?"

She hesitated a moment. "I didn't see him there."

So much for alibis, although maybe… "Did you see him right after?"

She shook her head. I should've expected it. The cops already knew all of this. They wouldn't be questioning Ted again if Jennifer had been with him after the talk. "Did he say where he was afterward?"

"No. He said he ran into someone, but he wouldn't say who." She paused for a moment and looked puzzled. "I hadn't thought of it before—we've stayed pretty busy—but that's odd. Ted's not usually so…what's the word?"

"Evasive?" I suggested.

"Yeah, that's it. Evasive. He's pretty much a what-you-see-is-what-you-get sort. Says exactly what he means." Her lips twisted in a wry smile. "It's one of our best selling techniques. Let Ted talk to the customers about the products he helped create. His enthusiasm and openness are very persuasive. But…" The smile disappeared, replaced by a thoughtful frown.

"What?"

"I don't know. Ted hasn't been quite himself, ever since Chase's death. We're all pretty shocked about it. Sad, even. I mean, he was a jerk, but still. But Ted's seemed more affected than I would've expected. Larry, too. Maybe even more so. He's been really down, and that's not like him at all. Anyway, it worries me."

That kind of worried me, too. It worried me even more that I got the feeling Jennifer had started to say something else and thought better of it. I wished I knew what it was. I hadn't seen anything in Ted that made him seem worried, but again I didn't know him as well as she did, and he almost certainly edited his behavior when I was around. I didn't want to add to her concern by pressing her.

"Is Larry here? May I have a word with him?"

Her lips twisted and she blinked a couple of times. For a moment I thought she might actually break down in tears. "No, he's not. And that's another thing. I don't know where he is. He said he had to talk to someone and went off. That was more than an hour ago." She sighed. "I'm going to kill him myself next time I see him." Her eyes widened. "Ohmigod. I didn't really mean it. Not that way. I wouldn't—"

"Easy. We all say things like that when we're upset. No doubt he got distracted by something or stopped to talk with someone and couldn't get away."

Her lips relaxed and the lines around her eyes eased a bit. "I'm sure you're right."

I felt my phone buzzing, which probably meant another assignment from Janelle.

I tried to sound reassuring when I said, "The police do know how to do their jobs, so I doubt Ted has anything to worry about. But let me know if you need anything. We'll do everything we can to help."

Jennifer offered that tight smile again. "Thanks."

I stopped a couple of booths down to take the call. It was indeed another complaint that required some feather-smoothing. The booth was several aisles over and I hustled that way since I was supposed to meet Joel for lunch in forty minutes. My destination threatened to be a huge distraction, however, featuring an extensive display of promotional merchandise. The imprinted key chains, luggage tags, folders, and other cheap giveaways didn't impress me much. The notepads would serve for scribbling on. The pens, however, tempted me to try out every single one. Well, okay, maybe not the really cheap stick pens in the bins in front. But there were some definite beauties behind those.

"What kind of promotional items do you buy?" The voice jerked me out of my preoccupation with some promotional pens. "We've got everything from inexpensive key chains and money clips to fine leather portfolios and superb pens. They can all be imprinted with your logo and text."

I looked up at the woman manning the booth. In her forties, she stood a little shorter than me and had hair dyed flaming red. Her lipstick matched her hair and the big, sparkly frames on her thick-lensed glasses completed the impression of a human firecracker. The brassy tone and attitude behind her words suggested a personality to match.

"I'm sorry," I said. "I'm not a customer. I'm Heather McNeil, assistant to the director of the Market Center. You have a problem?"

"Honey, don't you apologize. My mistake." She reached out a hand. "Michaelene Maxwell. Hell of a mouthful, isn't it? Most people call me Mimi. This is my company, Andover Promos. My life, in fact. *Tchotchkes*. But good quality ones." She looked left and right before she added, "Mostly." She rolled her eyes at the irony. "Anyway," she continued. "I guess you're here 'cause of my call earlier."

"Yes, Ma'am," I said.

She broke into loud laughter. "Aren't you the polite one! Wish I could teach my kids to be like that. Yes and no are the only answers I ever get from them, and a lot more no answers than yes answers at that. Kids got no respect." The woman shook her head, laughing at herself.

"Do you have a problem with the booth?" I asked.

"Not my booth. Them." She pointed back over her shoulder at one of the two booths behind hers. "They're a mess. They got these pyramids of boxes that look like they'll fall over if someone breathes hard on them. Add to that someone back there is an incredible klutz. They keep tripping over things, banging into the wall. Once they hit it hard enough to jar one of my shelves and the bins fell off. You can imagine how much fun it was sorting all those key chains and candy tins again."

I followed her line of sight. At least a dozen bins on temporary shelving held sample key chains, pins, and metal boxes in various shapes and sizes. Under the overhead fluorescent lights they winked and gleamed in metallic splendor.

"I don't know how much I can do," I admitted.

"There's no real cure for either klutzy or messy. I'll talk to them, see if they can move some of their stuff so it's not so close to the back of your booth. Ask them to be a bit more careful."

"I'd appreciate it. I almost came to words with one of them yesterday. Brash young man tells me it's not his fault my stuff gets jarred every time he bangs into the back wall. All I could do to keep from telling him to mind his manners. Love to see how much he'd get jarred if I happened to 'accidentally' fall into him."

I couldn't help it. I had to smile at the mental picture that evoked. But… "That wouldn't be a good idea, for several reasons."

Her laugh was harsh, almost raucous. "Oh, I know that. Wouldn't actually do it, but I got some satisfaction from thinking about it."

I couldn't quite smother my own grin, until I thought about the talk I'd need to have with the guys in the other booth. And… "I have to meet someone for lunch now," I said. "But I promise I will talk to them later today."

"Thanks. Hey, I saw you looking at the pens." She took one of the nicest pens out of a basket in the back row and handed it to me. When I hesitated, she said, "Might as well take it honey. I gotta give all this away. Don't plan to ship it all back again. Unless the company has a policy about taking gifts?"

"We can't accept anything worth over fifty dollars."

She cracked a loud, brassy laugh. "Take it, honey. I'm not saying any of our stuff is cheap, mind you, but that thing ain't worth anywhere near fifty dollars."

I thanked her, took the pen, and headed for the exit. I had two minutes to get to the restaurant down the street.

I needn't have hurried. Joel Halloway called as I was

trotting down the sidewalk toward the café and said he was running late. He swore it would only be about ten minutes and asked if I'd get a table in the most private corner I could find. *Paranoid, much?* I wondered. Of course he might have good reason for that caution, which meant I had good reason to reconsider whether this was a smart thing to do at all.

"You mind if I go ahead and order?" I asked. "With the show going on, I don't have a lot of time for lunch."

"Go ahead," he said. "I'll get there as quickly as I can."

I'd set to work on roast beef and Swiss cheese on a baguette by the time he entered twenty minutes later. He looked so different in jeans and a tee shirt it took me a moment to recognize him. If it weren't for the wild strawberry blond curls, I might not have. I waved at him since he had to pick out someone he barely knew. Before he joined me, he did a careful survey of the room. Checking for spies or enemies?

He was starting to creep me out, but he wore a cheerful smile by the time he sat and said, "Hi. Heather. I'm Joel. Thanks for coming. And for staying. I'm really sorry I'm late. I got delayed on the Metro. Glad to see you ordered." The words tumbled out in a rush that only stopped when a young waitress approached. Without consulting the menu he asked for a Reuben sandwich and a Coke.

"You sounded like it was pretty important that we talk," I said after swallowing a big bite and almost choking as I got a mouthful of horseradish along with the roast beef and cheese. I had to take a long drink from my own soda to soothe the burn.

"You okay?" he asked, seeing my distress, then continued before I could explain my singed taste buds. "It is important. To me, at least. There's some strange stuff going on at SteadySafe and I don't want to end up being the fall guy for whatever shit comes down as a result."

"What kind of stuff?" I asked. "And what do you think I can do about it?"

"I don't actually know what kind of stuff," he admitted. "I was only there for a few hours, but I definitely got the idea there were things... Well, like there were these awkward breaks in conversation whenever they realized I was close enough to hear them. Guys would just quit talking. And there were some papers they didn't want me to see either."

He paused while the waitress set his drink on the table and promised his sandwich would be out shortly. "But all that could be okay. I mean I realize they might have business secrets to keep. Right? But then that guy was killed, and they... I don't know, exactly. They just sort of flipped out."

"A lot of people did quite a bit of flipping out," I pointed out. "Me included. Murder tends to upset people."

"Yeah, I know, but their reaction just seemed too... too much, somehow. I mean, first of all they were all over me for not paying attention to the booth and letting it happen, but it's not true. I was never more than a few feet from the booth all day, but mostly I was right there in it. I was never so far away I wouldn't have heard, like, a fight or something."

"I'm not sure there was much of a fight," I said. "And it was incredibly noisy in here that day."

"True that, but still..." He stopped long enough to take a drink. "He was strangled, right? If there wasn't a fight, then someone must've snuck up on him. I mean, even if he knew the person, if he saw it coming, he would've struggled and fought back. Things were knocked over back there, so there must've been something."

"There's that," I agreed. "And he did struggle some, but not much. I don't think he saw or heard it coming until whoever did it was right on top of him. Or behind him." Thoughts clashed, one piece of knowledge trying to connect to another.

"But it did look like there was a fight in the back space," Joel reminded me. "Things were knocked over. How did I *not* hear that?"

"It was pretty loud in here. But there *were* noises when he was killed. A couple of loud ones."

Joel gave me a sudden, surprising smile. "So it's true. You were on the phone with him when he was killed. I'd heard that rumor. That's why I wanted to talk to you."

"And you were the person closest to the body when I found it. That's why I wanted to talk to you." I gave him a sharp look. "I'm willing to trade information, but I'm also suspicious. You tell me the real reason you're here, and I'll share my hidden motivation."

He laughed harshly. "Look, I'm not into playing amateur detective or anything," he said. "Don't have time and don't have the interest. My bottom line is I worry they're going to complain to the temp agency that I wasn't doing my job and watching the booth. I've got a good thing going with this temp company, and I don't want Steady-Safe messing it up. I can prove that I was there the entire time, but my witnesses are people at this thing who'll be going home in a week. I need someone local who can verify it for me."

As motivation went, it made sense, although I had

an idea there was more to it. Maybe ensuring that he wasn't considered a murder suspect himself? "Okay," I said. "Here's my secret agenda. I *am* playing amateur detective."

His eyes widened and he opened his mouth to say something, before I laughed and added, "Kidding. Mostly. The serious part is that the Center wants to do everything we can to help the police catch the killer. Fast, because there isn't much time. The show ends on Sunday. It looks really bad for us if there's no arrest or anything by then."

"Yeah, I can see that," he agreed.

"So what do we know now?" I asked.

"Not all that much, really. You heard a noise on the phone, right? And the cops honed in on where I was in the booth between three and three twenty, so I'm assuming that's when it must've happened. The thing is, I was in the booth, and yes, it was noisy, but it wasn't so noisy I wouldn't have heard a fight in the back. There was a chair flipped over. I should've heard that even with the carpet. Why didn't I?"

An idea began taking shape, growing in my mind. "It doesn't add up, does it? Something crashed pretty loudly, and I'm pretty sure it was metal against a hard surface like a chair hitting the floor or a table collapsing. Only there's carpet on the floor in all the booths. And then there was another noise that I think was his phone hitting something when he dropped it. And you didn't hear anything, even though you were nearby at the time. I'm sure the police asked you this and checked on your answer. You said there are people who can vouch for your being in the booth at the time."

"They asked. I answered. You probably don't remember this, but there are two booths across the aisle from the open side of SteadySafe. There was someone in each of them all afternoon. I even talked to them for a bit. They could see me the whole time."

"Did you go into the back area any time while the others were gone and you were watching the booth?"

He waited while the waitress delivered his sandwich. He took a big bite, chewed and swallowed. "Before you got there, I only went in the back area once, to get a book out of my bag and a bottle of water. That was a bit after two. There wasn't any reason to go back there again."

I was kind of thinking out loud when I said, "There was carpet on the floor so it would have been hard for almost anything to make the crash I heard on the phone, unless it was the chair hitting the table, which I don't think was that first sound I heard. But you didn't hear anything at the time, which is pretty unlikely when you were so close. Since there are witnesses that you were in the area, then the only conclusion is that he wasn't really killed there."

"That's my suspicion."

"Gilmont already figured that out," I said, mostly to myself. "That's what he was hinting at. He must've seen right away that the scene didn't match my report of the phone call. Come to think of it, the whole set up did look a bit staged. Everything was kind of neatly placed on the floor, but it didn't really look random. Dang. How did I miss that?"

"You were a little upset at the time," Joel pointed out. "But the real question is, if he was killed somewhere else and dumped in our booth, where was it, and how did they get him to the SteadySafe booth without anyone seeing it?"

"Actually, the second one's not hard at all. I wonder if Gilmont figured that out, too?"

Joel frowned at me. "Explain how someone could drag the dead body of a grown man around the show floor in the middle of the day and sneak it into the back of my booth without anyone noticing?"

"Big box and a hand truck. There were plenty of both around on Monday. Wherever the murder happened, the killer must've stuffed the body into a box and then used a hand truck to transport it to your booth. He got in by one of the flaps in the back. I assume there are flaps in the back. I didn't really look too close, but most booths have them. He just wheels the hand truck over to the side on the back aisle, out of your line of sight, and slides the box in quietly on the carpet, arranges everything so it looks like there was a struggle there and leaves. He could've done it in five minutes. Maybe less."

Joel nodded. "And given all the noise that day, he could easily have done it without my hearing a thing."

"I wonder if the choice of the booth was random."

"It's handy. On an end, and two blocks wide. Easy to get in on the back side with no one on this side seeing anything."

"And if anyone else saw it, they wouldn't have given it a second thought. People were transporting stuff all over the floor. I'll bet the cops have already asked. But what if it wasn't random? Maybe someone had a reason to throw suspicion on the SteadySafe people? Some of them knew Chase. And didn't like him."

"Maybe that's why they're freaking out about it so much," Joel agreed.

"Can you remember specifics about what they said or what they were worried about?"

"Not really. Some of it was just that they were worried because people knew they hadn't liked the dead guy.

Particularly Shawn. Apparently he'd said some things about the guy that made him look bad. And then there was some technical deal—no idea what it was all about, but there was some connection between Shawn and the dead guy that had him worried."

"You told all this to the police?"

"Hell to the yeah, I did. I was afraid for a while they were suspecting me. I was there and I claimed I hadn't heard anything but there was a dead guy back there on my watch. Don't even blame them for looking at me, but then it wouldn't make sense. I didn't know the guy at all. I was a temp. I didn't even know what most of those people were talking about half the time."

"You live around here?" I asked.

"Just off Van Ness. I'm working on a doctorate in history at American University. I've got a grant but I pick up temp jobs to pay for gas and rent. This one was definitely not worth it. I'll bet those assholes try to worm out of paying the agency for my time."

"It wouldn't entirely surprise me," I admitted.

"But the police know there were witnesses who can confirm I was there the whole time," he said. "And now you do, too. So if there is a complaint, I can refer them to you."

"I'll have to check it out with the cops before I can verify anything," I warned.

"Sure." He looked around again as though checking to see if anyone watched us. "You should keep this in mind. Those guys at SteadySafe? Wouldn't want to say any one of them killed him, but I'll bet Shawn knows something about it. Maybe something about why he was killed. And he's really, really worried."

TWELVE

I HAD A lot to think about on the way back to the Center, but I also had three messages on my phone for things that needed following up on, and one from Scott, wanting to be sure I was okay. I returned that last call on my way back and filled him in on the gist of the conversation with Joel. Scott pretty much agreed with the conclusions we'd come to and urged me to let Detective Gilmont know, even though he had likely already figured it out.

I assured him I would and made a mental note to call Gilmont later. On arriving back at the Center, I plunged right into the chaos of the Business Technology Expo. After a stop to check that a wonky electrical connection had been repaired, I was on my way to Mimi Maxwell's booth when the phone buzzed.

"We've got interference again," Ted said. "I'm near the twelve hundred aisle."

"I'll meet you there," I told him, and reversed direction. The show floor had gotten emptier and quieter, which puzzled me until I remembered that NovaCyn was doing their product introduction assisted by Lilya. I was betting security was a lot better prepared for today's event. I was also betting that ninety percent of the people attending that announcement weren't especially interested in whatever NovaCyn was debuting. But that wasn't my problem, thank goodness.

I met Ted at the twelve hundred aisle. He was staring down at the instrument he held and would have walked right into me if I hadn't side-stepped and grabbed his arm. He jolted out a reverie that might not have much to do with the readout on the device he watched.

"Sorry. Not paying attention. Oh. Heather. Yes, sorry." He shook himself and tried for a smile, but it looked more like a grimace. "We've got interference again. Or at least we did. It's gone now."

"Already?" I sighed. "This is so frustrating! The show's almost half over and people are griping. I hope we can find it before the end."

"I've got it localized to this block," he said, pointing toward the large booths between the one thousand and eleven hundred aisles at the back of the hall.

I stared down the row. A mid-sized telecom, a distributor of printers and fax machines, an IT services group, a couple of other small software vendors, and Schwartz-Mann GmbH, my current least-favorite German company. "Is there any way to tell this close?"

"Not until it starts up again. But next time we should be able to localize it." He stared at the little machine for a moment more, then looked up at me. "Heather…"

I waited, but after a few seconds he shrugged, which drew my attention to his chest. Today's tie was blue with an odd, asymmetrical pattern of strings of letters. No, they were numbers, I realized on a closer look. Ones and zeroes.

I pointed to the tie. "I'm totally a non-geek, but even I know that's got to be binary."

His grin was more subdued than before.

"Does it mean something?"

His grin broadened. "Yup. It says, 'Ties suck.'"

I laughed. "Wonderful." And then after a beat, I added, "What's wrong?"

"Nothing. I'm fine. Oh heck, no, of course, I'm not fine. I'm pretty sure the cops think I killed Chase, and I don't know how to convince them I didn't."

I considered for a moment before I said, "I need a cup of coffee. I'll bet you could use one, too."

We followed our noses to the nearest booth with coffee, which was only an aisle over. Once we each had a cup of a wonderfully aromatic Colombian, I took him to a small conference room down the hall from the show floor.

"You know technically you don't have to prove anything to them. They're supposed to be the ones doing the proving," I said.

"I know." He stared into the coffee cup for a moment. "But I think they're pretty satisfied that they can."

"Why?"

He took a drink of coffee and his face tightened. "I had a fight with Chase the day he was killed."

"Seems like Chase was doing a lot of arguing that day. What was it about?"

"It started about Jen and his hitting on her. But then it got into…this is kind of a trade secret thing, so I have to ask you not to share this with anyone." He waited for my response.

"Do the police know?" I asked.

"Yes."

"Then I don't see why I should have to tell anyone else."

He took a deep breath before he said, "I knew there

was a flaw in one of the communication assemblies he'd designed."

I considered that for a moment. "Obviously that's not a good thing, but just how bad is it?"

"I don't know, exactly. I don't know what it was installed in. I'm not even sure what it would do. I have my suspicions, but nothing I can prove."

"Say it was installed. What kind of harm could it cause?"

"Again it depends on what he's done with it. It might not cause any problems, or it could cause a catastrophic failure. One that would be hard to diagnose because it would probably cause a cascade of problems. I suppose it could represent a potential security breach, too, if someone knew about it."

"How do you know this?"

"Larry worked with him at Timmer, and he introduced us at one of last year's shows. We'd talked about the system. He even asked me about the problem and we talked about possible solutions. He'd started it when he was with Timmer, though they didn't accept the design he proposed then. When I heard what he'd done at Silo-Systems, before RTX bought them out, I figured it had to be the same thing or at least based on the same ideas. I asked him if he'd worked out the processor communication issue, but he kind of evaded the question. Said the issue wouldn't come up now. I wasn't sure what to make of that. Did he find a way to circumvent the problem rather than fix it?"

"Why'd you argue with him about it?"

He hesitated. "I thought it was irresponsible to use a design he knew was flawed. Even if it was a really good idea. Pretty ingenious, in truth, and brilliant if he could work out that last communication issue, but…"

I watched him sip his coffee. I liked the guy and didn't want to think he might've killed Chase Markham. I couldn't see the technical angle as a motive, but I rather suspected his feelings for Jennifer were stronger than he wanted to let on, and that could provide one. I was willing to bet Gilmont had picked up on that as well.

"So you argued with Markham about a design flaw, and you don't have an alibi for the time he was killed. That would make the cops take a closer look, but I doubt that it's enough for them to do any more."

"It was a pretty loud argument and a lot of people heard it. Come to think of it—" He stopped abruptly and set down the coffee sharply. "One of the people who overheard part of the argument was his boss at RTX. Can't remember his name, but I have this picture of a dragon in my mind."

"Drake Galloway?"

"Yeah, that's him. I knew there was some kind of link to dragons. Anyway, I looked up and he wasn't too far away. I think Chase saw him, too. Galloway looked kind of blank, shocked maybe, and Chase got sort of gray. Not sure why. Galloway must have known the thing had issues when he bought the company, but he kept Chase on. I understand he was the only one from Silo they did keep. Chase said loudly, and now that I think about it, I'm sure it was for his boss's benefit, that he'd found a solution to the problem. I kind of left it at that. I didn't like having everyone see me argue with him. And…" He shrugged. "Never mind."

"What?"

"He and Larry had some kind of falling out. I don't

know what all of that was about. Larry won't talk about it. But I'm sure he told the cops. Maybe it was about Jennifer, too."

Something in his tone on the last couple of sentences told me he didn't think that was it at all. In fact I'm not sure any of that was what he'd originally started to say.

"Okay," I said. "It still doesn't sound like something that would make the police suspect you any more than the other people he spoke to that morning."

"I hope you're right."

He sounded so dubious I was even more convinced there was something he wasn't telling me. "Ted, I need to know the whole truth if I'm going to help."

"There are some things I suspect, but they concern other people and I don't have any evidence, so it's not fair to point fingers."

I gave him a raised eyebrow, but he shook his head.

"Okay." I sighed to show him I wasn't exactly happy about his reticence. "We'll do what we can to help, but that may not be much. But if that's all the police have to tie you to the murder, I don't see them pursuing it. Do you know how Chase died?"

"I've heard he was strangled. I'm… I'm not sure what to say about it. I didn't like him much, but I'd never do something like that."

"Can you think of someone who might've hated him that much?"

"Plenty of people didn't like him, but it seems like it would take something more than that to drive someone to kill him. We had an argument, but even his harassing Jen wouldn't be enough to make me strangle him." He paused. "I'm not sure I could do it if I wanted to. Doesn't it take a good bit of strength to strangle someone with your bare hands? And wouldn't he fight and struggle?"

"I suppose so." I wondered if he was being disingenuous, pretending he didn't know how Chase had died. But it occurred to me that there were a couple of angles I hadn't considered, including the possibility that the motives for Chase's murder might not have been as straightforward as him having a fight with someone. I'd assumed killing him was a spur-of-the-moment sort of thing— at least until I realized the body had been moved. But even that was possible for someone who'd gotten so fed up he couldn't take any more. And I supposed that was still possible. But it was beginning to feel like the killer had spent some time planning it. I remembered Chase had seemed surprised to see the person who'd arrived at wherever he was. And since he'd just returned my call, he likely hadn't expected anyone. Or maybe he had, but the person either wasn't who he expected or was early for a meeting.

He'd honked off a lot of people, but being irritated with someone still isn't a good motive for murder. Heck, there wouldn't be many people still alive if people went around killing everyone who bothered them. So what would've caused someone to go to the trouble to murder Chase?

"Anyway, Chase was skinny, but he was taller than me and probably stronger," Ted added.

The words startled me out of my introspection. I finished the last of my coffee. "There's a lot we still don't know about Chase and why he was killed. I keep getting hints that there was more going on with him than most people knew about. Some people were afraid of him and others really angry with him. No one's been very straightforward about why."

Ted looked startled. To hide his reaction he picked up his nearly empty cup and drained the dregs. He grimaced at the bitter taste. "Chase was a disruptor. In a bad way. He liked to shake things up, but he tended to leave things worse rather than better once the dust settled."

"That's not the way I'd want to be remembered," I said.

"Me either," Ted agreed.

"One thing more. I understand Larry had words with him, too, that morning."

He gave me a wary glance. "Yeah. Chase came by the booth not long after the floor opened Monday morning. I don't exactly know what that was all about. Some kind of deal left over from when they worked together before, I think. Larry wasn't very happy about it, whatever it was."

My intuition was buzzing, telling me this was the something that Ted didn't want to talk about and he might be lying or at least not telling the whole truth. "Larry's not a tech guy," I said, speculating out loud. "So what kind of deal could he have going with Chase?"

"You'd have to ask Larry about that. It's probably another of Chase's crazy schemes he was trying to get Larry to buy into. He wanted to form his own company when SiloSystems was bought out, but nobody would sign on, so he gave it up and stayed with RTX. Maybe he was trying again with that. I know he wasn't all that happy with RTX." He sighed and stood up. "I'd better be getting back."

We walked back to the show floor and went our separate ways. I needed to find some way to have a private talk with Larry Barnes. I really wanted to have a talk with Sandy, too, but when I went by the RTX booth, she and Galloway were both involved in demonstrating something to a client.

A quick check of my phone showed no new messages so I headed for Mimi's booth, but turned to the one behind it on the right.

The booth was a mess—sloppy, disorganized, and scruffy looking. Most exhibitors go to great lengths to make the best possible impression on potential customers. Their booths tend to be gorgeously designed, beautifully decorated, and pristinely organized. In fact, spots on the carpet and banners not hanging straight are the most common complaints I deal with.

The Culbert and Braithwaite area had a professional looking backdrop. Sweeping images of gadgets glided across its surface, looping in and out of the company logo, which was the name in a fancy, curvy font. Beyond that, though, the space appeared to have been thrown together at the last minute, with emphasis on "thrown." The one long table that fronted the booth had no cover and only a couple of racks for papers on it. Boxes, small display cutouts, papers, and parts lay scattered haphazardly across the surface. Around the table, stacks of extra sell sheets, manuals, and brochures rose in various places, with several leaning against the backdrop, others at the side barriers and a few randomly dropped wherever the person moving them happened to be standing at the time.

Against the side wall that stood between their booth and Mimi's, three towers of boxes teetered in irregular, ragged shapes. The one on the left tipped to the side like the leaning tower of Pisa, and the other two appeared only slightly more stable. Boxes stuck out from the sides of each in random cantilevers. We didn't tell anyone how to decorate their booth or what it had to look like as long as they abided by the Center's rules, but I'd never seen one this messy before. Water bottles and coffee cups, some empty, some still holding liquids, sat on the table and floor, as well as on two blocks protruding from the stacks of boxes.

I stood there for several breaths before the lone young man sitting on a folding chair near the back wall looked up from his book and noticed me. He stood so fast the chair almost tipped over backwards. He grabbed it before it could teeter into the closest stack of boxes, and in the process came within a fraction of an inch of knocking over the water bottle on the floor beside the chair.

"Miss…er, Ma'am," he said, pushing hair back off his forehead while the color rose in his cheeks. "Sorry. I was…er, distracted. Are you interested in hearing about our services?"

"No, I'm sorry." I explained about being Center personnel and he managed not to look too crestfallen. A bit of worry crept in, though.

"Are you here about the booth?" he asked. "I mean, I know it's a bit of a disaster. But we've had some issues. Hell, more than issues. Everything that could go wrong has. The director of marketing was supposed to be here to supervise, but he took another job two weeks ago and last Friday was his last day. Then his assistant was supposed to take over but she came down with the flu over the weekend, so it's been me and one of the inside sales guys. We were the only ones who could manage to come at the last minute. We didn't even know how to set up the booth. Those guys across the way helped us out and showed us how to unfold it and put it all to-gether. And we've got twenty of each of our four models of routers, six varieties of ports and two switchboxes, all in their boxes, and we're not sure what the hell we're supposed to do with any of them. Let's don't even talk about all the brochures and sell sheets and order forms." He shrugged. "Hey, at least we did figure out we were supposed to dump the candy in the dishes and put them on the table to attract people. Wish someone would've told us what to do with the rest!"

Without bragging, I think I can safely say that I'm rarely speechless. I'm used to dealing with all sorts of ar-guments and problems. I'd never heard anything like this before, though, and for a couple of moments I couldn't think what to tell him.

"Have you tried calling whoever's taken over your marketing department for suggestions?" I asked.

"There is no marketing department." The words got louder as his frustration boiled over. "It was just the di-rector and his assistant. I suppose the assistant will take over, but they tell me that yesterday she was in the hos-pital getting extra fluids or something. I've been trying to reach the head of sales for two days but he's on the road and hasn't returned my calls." The last few words were loud enough to echo along the aisle.

"Hey!" I put a finger across my lips to try and quiet him down. People around had turned to check out the disturbance.

He looked chagrined. "Sorry. I'm just so way out of my depth here. I mean I can give you a run-down of our services and products, if you want, and really, they're pretty good, but figuring out how all this sales stuff is supposed to work is not in my job description. Not even in the same zip code. And then we've got that witch in the next booth who keeps complaining about our stuff falling on her side and bumping her shelves full of junk."

At least he'd lowered his voice, so probably no one heard that but me.

"About the witch next door," I said. "And everyone in all the other booths around you. They're exhibitors here, too, and they paid for their booths just like your company did. They deserve the courtesy of being able to conduct their business without your problems interfering. I totally understand and sympathize with your issues, but you can't let those affect the people around you."

He looked angry for a minute and I expected to be blasted, but then he drew a long breath and let it out slowly. "In other words, we need to clean up our act. And our booth?"

"More or less. The Center doesn't really care how you choose to decorate your booth—or not decorate it in this case. As long as what you're doing doesn't violate the law or safety codes, and doesn't interfere with anyone else, it's not our problem. Having stacks of your merchandise falling on your neighbors' booths is, though. Having your papers flying away and scattering all over is. You get the picture."

"I guess I do." He gave me a wry grin. "I wonder if you can maybe recommend someone we could hire really quick to help us out? A temp who would maybe know how to set up a booth like this? Or at least someone who could help us keep up? We really need one more person here. My bud over there and I have to trade off lunch and bathroom breaks."

"I don't know how good he is with displays, but I do

know someone who may be available to help out. Hold on a moment."

I found Joel Halloway's number on my phone and gave him a call. He was interested in the job, so I gave the number to the frustrated young man. I walked away a couple of minutes later, feeling like I'd at least done something to help them out. I hoped they'd take my warning about interfering with their neighbors seriously.

As I turned away, I had an idea. I passed Mimi's booth, going around the center end of the aisle. When I got to the other side, out of sight of the guys I'd just talked to, I caught her eye and gestured for her to come over.

"I talked to the guys behind you on the other side," I told her. "They've got problems." I filled her in on what they'd told me. "Don't let them know I talked to you about this, but if you get a chance and they'll let you, they'd probably be grateful for some suggestions about better ways to organize and decorate their booth. They're not marketers and they're pretty much at sea here."

I could see the wheels grinding behind Mimi's sparkly glasses. A customer stopped at her booth, so she had to cut it short, but she said she'd see what she could do for them.

I looked at the time and was stunned to see that it was almost four and that there were no new messages on my phone. I headed back to the RTX booth. This time I found Sandy in the booth, apparently by herself.

She gave me a strained smile. "It's Heather, isn't it?" she asked, trying to focus on my badge. "Sorry, I'm terrible with names."

When I asked if she had a few minutes to talk, she hesitated and glanced toward the opening to the back area of the booth. I guessed that meant Galloway was back there and could possibly hear us. I lowered my voice when I asked, "Do you get a break? Could we go get a drink?"

She nodded, but asked very quietly, "Can I meet you in the lobby in ten minutes?"

THIRTEEN

Thursday

"It is Heather, right?" Sandy asked after she sat down opposite me, holding a large iced tea. Her brown eyes were both wary and eager. "Thanks for this. I really needed a break. This is my first time at something like this, and I had no idea what it would be like. What a zoo! In a good sort of way, I guess. Except for Chase. That's… I don't even know what to say. I didn't know him all that well, but it's still shocking and sad. And having the booth trashed. If it hadn't been for all of that, I might have enjoyed the show. I think. It's exciting, but kind of overwhelming. I walked around the whole thing yesterday and my head was swimming by the time I got halfway through. I don't know how you handle this day after day, week after week." She rocked from side to side and rolled her eyes in a good imitation of someone getting a bit loopy.

I laughed. "It can be like the proverbial three-ring circus, only with dozens of rings. It isn't always this crazy here, though. Most of our events aren't this big. But you need to take those breaks or it will wear you out. How's business been at your booth?"

"Pretty good, I think. We've written several good orders. But I wonder if people aren't coming by more out of curiosity than anything else. I mean, everyone asks about Chase and what happened, and what do we know, and what are the police doing. I think some of them give us an order just because they feel guilty or something for taking up our time." Her expression changed, darkening into something more serious. "Do you like working for the Center? I imagine it can be a pretty hard job."

Change of topic or a segue into whatever she really wanted to say? "Most of it I like very much, but it has its share of not-fun stuff. What about you?"

She fiddled with her cup, pushing the straw down through the plastic top and then pulling it up again. "Mostly the same I guess. It's been kind of tense, lately, though, and I'll bet that's what you want to ask me about." She looked up at me, her eyes silently begging me to pursue it.

"It is. I got the impression not everything was going too well at RTX."

"Do you work with the police?" she asked, the question oddly abrupt.

"As much as we need to."

"If I told you something, something that I maybe should've told them but didn't, would you have to pass it on?"

"It depends. I can't withhold information crucial to the investigation of a murder. But if it's something that's not relevant, then I don't see why I'd need to share it."

She pushed the straw down again and took a short drink from her tea. "I'm not sure if it's relevant or not, and I could get in a lot of trouble even for talking about it. But someone needs to know in case it has something to do with what happened to Chase."

"How about this? Whatever it is, I'll tell the police only if I think it's relevant, and then I'll just say that someone else told me. I won't tell them who told me until we know if the information is important enough to need confirmation."

Sandy bit her lip. "Okay." She glanced left and right and even twisted to see who was behind her. "There was a lot of tension between Chase and Drake after RTX bought out SiloSystems. Most of it was over money, of course. The thing is, we work in a small office, and I can hear pretty much everything that goes on. I don't mean to eavesdrop; I just can't help it. Anyway, from the arguments I heard, I think SiloSystems had promised Chase a pretty big bonus once his design was approved and went into production. But it must have been a verbal promise. I don't think there could've been a written agreement or Drake would've had to pay out. So Drake bought the company before the thing went into production, and maybe he didn't even know about the promise…"

It didn't sound like she really believed that, but she had to give her boss some benefit of the doubt.

"Anyway, the bonus wasn't paid, or at least it wasn't near as much as SiloSystems had promised, and Chase was seriously pissed off. He and Drake had a huge, shouting fight over it. I guess Drake must've offered something to calm him down since Chase didn't walk out or hand in his resignation. I have no idea what. And it didn't really make either of them very happy. The tension between them was like a cloud of smoke or something. You could practically see it every time they even looked at each other."

"But there wasn't another fight?"

"Not exactly. A lot of snide words, though. Mostly from Chase. I think Drake was relieved that they managed some kind of accommodation, but Chase really wasn't happy about it."

I waited to see if she'd add anything, but that was it, so I said, "You already know the cops are going to consider this relevant to their investigation, don't you?"

She sucked in a huge draft of air and let it out. "I guess I do. Is there any way you can keep my name out of it?"

"I don't know. I'll try. If I do have to tell them the source, I'll try to let you know about it first."

"I hope you don't have to, but I'd appreciate the warning if you do."

"Okay. How did *you* get along with Chase? He had kind of a reputation for hitting on female co-workers."

Vivid color flamed in her cheeks. "Yeah, he did at first. But I already have a guy, and when I told him that, he backed off. I got the idea there's someone else he's really hot for, and I'm pretty sure she's here."

I was pretty sure of it, too.

"Did Chase have any other friends among the people here? I know he argued with several people, so he knew some of them, but was there anyone he was friends with?"

Sandy looked blank for a moment. "He mentioned a couple of people he needed to talk to. I don't know if they were friends or not, and I only know their first names, but he mentioned someone named Shawn and someone named Larry."

"I have no idea." I didn't want to mention that her boss seemed like a better candidate. Drake Galloway had a possible motive for killing Chase. Maybe there was some kind of written agreement about the bonus, or witness to it, that Chase could drag in. He might be able to bleed Drake dry. Or if there wasn't a written agreement about ownership of Chase's brilliant but flawed design, Chase could threaten to sell it to someone else.

Then I remembered what Ted had said about Galloway overhearing part of their argument. If Galloway hadn't known that the design was flawed before, that could explain his apparent shock at what he'd heard. It might even be a stronger motive.

"Did you and Drake go to the MegaComp announcement on Tuesday?"

"Drake did. He'd heard about the argument Chase had with Tom Hovey and said he'd better go check out what the competition had stolen." She stopped and thought about it. "That's interesting, isn't it?"

I nodded and asked, "Did he come right back? He wasn't there when I came to ask you for Chase's number."

"He came back, but he got a message on his cell, and left again. Said he had to talk to someone. I didn't see him again until about twenty minutes before the police arrived to tell us Chase was dead."

"I'm sure they had some questions for both of you."

"A lot of them. Drake spent more time with them than I did."

"You didn't tell them about Drake's argument with Chase, though."

"I didn't think…" She stopped and sighed. "No. I'm not even sure why I didn't, except that I was pretty sure Drake wouldn't want me to, and the whole business was kind of a company secret. I realize now that was a mistake."

And I'm the way you're clearing your conscience, I thought.

She looked at her watch and jumped. "I'd better get

back to the booth. Thanks for listening! Please do let me know if you have to give them my name."

I stayed seated while she walked away. I pulled out my phone and checked time and messages. Four-forty and there were two texts from Janelle. Neither looked urgent, so instead I searched for Detective Gilmont's number. I'd just found it when the phone startled me by buzzing to announce an incoming call from Scott.

"Heather? Better get over here. Twenty-two ten. We may have another missing person."

FOURTEEN

Thursday

THE BOOTH NUMBER sounded familiar but it wasn't until I turned into the aisle that I realized why. It was Gryphon-Loyall.

Ted, Jennifer, and the older man I'd met on Monday were gathered in a circle near one side of the open area, along with Scott and Janelle.

"We haven't seen or heard from Larry since this morning," Ted said as I joined them. He got up and brought over another chair for me.

I sort of remembered the older man was the chief marketing officer for Gryphon-Loyall, but didn't remember his name was Ross Campbell until Janelle introduced me. "We've met," he acknowledged, thumbing through a stack of papers he held. His gray-streaked hair stood up in tufts, suggesting he'd run his fingers through it more than once.

I sat beside Scott. Janelle was on the other side of him. In that back corner of the booth, we were out of voice range of others, but still in sight. Only one other person was in the booth—the very young man I'd seen that morning was talking to a client on the other end of the space.

Scott had a pen and pad in hand and consulted his notes. "You last saw him yourself at ten-fifteen, Jennifer at ten forty-five, and no one else here has seen him since. You've called his hotel and one of your people knocked on the room door but didn't get any answer. He's not answering his cell phone either."

Campbell shook his head and heaved a deep sigh. Jennifer bit her lip and dabbed at her eyes with a tissue.

"Did he get a call or a message that you know of? Anything that might have caused him to leave?" Scott asked.

"Not that I know of, but even if he had, he would've told us he was leaving and why. He wouldn't just walk off and leave us in the lurch."

"Larry loves the job. He wouldn't just walk off without a really good reason," Jennifer added on a hoarse gulp.

"Did he seem upset when you saw him this morning?" Scott asked. "Or unhappy? Worried? Anything unusual?"

Campbell pulled at his tie while thinking about it, then shook his head. "He seemed pretty normal to me. Maybe a little worried, but then he's been worried a lot lately. Personal issues, I think. Wife of his…well, that's not relevant."

"Probably not," Ted agreed. "I saw him this morning too, and thought he seemed kind of upset. Of course, we've all been a bit knocked back by what happened to Chase."

"He did seem unhappy this morning," Jennifer added. "But he wouldn't tell me what was going on. I got the impression it was something happening here, though, and not at home. Still, he didn't say anything about taking off."

Scott said, "Did he mention meeting someone or doing something particular today?"

Campbell shook his head.

"Did he argue or fight with anyone this morning?"

"Not that I know of," Campbell answered. Jennifer and Ted both shook their heads when he glanced at them.

Scott thought again for a moment. "Did he leave any of his things here?"

"Not here. I haven't checked his hotel room."

Scott scribbled a couple more notes on his pad. "Where is your company based?"

"New Orleans."

"All your people flew in from there? Do you know if Barnes has any relatives or friends in this area? Someone he might've gone to visit?"

Campbell ran his hands through his hair. "Not that I know of, but then I probably wouldn't know. They might." He glanced at Jennifer and Ted.

"I don't think so," Ted answered. "But I don't really know. He never mentioned anyone." Jennifer shook her head again. Her fingers were laced tightly together and she squeezed spasmodically.

"I'd like to talk with all the other people you have here," Scott said.

"We're it. Just the four of us—three now—and Jake." He nodded to the young man with the customer.

"Larry didn't give you any reason to think he was concerned about something?"

Campbell moved a stack of papers off his lap, pulled a sales sheet from his pocket and began to roll it up. "He's seemed a bit distracted the past couple of days, but then he was kind of friends with that man who was murdered. I know it upset him."

Ted glanced at me with a worried look. "Heather knows that he and Chase had some kind of discussion or argument on Monday morning. We don't know what it was about, but other than being shocked by the murder later—like the rest of us—he didn't seem too concerned about it."

"Larry claimed it was just a disagreement over how to handle some paperwork from one of their former employers," Campbell said.

He didn't really believe that. Did he know that Markham had been pursuing Jennifer and was he trying to protect her?

Scott took a moment to look at his notes. "Larry Barnes being away leaves you short-handed."

"A bit," Campbell admitted. "But we can handle that. It's just that this is so out of character for him. And given that someone he knew and interacted with has already—"

"Oh my God," Jennifer burst out. "Don't go there. Don't even—"

Scott held up a hand. "It's too soon to get too worked up. Things do happen. He might've gotten lost. Or got stuck somewhere unexpectedly. One of you needs to knock on the door of his hotel room again, make sure he isn't there. Keep trying to call him. If he doesn't show up by tomorrow morning, though, we need to call in the police. You realize this isn't going to look good to them."

Jennifer's drooping head shot up as she caught the implication. "No way. Larry wouldn't. They can't think he could possibly have killed Chase, can they?"

Ross Campbell drew a deep breath. "They can. We know they're wrong, but his disappearing like this certainly throws suspicion on him." The client who'd been occupying the other young man in the booth finally left and Campbell motioned for the young man, Jake Rogers, to join us.

Jake dragged over another chair, but he had a hard time sitting still. His legs swung and he picked at his cuticles or wove his fingers together while Scott asked the same questions about Larry we'd asked the others.

"I didn't know him very well," Jake said. "Not like Ted and Jennifer did. I've only worked for the company for four months. He did seem a bit… I don't know. Worried or something. Not like his normal self? But he didn't say anything about why."

Some instinct was ringing a bell in my head. Jake knew something he wasn't telling. If the others realized it, no one said anything, but I was betting Scott picked up on it, too. Following his lead I didn't press. We'd probably both be having a private talk with Jake Rogers in the very near future.

Scott looked at Ross Campbell again. "Do you want to call in the police now?"

Campbell's mouth worked. He stared at Ted and Jennifer, looking for their input.

"If he did get stuck somewhere or had something else to do," Ted said, finally, "he won't appreciate it."

Janelle looked at Scott. "If we did call them, what would the police do?"

"It's borderline. Normally when adults go missing, they won't do much but take the report unless there's reason to suspect a crime has occurred. It's not against the law to disappear if you're not on bail or parole. In this case, given the circumstances, however, I'm betting they'd put out a BOLO for him."

"What's a bolo?" Jennifer asked.

"'Be On the Look Out,'" Scott said. "They'd want to pick him up for questioning."

"You mean *arrest* him?"

"Not necessarily. But they'd certainly want to ask some hard questions."

Jennifer's eyes were wide, her face distressed. The others looked uncomfortable.

"Maybe we don't want to do that just yet," Campbell said.

"Your call for now," Janelle said. "But if we don't hear from him by tomorrow, we will notify the police."

She and Scott exchanged a glance and both stood up. "Let us know as soon you hear anything," Scott said as we moved away. Janelle hung back. "I'm going to have a private word with Mr. Campbell."

Once we were away from the booth, Scott gave me a look that combined exasperation and admiration. "Okay, how'd you know our missing boy had an argument with Chase Markham?"

"See the booth down there on the right with the bright green backdrop? One of the men there told me about it yesterday. He saw it. Only he wasn't sure if it was really an argument. It might've just been a forceful discussion. But Jennifer and Larry both worked with Chase Markham at one time." I chewed my lip. "Should we file a missing person report right now? I have a bad feeling about this."

Scott thought for a moment. "He's only been gone a few hours that we know about. That's not really very long. It looks bad, but there are an awful lot of possible explanations. I think for the moment we should go with Campbell's decision."

I looked at my phone, more by reflex than interest,

before I added, "I was planning to call Gilmont this afternoon. I've got a couple of things to tell him."

"He's probably off by now, but if you have his cell number, give him a buzz. I'd like to be there if you don't mind."

As Scott had predicted, Gilmont was at home, but said he'd meet with us the next morning at seven thirty. Janelle rejoined us as I ended the call.

"I warned him again that we might have to call the police in," she said. "He wasn't thrilled about it."

"We already have."

She raised an eyebrow at me. I envied her the ability to draw up a single eyebrow. I'd never been able to do that. However hard I tried, both eyebrows insisted on rising.

"We're meeting with Gilmont tomorrow morning at seven-thirty."

"It's more than just Larry Barnes's disappearance, isn't it?" she asked.

Scott said, "Heather's learned a few things she needs to share with him."

"Of course." Janelle glanced at her watch. "It's past quitting time. Go home, both of you. Or go get dinner. Then get some sleep."

We all headed for the elevator upstairs to clock out, and while it ascended Janelle gave me a sharper look. "You look drained, Heather."

I shrugged. "Long day."

"When this show is over, you need to take some of that personal time you've been accumulating. Next week is the orthodontics convention. We can handle it without you."

"I'm okay with that. All those dental appliances give me the heebie jeebies."

"We've got the farm equipment show after that."

"Ooh, that one's always fun. I love it when they let me sit on the big machines." I turned to Scott. "One time they even let me drive one of the balers onto the floor."

"And it only cost a few hundred bucks to repair the wall you hit," Janelle observed.

"At least it didn't dent the machine. They forgot to tell me it didn't have power steering."

A grin lightened Scott's features. "I can picture it."

"Please don't," I begged. "It was fun, but it wasn't my finest hour."

"It's going to be hard to scrub that image out of my brain. I'm feeling Mexican tonight, Heather. You up for it?"

"Sure," I said.

"Janelle?"

"Sweet of you, but I'm not into being a third wheel. Anyway, I already have plans for the evening." The elevator dinged and opened. Janelle got off first, content to leave that as her exit line.

Forty minutes later Scott and I settled into seats at a Mexican restaurant about halfway between the downtown Market Center and my apartment in Bethesda.

"It's been a crazy day," he said, once we'd ordered food.

"How'd the event with Lilya go?"

"Better today. At least we were better prepared for it. Still had a huge crowd in the ballroom, but it was under control and we didn't have mobs swarming the stage. I'm betting NovaCyn's never had more people at a product introduction."

"No doubt. I didn't hear about any more shoplifting episodes. Any developments there?"

"I didn't hear of any, either. I went back and talked to each of the people who'd had something taken to get more details. I have an idea I'm working on, a possible connection between the items taken. It may even tie in with Markham's murder."

"You're kidding. Really? How?"

"It's only a theory," he reminded me. "But all the devices taken were MegaComp products. Some were rebranded but the basic system was MegaComp. I'm still checking on this, but at least two of them likely used some of the technology Chase Markham claimed they stole from him. I think, anyway. The technical details are a bit confusing."

"More than confusing. Mind-boggling. But Ted might be able to help if you need it. Of course, he might be involved in other ways, too."

Scott gave me a look. It's hard to describe that look. It's not really a frown or anger. In fact, not much about his features changes. The hard mouth stays pretty much the same and the lean jaw doesn't move. The only difference I can see is a slight tightening around his eyes, a change so small you have to look closely to notice it. But he stares so steadily and with such purpose that it's hard to sit still under the glare, so I wiggled a bit.

I'm sure he honed that stare as a cop, and probably it got all sorts of admissions from the people he turned it on. I knew what he wanted from me and it was annoying as all get out.

"Look, I'm not playing girl detective here," I said. "I can't help it when people tell me things. I can't help it that they want to talk about the most exciting thing that has happened at the show. And I can't help it that my brain tends to latch onto those things and work on them.

It's part of my job to solve problems that come up at the show, whether it's dirty carpet in a booth or the murder of an exhibitor. And I like to think I do my job well." I realized my voice was rising when I noticed a couple of people at the next table were looking my way.

I drew a deep breath and calmed myself. "Anyway, you already know I plan to tell Gilmont everything tomorrow morning. If he could've met me tonight, I'd be telling him right now, just like I'll tell you if you're willing to listen and not glare at me like I'm some kind of criminal you're grilling."

"Grilling?" He blinked a couple of times, then leaned back in his chair, deliberately relaxing his entire body. "I'm sorry. Maybe you're right. And I should know better. You can't help being who you are."

The waiter showed up with plates of burritos and enchiladas for us, along with two mugs of beer. I used the small respite to consider his words and what they meant.

Once the waiter had departed I said, "That's rather condescending."

Scott looked surprised but didn't say anything right away. He took a bite of food, chewed and swallowed, but I'm not sure he really tasted it. "You're right, and again I'm sorry. I just keep putting my foot in it, don't I? I don't think I meant that the way it came out. What I really meant was that being the person you are, you're going to find yourself in situations like this. It worries me because I am who I am."

"A cop?"

"Ex-cop." He gave a brief, wry smile. "And I hope it's broader than that. It better be more than that." He took another bite and chewed slowly.

"Yeah, it is. You have those 'protect and defend' instincts. Just like I have that 'let's figure out a solution to the problem' instincts. Both are good in theory but they can lead you into dangerous situations."

"And we're both going to have to figure out how to live with it in each other if we're going to have a relationship that works."

"I don't think I'd have a problem with it in you," I said.

"You already do," he pointed out, with irritating logic, "when it comes to me wanting to protect you. And you haven't seen the whole of it in action yet. Cops don't have a very good track record when it comes to marriage."

"Are you warning me off or something?"

"Bit early in the relationship for that. But no, I'm just pointing out the difficulties."

"Okay, fair enough." I took a drink of beer before continuing. "So, what does this mean for us? Are you trying to call it quits already?"

He looked stunned. "Hell no. Just looking squarely at the challenges."

He put down his fork, reached over and took my free hand. As always seemed to happened when he touched me, every cell in my body went on high alert and began zinging around bits of electricity.

"We've only known each other a few weeks," he said. "It's a bit early to make any decisions or commitments. But I'll say this right now. It's special. Okay? We've got time to figure out the rest."

It was fascinating to watch the subtle changes in his expression and body language, and especially the way the color of his eyes seemed to shift from blue to gray, with shadings of green at times. And shallow as it is, I liked the way something seemed to light up in those eyes when he looked at me. I liked *him*. A lot. I've dated my share of guys, but they all seemed a bit shallow and juvenile compared with Scott.

And then there were all those hormones or whatever they were cartwheeling around my body shouting, *More!*

It took a minute to catch my breath enough to talk. "Yeah, it's special," I agreed. "That doesn't automatically make it easy."

"Maybe just the opposite." He withdrew his hand so he could grab his beer glass. "But that just makes it more worth working for." He held the mug out toward me. "To us."

I lifted mine and clinked it against his. I felt the heat rising in my face so I was probably blushing as well as grinning like an idiot when I echoed, "To us." His smile was a work of art.

We ate in peaceful, happy silence for a few minutes. Once we'd taken the edge off the hunger, he said, "Want to fill me in now?"

So I did. He listened without interrupting as I told him about the various conversations I'd had during the day and conclusions I'd drawn. He seemed most interested in the talk with Sandy. When I finished, he sipped thoughtfully on the beer for a couple of minutes.

"I'm glad you've called Gilmont," he said at last. "Some of that puts a new light on the motivation."

"Drake Galloway might well have had a good reason to kill him," I ventured.

"Another talk with him will certainly be on the to-do list. But it also raises some questions about Markham and what he was up to."

"There were already plenty of questions. He seems to have made enemies everywhere he went."

"Almost like he was trying to," Scott mused.

"Why would anyone try to make enemies?"

"Lots of possible reasons. Create bad feeling toward his employer. Given their relationship, that's at least possible. Some people like being hated. It's better than being ignored. Direct attention away from something else he was doing? Make problems for other people? Who knows? Some people seem to thrive on drama. If there's no chaos in the area, they'll create some. I'm getting an idea Markham might've been that type."

"And he's not around to ask." I shivered a bit, remembering finding his body.

Scott reached out for my hand again. "That's the kind of experience I wish I could spare you. You've already had more of it than you need."

"And I appreciate it. But don't cops have those kind of experiences pretty frequently? Are they really any better prepared for it?"

"Yes, they are. They know what to do."

"Not what I meant. I know what to do, too. Call the cops. I meant are they any better prepared personally for that kind of experience?"

"Probably not," he admitted. "But they know it's part of the job when they sign up for it. And police academies are doing more to try to prepare people for it. But I'm not sure anyone's ever really ready, which is why we have traumatic stress debriefings."

"When I was a kid my dad used to say that growing up meant learning to face life's realities and figuring out how to deal with them. Not relying on someone else to take care of everything for you."

"I can agree with him about that."

"So, is there anything we can do about the reality of Larry Barnes being missing?"

"Not really, unless you think he might be hiding out somewhere in the Center building itself."

"Not likely," I admitted. "Ohmigod, the last person who went missing turned up dead." The vision of finding a body in the trash bin at the Gifts and Home Decor Show a few weeks back suddenly rose up in my brain and made me shiver.

Scott's hand was on my arm again. "That's not the usual outcome when people go missing," he assured me. "My guess? He knows something important about why Markham was killed and he doesn't want the killer to find him, too, so he's removed himself from the vicinity."

"That makes sense," I admitted.

"In any case, there's very little we can do about it. Tomorrow we'll tell Gilmont and he'll take it from there. The police can search for him much more effectively than we can."

A waiter showed up to remove our plates. We decided against dessert, paid the bill, and headed for home. I invited him in when we got to my apartment. He debated about it but declined.

"We both need to be up early, so we need sleep." He must've seen my expression even in the semi-darkness. "Heather, next week, after this is over, I'm taking you on a real date. Dinner, movie, whatever, and when you invite me in afterward I'll take you up on it, but you have to understand that if we do that, I won't be leaving again an hour later. It's a pretty big step. I want you to be sure you're ready to take it. And I want to have the time to do it right."

"All right."

He pulled me to him, wrapping his arms around me, making it seem easy and natural even in the confined space of his car. And then he kissed me, and we didn't talk again for quite a while. The kiss was—there's no way to describe it. All the words I could think of later, when I could think again, were so totally inadequate for the way that kiss burrowed into me, down to my soul and set off all sorts of turbulence inside. It went on and on, and I didn't want it to stop, ever.

When Scott finally broke it off and pulled back, I could barely breathe. My heart pounded, blood raced through my veins and those hormones were shouting *yes, yes, yes*!

He sounded a bit breathless himself when he said, "If I don't leave you wanting more, I'm not doing it right."

"You're doing it right."

His mouth curled into a wicked smile.

FIFTEEN

Friday

THE NEXT MORNING Scott and I arrived at almost the same time. Since the building was locked before eight and Gilmont would have no way to get in, we waited outside for him. Even in the early morning, this area of downtown Washington, D.C., wasn't completely quiet, but I enjoyed the relative peace. A garbage truck up the street clanked and huffed, and a few cars zoomed by, but the noise level was well below what it would be in an hour or so.

The detective showed up and I led the way inside and up to the conference room. Janelle was already there and joined us. Scott—bless him, multiple times!—had stopped at Starbucks and brought four cups of coffee. Gilmont's odd attitude toward Scott didn't extend to gifts containing caffeine. He accepted a cup with enthusiasm.

He gave each of us a sharp glance as we all took those necessary first sips in silence, but he zeroed in on me when he put the cup down, pulled out a pen and pad, and said, "Okay, what's up?"

I told him everything, withholding only the name of my source for the information about Drake Galloway and his argument with Chase Markham. He stopped me briefly to ask why I wasn't saying who told me about it, but didn't press for a name when I told him the person wanted to remain anonymous. Of course he didn't. How likely was it someone outside Galloway's company knew, unless it was someone already closely acquainted with Chase Markham? He'd talked to everyone here who qualified. And he already knew there were only two people from the company here now.

He let me go on and didn't say anything more until we got to the missing Larry Barnes. His expression pulled up into a harsh frown. "Have you reported this yet?"

Scott answered. "We're reporting it right now. We didn't hear about it until late yesterday afternoon, and he'd only been missing since late morning. For all anyone knows, he might've decided to take a day off and go tourist."

"You're not buying that," Gilmont said.

"Would you? Given that his name keeps coming up in a murder investigation?" I asked.

"No. If he doesn't show up here this morning we'll start looking for him."

"The show only has a couple more days to run. There's not much time to solve this."

Gilmont glanced at Janelle before he asked, "It ends on Sunday?"

"Technically," she answered. "The big awards banquet is Saturday night. Some of the exhibitors pack up and leave on Sunday morning, although the show officially goes to noon."

"So time is short."

"Chase Markham's phones," I said. "One of them was on the floor by him. Supposedly he had two others. Have you found them? I have to assume they didn't help you track down the killer, though."

"We have two phones. The one on the floor and another we found in his hotel room. We haven't located a third, but we do have the two that had service plans. The other one may have been left at home since it had no cell service."

"And you didn't find any incriminating calls on either of the two phones? One was kind of carefully smashed."

Gilmont actually grinned. It was startling and surprisingly attractive. "I've had guys running down all the calls he's made over the last few weeks. We've also checked his text messages, including deleted ones. There were a lot of both and quite a few to people who are here. So far none of them have produced anything to suggest a motive or opportunity for murder."

"No 'Meet me in the men's room outside the fourteen hundred aisle door at three o'clock' sort of messages."

"Obviously not."

"But you know…" I was kind of musing out loud on this. "There should've been something like that. Wherever he was, I think he was expecting to meet someone. Maybe just not right then."

"We had the same thought," Gilmont said, "So we've been looking for it. Nothing so far."

"Do you have any suspects?" I asked.

Gilmont's eyebrows went up. "Right now, I'd have to say that unless he's back in the booth this morning, Mr. Barnes has just taken himself to the top of the list."

He set down his coffee cup and looked at Janelle again. "Shall we go see if Mr. Barnes has put in an appearance?"

Scott and I stood up after they'd left. "This is too damn complicated," I said. "Chase accuses MegaComp of stealing his…whatever. Ted tells me Chase knew that the 'whatever' didn't work right but he'd found a way to fix it. Sandy says her boss and Chase had words over the bonus he should've gotten for the 'whatever.' Why did Galloway seem stunned when he heard Chase admit it had problems but he'd fixed them? Surely he knew that already. Or did he? Maybe that's why he didn't want to give Chase the bonus."

"Why would he withhold it if the problems were fixed?" Scott asked.

"Most likely because he couldn't afford to pay it. I suspect the company's in financial trouble. But still, you think they'd do whatever they could to hold onto their most brilliant engineer. Stock options or whatever in lieu of payment."

"I have no idea, but I need to get to work."

"Have you heard from your friend who was looking at the video?"

"Not yet. I'm expecting a call from him shortly."

We parted. I took a quick stop by my desk to check for critical messages, then went down to the show floor. I took care of a couple of minor issues quickly, then headed for the thirteen hundred aisle and the Steady-Safe booth. Luck or fate or whatever was with me this time. Shawn was there and not involved with a client.

He didn't look happy to see me approach, but he didn't duck away either. Dean Lee stood at the other corner of the booth, but fortunately he was engaged with a customer. Frank Merrimon was nowhere in sight.

"Things back to normal here now?" I asked. "Is everything going okay?"

Shawn shrugged, which managed to emphasize the tight way he held himself. Although his suit and tie were neat, and his curly, dark hair combed into temporary submission, up close I could see the lines of strain on his face. Dark half-circles sat under his eyes like bruises. He held one of the company's flyers, and he rolled and unrolled it almost spasmodically.

"Business off?" I asked. "Traffic seems to be strong this year."

He stopped unrolling and tapped the rolled-up flyer against the other palm. "Traffic's pretty good," he answered. "We've had plenty of inquiries and signed up some new clients."

"How is everyone managing the trauma?" I asked. "I'm sure I'm not the only one having nightmares about finding a body in your booth."

Shawn winced and said sharply, "I don't really want to talk about it."

"Okay. Can you talk about Chase Markham's work for a minute? I understand you were friends and I'd like to know a little more about what drove him. I'm told he was brilliant but tended to sabotage himself with his attitude."

For a moment I thought he might not answer at all, but after an awkward pause he said, "I wouldn't call Chase a friend. Acquaintance, co-worker, occasional drinking companion, and sometimes an irritatingly persistent annoyance. Chase's own ego stood in the way of his having any real friends. He never saw that, though. Never understood that he was his own worst enemy. I tried to tell him. Tried to make him see that he had to learn to work with others. Compromise. I told him more than once that he had to be more flexible. He never got it. He was brilliant. His designs were brilliant, way ahead of everything else. He couldn't understand why that didn't automatically make them the best solution for any situation. Why it didn't make him the most sought-after engineer in the business."

"Okay. Keep in mind that I'm not an engineer. Explain to me why the most brilliant solution isn't automatically the best one."

"Okay." He reached into his shirt pocket and pulled out a smartphone. I wasn't savvy enough to know what brand it was, but it looked sleek and shiny. "Take this. If I were to take it apart, you'd see that it's made up of lots of different components, from several different manufacturers. They all have to be able to work together or the whole thing won't work."

I nodded.

"But it's more than just fitting together physically," he continued. "They have to be able to connect to each other, of course, but they have to be able to communicate information to each other in ways both understand, and they have to share resources, like the computer's memory and power. If one of them hogs too much, then the others aren't going to work as well."

"So if a design is totally brilliant but doesn't play well with others, then it's not going to be much use."

"Right. But it can be even more subtle than that. Suppose you have something like a program on a chip that facilitates moving information in one format, say from a camera, to another format, suitable for storage or uploading to some social media site, and it has a really ingenious way to do the translation, but it feeds the information back out faster than the other pieces can keep up with. If it's way too fast, you'll realize that pretty quickly and either find a way to fix it or decide not to use that piece. But what if it's feeding it out just a little, tiny bit too fast? It might not be obvious on testing, even with a lot of testing. Small, infrequent errors can be hard to find. But get millions of people using a device with that tiny error and eventually there are going to be some 'uh ohs'. Of course all of this is an over-simplification, but you get the idea."

"I think I do. So Chase's brilliant ideas were genius but didn't always work well with other things. And he didn't want to compromise his own cleverness."

"That's pretty much it."

"I guess that's why companies would keep hiring him. They hoped he'd come up with that brilliant idea that would work well."

"In fairness, he already had. In fact, one of his ideas worked so well, the company ended up licensing the technology to several others. They made a pile of money on it."

"Did Chase?"

"He got a raise and a really nice bonus, but not as much as he thought he should've."

"That was kind of a theme in Chase's life. But why didn't he just go somewhere else? I'll bet there were other companies that would want his next products?"

"He did. He changed jobs several times."

"You mentioned, or at least hinted, that he wanted to work for MegaComp?"

"Did he ever. They hire the best engineers around and pay well. But by then he had a reputation as a diva and MegaComp doesn't like divas. They only have room for one and Hovey already has the job. In fact, I understand Chase's second application caused something of an uproar. Their CTO wanted him, but HR vetoed it."

"CTO? Chief Technology Officer?"

"Right. Jim Driscoll. You may have seen him around.

He tends to cling to Hovey's right-hand side. Has visions of changing the 'T' to an 'E' someday, when Hovey retires."

"I met him a couple of days ago."

"He's ambitious and I'm sure he thought Chase's ideas could contribute to their next 'insanely great' product. HR probably thought he was a bad bet or a potential liability."

Dean Lee appeared to be finishing up with his customers. I expected he'd be over as soon as they left. "Can I ask you one other question? Did you know Larry Barnes? I understand he's here and he is, or was, a friend of Chase's."

"Know him, sort of. It's not like we're close friends or anything. I think he was a bit closer to Chase. Larry's ambitious. He's more salesman than technical, though."

"He may have had some kind of argument or at least an urgent discussion with Chase on Monday."

Shawn rolled his eyes. "Apparently lots of people did."

I took out my phone. There weren't any messages, but Shawn didn't know that. Dean Lee's customers had just left and he was turning this way. "I've got to run," I said. "Thanks for the help."

I waved at the booth in general and made a quick getaway. Once I was out of sight a couple of rows down, I dialed Janelle to ask if Larry Barnes had shown up.

"No," she said. "They're pretty worried about it, too. No one has heard anything from him, including his wife and parents back home. Gilmont's got his guys checking his credit cards, airlines and such, but it will take a while."

She gave me a couple of booths to check for various issues, which kept me busy for the next half hour.

The last of those left me only one aisle over from the Gryphon-Loyall booth, so I stopped by there. Ted saw me and came over, shaking his head. "No sign of Larry. No word from him, either. Jen and I knocked on the door of his room last night but got no answer. We talked to a police detective this morning. He didn't say it outright, but I'm pretty sure he thinks Larry killed Chase. They've put out that Lookout thing for him and I think they're trying to trace his credit cards. Sounds like they'll arrest him if they find him." He sighed heavily. "I don't believe it. Larry wouldn't have killed Chase."

"We don't always know other people as well as we think we do," I reminded him. "Sometimes people do react violently when they're threatened or cornered."

"I get that. But still—"

"Ted, enough futzing around. Dish the dirt. You know something about this you haven't been telling anyone. It's past time to let it go."

His face went almost blank. It was frightening, but only in the sense that he seemed so unsure and even scared, himself. Then he sighed and his features went back to the worried frown of earlier. "That's the thing. I don't really *know* anything, so I didn't want to talk about something that might not even have happened."

"Spill it," I said.

"I think I told you Larry and Chase had some kind of deal going. What I didn't tell you is that I'm pretty sure it involved MegaComp. And something about it was going wrong. But I don't know what the deal was or the problem. I tried not to listen in when Chase and Larry were talking on Monday, but I thought I heard the word 'MegaComp' and I could tell by the tone that things weren't going smoothly. I asked Larry about it later, but he brushed me off. He hasn't said anything about it since, but he hasn't been a happy camper. He's been distracted and kind of distant, which isn't like him."

Ted stopped to draw a long breath. "Here's one other thing that might be relevant, but isn't something I know for a fact, either. I think Larry had money issues. And of course that could account for why he's unhappy and distracted all by itself. But all of this is speculation on my part. I couldn't tell the police because it would make Larry look bad, and I'm not sure about any of it. And Larry is kind of a friend. Not a close one, but we've had a few beers."

"What do you think happened to Larry?"

"Best case? Chase was murdered, Larry knows who did it, and is hiding out until the show's over and he feels like he can come forward safely."

I didn't need to ask about the worst case scenario. That was a little too obvious, and maybe a little too possible. "You really don't know where he is?"

"No. I'd feel a lot better if I did."

The words sounded pretty sincere to me. "I'm with you on that." I sighed. "Listen, before I go, I need to talk to Jake for a moment privately. Can you make that happen?"

"Sure. You think he knows something?"

"Maybe."

"Go easy on him," Ted said. "He's very green." He beckoned the younger man over.

Jake Rogers didn't look happy to see me. I had to hide my amusement as he glanced around wildly for a moment, clearly searching for an excuse to avoid me. Lucky for me he didn't find anything.

I took a minute to re-introduce myself, though he

clearly remembered me from the previous day. When I asked if we could talk, he sighed audibly. He glanced at Ted, who said, "Okay." We moved to a back corner for privacy.

I dove right in, hoping to catch him before he could think up a good story. "I'm not a cop, just a lowly assistant here at the Center, but we're trying to straighten out some issues with Chase Markham and other vendors, so I have to ask. What did Chase and Larry argue about on Monday?"

"What makes you think they argued?"

"The way you reacted yesterday when we asked about him. I could tell you knew something and it was bothering you. A lot."

"Hell." He sucked in a breath and looked around. No one was near enough to overhear. "Look, you can't tell *anyone* about this. No one knows I told you this. Promise?"

"I promise I'll do my best to keep it confidential. I'll only tell someone else if it's clearly relevant to the murder of Chase Markham, and then I'll do my very best to keep your name out of it. You don't know me, but I've been in this job as long as I have because I'm good at keeping things confidential when needed. And if I can't keep your name out of it, I'll tell you before I tell anyone else. Will that do?"

He chewed on that for a moment, literally working his lower lip with his teeth. "It's honest," he said. "I guess it'll have to do. And I don't really know anything very specific anyway."

"So...?"

He took another peek to either side before answering, "They don't know it, but I overheard part of Larry's talk with Chase Markham on Monday. They didn't see me and I couldn't hear all of it, but I got a few words. It wasn't really an argument, more like an urgent discussion, and they kept their voices really low. But I heard a few things. I don't really know what it all means. Maybe it was more the tone. They both sounded worried, maybe even scared. I think that's what caught my attention. They were sounding tense. And after we heard about Chase Markham being killed, Larry got kind of weird. Fidgety and scared. He and Markham had something going and I suspect it was something kind of risky. I think it involved MegaComp. I heard them mention the company, and then something about how someone was suspicious. And after Chase's argument with Hovey, I just got a bad feeling about it."

Apparently Chase and Larry hadn't been keeping their voices down very well. "Can you tell me exactly what you remember them saying?"

'Well, first Chase said, 'We've got a problem.' That was loud enough for me to hear easily, but I'm guessing Larry shushed him or he realized he was too loud because their voices got lower. The next thing I heard was 'fell through,' then 'MegaComp,' 'they didn't,' and finally 'he's suspicious.' Of course there were a lot of other words between those, so I don't really know what it all meant. It just didn't sound good, and when Larry started getting all nervous, I knew it wasn't good. Then we heard Chase got killed, and I kind of got scared, too."

"Understandable," I said. "Did Larry say anything to you about it later on?"

"Nope. Not a thing. But he's been looking kind of green most of this week."

"He didn't say anything to you about leaving or going somewhere else?"

"Not a word. But…"

"But?"

"Yesterday morning, I got here kind of early." He blushed disarmingly. "I realized I'd messed up an order form and I wanted to fix it before anyone else could see it, so I got here as soon as the place opened at eight. Most days the others don't get here until a few minutes before nine. Anyway, I was surprised that Larry was already here. He was looking for something, and it seemed to make him frantic when he couldn't find it."

"Really? Any idea what? Did he ask if you if you'd seen anything?"

"No and no. But I think it might have been either papers or something small because he went through every stack of paper in the booth looking for it. When I asked him what he was looking for he just muttered something about losing a list he'd made and kind of brushed it off as not too important. But I could tell it was important to him."

"You have no idea what he was searching for?"

"Not a clue."

"Do you think he found it?"

"I don't know. The last time I saw him I'm pretty sure he hadn't, but he might've found it afterward."

"You think he disappeared because he was worried? He didn't leave right after Chase's murder, but when he couldn't find whatever it was he was looking for, could that have chased him away?"

"Maybe. It sure seemed to worry him."

I ran a couple of scenarios quickly through my brain. He found the papers or whatever and lit out, or he didn't find them and lit out. Either way I didn't have enough information to make sense of it.

"What was Larry like as a salesman?"

"The best. You know that chestnut about selling ice cubes to Eskimos? If anyone could, it's Larry. He's smooth and slick and great at finding ways to get people to see what he thinks they should. I'm told he's been the top performer for the last two years. Almost since he first started at the company."

"Did you like him?"

The question took Jake by surprise. He opened his mouth then shut it. When he finally spoke, I got the feeling I'd get the real answer and not the platitude he'd been ready to spout. "No," Jake said, "not very much."

I waited.

"He was a little too slick, a little too full of himself, too…slippery. He could sell pretty much anything to anyone and he knew it, but when you were dealing with him, or even just having a conversation about…well, anything, the car, the football game, the weather…you could never be sure he wasn't still trying to sell you something, if you know what I mean. The other day I told him he'd missed his calling. He should've been one of those sports agents who get athletes all those millions. He could totally do that. He looked a little funny when I told him that. Like maybe he realized he'd missed an opportunity or something."

Jake looked around and his expression changed. Following his gaze, I saw Ross Campbell approaching the booth.

"I'd better get back to work," Jake said.

I thanked him for the information. For a few minutes I wandered up and down aisles thinking about what he'd said. The bits and pieces of conversation Ted and Jake Rogers had overheard were suggestive, but little more. I couldn't put them together in any way that made sense of what was going on between Chase Markham and Larry Barnes. I mentally pushed those words up against the argument Markham had had with Hovey and the accusation that MegaComp had stolen ideas from him. It made even less sense in that context.

It sounded like Markham and Larry had been conspiring to do something—but what? Sue MegaComp? If that were the case wouldn't it be RTX's job to do it? And wouldn't they hire a lawyer to take care of it?

A bit of blackmail, maybe? That had possibilities. If Chase had in fact discovered that MegaComp had stolen an idea or bit of design, then he might've decided to bleed them for it. The very public argument wasn't really a good idea if that were the case, but it was possible that he'd blown his stack when he'd learned of it, before he'd realized the possibilities. He would likely have had to make some sort of public apology, but if the potential earnings from the blackmail had been strong enough—and with a company the size of MegaComp, that was entirely possible—he would have done it. Maybe he wanted Larry's help. He needed a salesman to work out details for him.

There were still pieces that didn't fit, though. If that were the scenario, I would've expected Larry to disappear or spill his guts as soon as he heard of Markham's murder, because if he knew the same things Chase did, then his life was in just as much danger. But he didn't do anything until he realized he'd lost or misplaced something.

Or maybe Chase and Larry had both known about

MegaComp's "borrowing" before they came and they already had a plan to blackmail them here. If Chase had just found out when he got here that they weren't going to go along with it, then the argument might have been a way to put pressure on MegaComp to come across.

That worked a bit better, though there were still holes. No one at MegaComp seemed particularly concerned about Chase's accusations. That could be good acting, of course, but I wasn't really buying it.

And I couldn't quite fit the whole business of Chase's argument with Ted and Galloway's reaction to whatever he'd overheard into that scenario.

I was so caught up in those musings that I almost didn't hear my phone buzz.

"I've got it," Ted said, when I answered. "You're not going to believe what it is."

"What?" I'd been so deep in my thoughts I had no idea what he was talking about.

"The interference. I've found out what's doing it. You've got to come see."

"Where are you?"

"Eleven hundred aisle."

I headed straight there. I found Ted near the back, staring at the booth of the Germans with the lights and the huge roulette-type wheel. My heart sank straight down into my shoes. From the way Ted was staring at that wheel, I knew. I just knew. And I so didn't want to have to do this.

"The wheel?" I asked.

He nodded.

"Will you back me up on it?"

"Of course," he answered. "We've got to get the interference stopped or fixed."

"Let's do it, then." I was already looking around for Dieter. We had to go around one of the displays to find him, talking to a group of customers in English quite a bit better than he'd ever used with me. He saw me and started to smile, but that faded quickly. He gave a quick nod before returning to the customers, but within moments, he had them signing his contact list and shuffled them toward the wheel. They spun it, the wheel made a couple of turns, then stopped with the indicator on $100.

While they cheered, Ted murmured, "That nailed it." I turned to find him staring at the meter he held.

"No question?"

He shook his head. "Absolutely no question. The minute that thing started turning, the readings jumped. When it stopped they fell back. Direction indicators match perfectly."

I looked at his tie. At first glance it looked like a normal, if somewhat loud, bit of fabric in burgundy and yellow diagonal stripes. Then I saw the crest. "A school tie? From where?"

"Check it out." He held up the end so I could read the single word.

"Gryffindor? Oh. Harry Potter."

"Right. I wish it had Hogwarts on it."

Dieter had handed an envelope to one of the members of the group and waved them off. "So, what's the problem?" he asked as he joined us. He was concerned enough to forget to exaggerate the accent.

"I hate to have to tell you this, but there's a problem with your wheel." I stared at the thing that took up most of the center of the booth. "It's emitting some kind of something that's interfering with the electronics of other exhibitors. I don't really understand it," I admitted, "but we've been getting a lot of complaints about problems with wireless communications, and we've traced the source of it to your wheel. Ted, here, can explain it better than I can."

My eyes glazed over as Ted tried to explain about electromagnetic frequencies and gigahertzes and other stuff that made zilch sense to me. Dieter's face looked just as blank as I'm sure mine must have. "Pardon, but I don't understand this," he said, after listening for a bit. "I need to get Erich."

Dieter returned shortly with a tall, thin man in tow. "This is Erich. Explain to him, please." So Ted explained and Erich asked questions, the whole conversation a muddle of English, German, and Engineer. But after a few minutes, Erich seemed to have some grasp of the problem. He turned to Dieter and they had a long conversation in German. At one point Erich swept his arm out in a near three-sixty arc, so I assumed he was explaining that the problem with their wheel could be affecting everyone in the building. Dieter wasn't happy, but finally nodded acceptance. Erich turned back to face us again.

"We need to shield it, yes?" he asked Ted. "This is not my...understanding. No, my expert."

"Area of expertise," Ted suggested.

The man pushed thick glasses back up the bridge of his nose, ran his hand through lank brown hair, and said, "How do we do this?"

"Can I take a look?" Ted asked. "First thing is to find out exactly where it's leaking from. Then we'll see what it's going to take to fix it." He turned to me. "This could take a while so you might not want to hang around, but I might need your help once we've isolated the leak. If it's something we can fix, we'll probably have to find some shielding material in a hurry. You'd have a better idea where to get that. I'll call you when I know."

"Okay. Ted, I owe you big-time for this."

He gave me that wonderfully endearing grin, dimples on full display, and said, "We've got to get this fixed. If I get geek points for it, all the better."

"Many, many geek points, I promise. Though I'm not sure what you trade them in for."

His grin faded abruptly. "Maybe some help for Larry if the police do find him?"

I'm sure my own smile went as fast as his. "You've got it. I'll do whatever I can."

I watched for a moment while Ted and Erich crawled under the edge of the big wheel to check out wiring underneath. Dieter stopped me as I was heading out of the booth. "I must thank you for the help," he said. "I have given you the headache, I know, before. And Erich tells me our wheel has caused problems for others. Your help in fixing it is appreciated." His tone sounded sincere, so I decided to take it that way.

"We appreciate that you co-operated in not using the sirens and making minimal use of the lights," I said.

"Erich said at the beginning you wouldn't like the noise. But our company said 'try it,' so ve have to try it."

"I understand. My bosses sometimes tell me to do things I'm not happy about." And I had a feeling I'd be hearing some of that again soon, given what had just occurred to me.

I made my way out of the booth and headed for the MegaComp booth. I still had no real clue what was going on with Chase Markham and MegaComp, but a bit of pot-stirring might produce some interesting results. And would probably also result in complaints to Janelle and a warning from her. I'd trod this path before.

Nonetheless, I slipped through the crowds to the castle of the MegaComp empire. I walked around the booth, searching for a familiar face among the people demonstrating the products, and hung around until one young woman noticed me.

I introduced myself and asked if Mr. Driscoll was around.

"I'll go and see," she said. I handed her my card to give to him. She disappeared into a space behind the theater area, then emerged a few minutes later. "I'm sorry. He's in a meeting right now. Do you want me to give him a message?"

"No, thanks. I'll try again later."

As she turned to an approaching pair, I backed away, thinking. Driscoll was there, but couldn't be bothered to talk to me. Not that I blamed him. He had no idea who I was or why it would be worth his time to talk to me. From his point of view, I was no one he needed to be concerned with. He probably didn't even remember our previous, brief meeting.

My best bet was to try to catch him either coming or going from the booth. I could hang around waiting for him for a bit, but if that didn't work, I'd just have to go for the squeaky wheel strategy. However, after just a couple of minutes of dawdling in the vicinity, my phone buzzed.

"Are you in the middle of something?" Scott asked.

"No."

"Good. Craig and I are meeting with Janelle in her office in ten minutes. Can you get here?"

"I'm on the way. What's up?"

"We may have a break in the thefts. I'll show you when you get up here."

SIXTEEN

Friday

I GOT TO Janelle's office in four minutes flat. Not that I was rushing or anything. Craig and Scott were already waiting. I took the one remaining seat.

Scott picked up an envelope from the floor next to his chair. "I told Heather a couple of days ago that I was going to ask a friend to look at the video we had of the thefts. He's an expert in reading videos and enhancing them as much as possible. He also thought of a couple of things we didn't, and the result is we have what we're pretty sure is a picture of our thief."

He opened the envelope, took out a stack of pictures and handed one to each of us.

The image was black and white and very grainy. But it showed features in enough detail to make the face recognizable. I nearly dropped it in surprise. "Holy cannoli!"

"My sentiments, exactly," Janelle said. She sounded as gobsmacked as I was.

"So you recognize him, too?" Scott asked.

"Oh, yeah. How sure is your friend that this is the person who lifted the merchandise?"

"Pretty sure. My guy followed our suspect out of the booth on the video, then he matched it up with video from other cameras until he found one that showed the person's face. He said it matched on clothing, size of person, the color tones, lighting, and some other things I didn't entirely understand. He was ninety-five percent sure this person was our thief. Unlikely as it seems."

"Wow, this is going to be awkward." I looked at Janelle for guidance. "What do we do about it?"

Janelle drew a deep breath. "Obviously we have to confront him about it. At a minimum he has to return the things he stole and perhaps provide some additional compensation for the worry and inconvenience he caused. If he'll agree to that, maybe we don't need to involve the police." She was thinking out loud and watching Craig and Scott for their reactions.

"This is an exhibitor, isn't it?" Craig asked. "An important one?"

"Yes." Janelle made the word almost a sigh.

"You know," I said, "I'm not sure we can keep the police out of it entirely. Scott told me a couple of days ago that he thought there might be a connection between the thefts and Chase Markham's murder. He was right."

"What's the connection?" Janelle asked.

"All of the items stolen were MegaComp products," Scott said.

Craig shifted in his chair. "Enlighten me. Who is that in the picture?"

"Drake Galloway," I said. "Owner of RTX and Chase Markham's employer at the time of his murder."

That produced a couple of quiet moments while everyone chewed over the fact and considered what it might mean.

"If he were considering a lawsuit against MegaComp for theft of intellectual property," I said, "you'd think he'd want to collect his evidence a bit more legally."

"Good point," Janelle said. "I suppose for now, it

doesn't matter why. Heather, you have the associate's number? Call down and find out if Galloway is there right now."

I did and got Sandy. "He's here," she said. "But he's meeting with some people. I think they'll be finishing soon, though."

"Don't let him leave until I get there. It's important. Very important. Keep him in the booth any way you have to. I'll be there in less than ten minutes."

Scott, Craig, Janelle and I were already hustling toward the elevator as she said, "Okay."

Sandy waited for us at the booth. "He's still at his meeting in the back, but they're getting ready to end it." She stared at each of us in turn, curiosity and worry showing on her face. "I'll go check."

She ducked back behind the backdrop. "Should we have someone guarding the back?" Scott asked. Before I could answer, Sandy returned, followed by two men and a woman I hadn't seen before, with Drake Galloway behind them, still talking to one of the men.

Sandy came to stand next to me and leaned over to whisper so only I would hear, "Are we in trouble?"

"There's a problem," I answered in the same low tone. "But it's not you." I lowered my voice even more. "Something else entirely. We need to talk to your boss privately."

As I was saying that, Galloway finished and saw the others off. Janelle approached him. "Mr. Galloway? I hope you remember me and Heather and Scott Brandon. This is Craig Vincelli. He's an employee of the Market Center as well. We have something we need to discuss with you in private. Can we go to one of the conference rooms to talk?"

A flash of panic swept across Galloway's face before he controlled it and tamed it into annoyance. "This is a very busy time. Could we do this later? Perhaps tomorrow?"

I wondered if he guessed why we were there or if he thought it related to Chase Markham's murder.

"I'm afraid not," Janelle said firmly. "This is something that has to be dealt with immediately. If we don't take care of it now, the consequences could be unpleasant. Or worse."

He shut his eyes for a moment, then shrugged with the air of a man reluctantly putting aside adult matters to humor children wanting to play. He turned to Sandy and gave her a list of instructions about what to do if various people came by. Janelle led the way off the show floor to the closest conference room. Silent, we all followed her inside. Scott positioned himself behind Galloway and kept his eyes focused on the man.

Craig closed the door. The area was small, with room enough for a table and chairs that would seat ten and a stand holding a water cooler and cups. Unfortunately, the water cooler was empty. Even before I sat down I wished I'd brought a coffee cup or water bottle. Something to sip on and fidget with. Galloway took a chair at one end. Janelle seated herself to his right and I sat next to her on the other side. Scott positioned himself across the table from Janelle, on Galloway's left, with Craig beside him.

"All right, what's the big deal here?" Galloway asked.

Janelle withdrew the picture Scott had showed us and laid it on the table. "This is a picture of you." She said it baldly and waited for his reaction.

He glanced at it. "So?"

"Moments before this image was taken by one of our surveillance cameras, an MC Hitell 2600 tablet was stolen from a booth. This is the person who took that tablet."

He glanced from the picture to her, then around to each of us, his face a careful study of blank incomprehension. "You can't seriously be accusing me of stealing a tablet! My own company makes and sells tablets. Why on earth would I steal one?"

"That's one of the things we'd like to know from you," Janelle said. "We have some theories of our own, but we'd like to hear about it from you. And what you plan to do about compensating the victims of your crimes. We know that this wasn't the first piece of equipment stolen."

"This is crazy! You can't really be accusing me of stealing from other exhibitors."

"Actually we can." She pointed to the picture.

He looked at it again. "That doesn't prove a thing. It's just a picture of a man walking up the aisle at a trade show."

Craig said, "On its own, it doesn't prove anything. But coupled with these, it's pretty convincing." He nodded to Scott, who pulled a few more video capture images from the envelope and spread them across the table. Craig pointed to the first three. "Take a good look at these, and note the time stamps on them. In the first one, you see a rack of tablets. In the second one, just seconds later, a man in a dark coat with an interestingly uneven collar is standing in front of the rack. Another image, again just seven seconds later shows the same rack after the man has moved away, and one of the tablets on the rack is no longer there." He put a finger just below the empty spot on the picture. "From here we have a series of images that show the man in the coat with the crooked collar leaving the booth. Another camera, pointing from the opposite direction picks up the figure, which we match to the other view through details of timing, clothing and position against the background, and now we have a pretty clear view of his face. *Your* face."

Galloway's shoulders slumped. He drew in a long breath and let it out on a slow sigh. "What do you plan to do with these? Why tell me before you take them to the police?"

"Because we'd rather not go to the police," Janelle said. "It inconveniences our exhibitors and doesn't make anyone look good. Don't mistake me, we will if we have to, but we're hoping you'll co-operate in setting things right and it won't be necessary."

His eyebrows rose and a hint of relief crept into his expression. "What do you want me to do? I can't return the devices, I'm afraid. They've already been shipped off site. I can arrange for replacements to be delivered, I suppose. But I don't know if they could be delivered before the show ends."

"Replacements to be delivered wherever the victims specify and additional monetary compensation for each of the people you inconvenienced," Janelle insisted. "Some of the devices were used to demonstrate the exhibitors' programs or functions."

I zoned out a bit while they discussed the details and mechanics of how Galloway would compensate his victims and how the Center would double-check that he had. As that discussion wound down, I voiced the question that was rolling around in my head. "Why? You could've just bought them instead of stealing them."

He looked up at me. His expression showed some light chagrin and amusement, but a lot more was going on behind the faux mirth. Some rapid-fire calculations, I suspected.

"I'm tempted to tell you I have a psychological problem, a compulsion to steal things, but I don't think you'd believe it." A slight, almost genuine grin briefly curved his lips.

I considered the possibility that he was telling the truth under the guise of an obvious lie. It didn't fit with anything else I knew, however. "I don't think so. You had a purpose in swiping those things. Taking from strangers things you could just as easily have bought doesn't seem realistic."

The grin faded and he eyed me more sharply. Again I wondered what was going on behind the expression. "Perhaps, but then everyone would know I had bought them."

"Why would that be an issue?"

"I don't want word to get back to MegaComp that I'm looking more closely into the technology of the machines. I hope that if I comply with your demands, you will keep this all confidential."

"Wait. Of course, if you do find that they've infringed on your patent, you can always buy a few machines legally to check."

The tense lines around his mouth relaxed a tiny bit. Why did he look a bit relieved at my words?

"And if they don't find anything," he said, "then I don't have to worry about MegaComp coming after me for implying Chase's accusation might have some merit." He stood up, signaling that he'd said all he would. Even more of the tension that had held him stiffly upright initially had drained from him in the last minute. It was unsettling. I was willing to bet he was still hiding something and had realized I didn't see it or didn't have the leverage to pull it from him. What was I missing? His last sentence sounded okay on the surface, but didn't stand up to close examination. MegaComp wouldn't care about someone like him making accusations. Or would they? If it were true?

"Hold on," Scott told him. "We have a few more details to iron out. Everyone else can go." Galloway settled down into a chair again. Craig stayed seated as well.

As Janelle and I left the room, I checked my phone and found a message from Ted asking me to call. He'd figured out where the problem was in the wheel and knew how to fix it, but he needed a couple of things. He'd already called around and located materials and tools, but someone had to go get the stuff. I spent a few minutes on the phone in a quiet corner of the corridor, arranging with a messenger service to pick up and deliver the equipment.

Once that was taken care of, I went back to the show floor and headed over to check on how Mimi was doing and whether she'd made peace with the guys behind her. She wasn't in her space, but I spotted her within moments, sitting in the booth behind hers, next to the guy I'd talked to there the day before. It looked friendly. In fact, they were both bent over a device that was either a large smart phone or a small tablet, working on something.

Mimi looked up, saw me, and gave me a big smile.

"I take it things are okay here?" I asked.

"Oh, yeah. The boys needed a bit of a hand getting their stuff in order, so I helped them out. Looks better, doesn't it?" I glanced around the booth. A new cloth shrouded the long table at the front. Brochures were neatly stacked in racks and the product boxes had been organized into attractive and more secure display towers along the backdrop, their tops following the curve of the logo on it.

"Much better," I agreed.

"And now they're showing me how to use this program that lets me video chat with my daughter and even see my grandson and granddaughter. I heard you could do that, but I thought you had to have special equipment. Turns out not. There's this program called Skype. Tyler is showing me how to use it on my tablet. I'm telling you, the technology today is amazing. He even showed me how I can do it without using up all the data allowance on my phone plan."

Okay, so this little kerfuffle, at least, appeared to have a happy ending.

My stomach chose that moment to emit a loud rumble, reminding me it had to be past lunch time, so I said goodbye and went down to the food court. I texted Janelle, Scott and Craig to see if they could join me and got a response from Scott saying they'd be there in ten minutes. Janelle was on her way. I was too hungry to wait, and was already well tucked into a gigantic slice of pizza by the time they arrived.

When we'd all gotten enough inside to keep the hunger pangs at bay, Janelle asked, "What's up?"

I told them about the talks I'd had with Shawn, Ted and Jake and what I'd learned. We tossed around a few ideas based on those thin facts. Craig and Scott both agreed the blackmail angle seemed to fit more of the facts than anything else, though we all still stumbled over the idea of MegaComp actually needing to steal an idea.

"Suppose they didn't actually steal the idea," Craig said. "It's possible their engineers heard about what he'd done and figured out a way to do the same thing. Reverse engineering. I've heard it happens a lot. But maybe Chase heard about it and realized that what they'd done infringed on a patent he held and was trying to extort money from them for it rather than filing a lawsuit."

Scott added, "That seems to fit. But if Chase had developed this thing while he was working at SiloSystems, wouldn't the company own the patent? And when they were bought out by RTX, the patent would transfer to the new owner."

I took a sip of my drink to wash down the pizza. "So RTX would profit from any lawsuit, rather than Chase himself. Maybe he was trying to earn a few bucks for himself on the side. Possibly with Larry's help. Maybe he promised he wouldn't tell Galloway about the copying."

"But how does Markham's argument with Hovey figure into that?" Scott asked.

"Good question. Maybe trying to tighten the screws?"

Scott frowned but didn't respond.

Thinking out loud, I said, "But why was Galloway surprised when he overheard Ted and Chase's argument? It couldn't have been that MegaComp was using the same or similar technology. Chase's row with Hovey didn't come until later, so Galloway probably didn't know anything about it at that point. He must've already known there was some kind of flaw in the technology that had been fixed."

No one had any suggestions for that.

Janelle's phone buzzed and she answered. Her tone changed almost immediately and it quieted the rest of us. "That's good news, but—" A few seconds later she asked, "What can we do?" Then, "Yes, we'll tell them." And after another couple of minutes of listening, "Let us know as soon as you've made a decision."

She ended the call and looked at us. "Highway Patrol in Virginia stopped a rental car driven by Larry Barnes about ten minutes ago. He agreed to return voluntarily, so they're bringing him back here, to the police station, but it will take a while. They want to question him, then they'll decide whether to charge him with something or release him. We need to go tell the people at Gryphon-Loyall."

We were pretty much finished with lunch at that point. Craig and Scott stood and said they had things to do, though Craig asked to be informed when Janelle got further word on Barnes. Before they left, Scott drew me aside.

"What are you planning to do next?" he asked.

"I'm not sure. Time's getting short. I'd like to talk to Driscoll at MegaComp, if he'll even talk to me. I want to follow up on what Shawn said about Chase wanting to work there. If it's true that he did and HR nixed it, that might give him even more motive to lash out at them. The problem is I can't really see any motive for anyone here to kill him. MegaComp pretty clearly doesn't care about any allegations Chase Markham might've made, and why would they? They're the eight-hundred-pound gorilla and even RTX was pretty puny compared to them." I paused then said, "I wonder if Galloway was thinking about blackmail himself rather than a lawsuit. Maybe he and Chase even concocted the scene with Hovey to set it up. That could explain why he seemed relieved when I accepted his explanation earlier. But, no, that doesn't really fit either."

"This isn't your problem, Heather." Scott's tone was cold with warning.

"I know. But what if they arrest Larry Barnes for it?"

"If they do, they'll have some other evidence that ties him to the murder. Having an argument with someone and then deciding to take off without warning anyone is suspicious, but it isn't probable cause for an arrest warrant."

"Oh, yeah, I guess that's true. What about Drake Galloway? If he didn't know before, he might've been so mad at Chase for hiding MegaComp's possible patent infringement that there was a fight and things...well, happened."

"It's possible, and the next time you or Janelle talks to Gilmont, you need to tell him about it. Don't go tackling Galloway yourself."

"We've had this talk," I reminded him. "Not too long ago. I don't plan to do anything stupid."

Scott's expression softened and got rueful. "You're right. It's easier to talk about it than it is to stop my gut reaction."

"Got that. And I'm not sure I want you to totally stop."

He rolled his eyes and said, "Mixed messages. Go. Be yourself."

There was too much warm affection on the last words for me to take offense.

I caught up with Janelle and we headed over to the Gryphon-Loyall booth. We found Ross Campbell, Jennifer and Jake Rogers there. When I looked around for Ted, Jennifer said he was off somewhere meeting with someone. Or he might still be working on the shielding on the game wheel. I let Janelle handle telling them the news while I watched their reactions.

Their faces all showed pretty much the same thing. Relief that Larry was safe came first, followed by concern when told that the police wanted to question him before releasing him.

"You mean they might arrest him?" Jennifer asked.

"It's possible."

"But they can't! Larry didn't kill anybody."

"Can you prove it?" I asked. "Can you vouch for where he was between three o'clock and three-thirty on Monday?" I looked around at the others. "Anyone?"

They all looked kind of blank. Finally Jennifer said, "No. I went to the MegaComp presentation and then on the way back I met an old friend and we talked for a while. I think it was nearly four when I got back to the booth."

"He wasn't in the booth," Ross Campbell said. "He'd said he was going to the presentation, too. Everyone did but Jake and me."

"So you two were here in the booth. What time did Larry get back?"

"Around four thirty," Jake said. "I remember it was pretty late in the day because I had a couple of questions to ask him about where to put things and by the time he got back we were almost done with everything else."

"I still don't believe it," Jennifer insisted. "Larry isn't the type who'd do that."

"You never know how other people will react when the pressure is really on," I told her. Did I ever know it was true, too.

She just sighed. "What can we do to help him, anyway? Get him a lawyer?"

"Let's wait until he gets back to D.C.," Janelle said. "I'll have one on standby."

A group of potential customers wandered into the booth. Jennifer turned her attention to them. We said goodbye to the others and left.

As we walked away, Janelle looked at her phone. She read off a message to me. "Twenty-four twenty-two. Something broken. Will you check on it?"

"Sure. See you—"

"Oh, in case I forget, the big award gala and fund-raiser is tomorrow night. I'd like both you and Scott there if you can manage it. Will you tell him? I'll leave the tickets on your desk."

"Will do," I answered. I'd seen it on the schedule, knew she'd want me to go, and still managed to forget about it until she mentioned it. I'd picked up a to-die-for Tadashi lace shift at a consignment store a couple of weeks ago and was more than ready to have an excuse to wear it. With Scott as an escort the gala would definitely be mixing business with pleasure.

I got to the booth at twenty-four oh eight and saw the problem before anyone approached. One of the braces holding up their backdrop had either broken or come loose and the banner hung sadly askew. I put in a call to maintenance and Mark showed up ten minutes later.

As I turned to go, leaving him to do the repair, he called, "Heather."

I faced him again. He set down the screwdriver he'd pulled out of his toolbox, walked toward me, and motioned me to join him out of earshot of anyone else.

"Listen, Heather, I know this isn't really a good time, but I don't know when will be. I gotta warn you. Scott Brandon? He ain't really what he seems, and I think he could be trouble. Maybe for all of us."

I stared at him. "What are you talking about?"

"Brandon. You know how he says he was once a cop? I don't know if that's true."

"Why not? I'm pretty sure Craig verified it before he hired him."

"I don't know. I just get this sense of something wrong about him. Why would a guy who was a real cop want to work here?"

I'd asked myself that question more than once. I'd even asked Scott about it. His answer was that he hadn't kept his mouth shut about something when he should have and it cost him his job. It wasn't entirely satisfactory, but it was all I'd gotten and I didn't think he'd want me sharing even that much.

"I'm still pretty sure Craig would've checked him out," I said. "And to be honest, I've got too many other things to worry about right now that are more important."

The words came out more sharply than I intended and Mark looked taken aback.

"Sorry, I didn't mean to snap at you," I said. "It's just that we've got so many major problems right now that I can't worry about the smaller ones."

"It's smaller now," he said. "But it may not stay small. I know you like him. I just want you to be careful."

I decided to take it at face value. I'd have to deal with all of it—Mark, Scott, and our relationship—eventually, but I just didn't have time or energy for it right now.

"I appreciate the warning," I told Mark. "I'll keep it in mind. Now, I need to get back to work. You got this?" I nodded to the sagging banner.

"Sure." He took the hint and went back to the repairs, while I moved away.

I was heading back toward the Gryphon booth, using the back aisle, then turning to cut across to the middle at the eighteen hundred aisle, along the far side of the MegaComp extravaganza, but as I rounded the far corner, I saw that Jim Driscoll and two other men had just left the booth by a back exit and I all but plowed into them.

I said, "Mr. Driscoll, I'm sorry to disturb you, but could I have a short, private word with you? I just have one quick question."

He looked annoyed and I thought for a moment he'd refuse, but he told his companions he'd catch up with them, then turned to me and said, "What is it?"

"It's about Chase Markham, of course. Rumor has it that he badly wanted to work for MegaComp, but his application was rejected. Can you tell me if that's so?"

"You should know I can't discuss company personnel issues. Markham was a very bright young man with issues that probably hindered him reaching his goals. That's all I can say. I would like to know who is spreading those rumors, though."

I returned his frown with the sweetest smile I could muster. "And I'm sure you'll understand that I can't discuss my sources either."

His eyes narrowed and lips compressed before he nodded. "Then if you'll excuse me." He turned and walked away before I could respond. Not that I had anything more to say anyway.

I thought I had my answer. Most likely the rumors were true, that Chase had applied for a job at MegaComp and been turned down. All the more reason he might want to try a bit of blackmail. But why would anyone at MegaComp actually care?

I rang Scott's number to remind him about the banquet the next night, then called Janelle to check on the status of Larry Barnes. She hadn't heard anything. By then it was ten to six and the place was shutting down. As I went upstairs for my purse, I realized I was totally beat and prayed nothing would delay me in getting out of there.

Somewhere in the middle of the night I had a dream about finding Chase Markham's body. But it morphed into one of those weird running in place things where I knew someone who meant me harm was coming closer and closer, but I couldn't manage to move a muscle. I woke with a start, panting and sweating, as though I'd been running for miles.

I got up for a glass of water. While I was drinking, it occurred to me that, although technically the show went through noon Sunday, most people departed Sunday morning, leaving only the low-level guys to handle whatever stragglers showed up and then dismantling and packing up the displays. Essentially there was only a day left. And while the police might still find out who killed Chase Markham, it got much less likely once everyone had dispersed.

We might never know who did it.

SEVENTEEN

Saturday

I DIDN'T HURRY into work the next morning. It was going to be a long day and I found myself curiously reluctant to get on with it. I love my job most of the time, so this was not the norm. Maybe I just needed that vacation Janelle had been urging on me.

There were no messages on my phone summoning me to any particular area when I arrived at eight, so I went upstairs to my desk to try to catch up on paperwork. Janelle came in twenty minutes later, looking even more beat than I felt.

"You look like someone who had a rough night," I said as she came in.

"I got a call to get a lawyer for Larry Barnes at two o'clock this morning. Broke up my beauty sleep and then I had a hard time dozing off again," she said. "Then I got a call at five-thirty from the lawyer, saying the police were releasing him." She yawned. "All in all, not the most restful night."

"Still, I'm glad they didn't arrest Larry."

"I gather he's a pretty likable sort? Everyone at Gryphon seemed pretty worried about him, too."

"He is. I wonder if he's here now? I'd really love to know what he told the cops."

She gave me a stern look. "It's not really our problem."

"I know. It's just that I like him and I'm concerned about what happened to send him running like that."

She gave me a crooked grin. "Of course. Just don't do anything that *I'll* regret later."

"*Moi*?" I widened my eyes and blinked a few times, working on charming innocence.

Her laugh was half-real and half-sarcastic. "That won't work on me. You have a history."

I gave it up. "And you're immune anyway."

"Just take care."

Her cell phone rang and she answered as she turned to walk away. I heard her say, "What?" then "When?" and finally, "Okay. We'll get on it."

She turned and came back to my desk. "You can talk to your boy after you check on this one. Coffee disaster at seven-fourteen. Sounds like an urn overturned. Call maintenance. Make sure no one was hurt. You know the drill."

I did. I called maintenance before I left my desk and got a promise that someone would meet me at the booth. I hoped no one was hurt. Something similar had happened a couple of months after I'd started here, where someone banged into a coffee urn hard enough to send it flying. We'd sent one person to the hospital with second degree burns.

This time the mess was greater, but the only injury was a man with a few small red patches where coffee had splattered him. Nice suits on two others might or might not be salvageable with dry cleaning. The clean-up, however, was going to take a while. Sam was already there, setting up a wet-dry vacuum and handing out cloths to the employees who were using paper towels to mop coffee splotches off the backdrop and table.

I headed toward the Gryphon-Loyall booth and found Ted and Jennifer there. Both looked much better than the previous day, their expressions lighter, although Jennifer still had dark shadows under her eyes. Ted was engaged with someone, but Jennifer smiled and came to join me.

"I heard the good news about Larry," I said.

"Yes, thank goodness," she said. "I knew he hadn't killed anyone. So glad the police agree."

"Is he coming in this morning? I'd really like to talk to him."

"Wouldn't we all? He's sleeping it off right now. I heard he didn't get back to the hotel until five this morning, so he's got a bit of a sleep deficit."

"Will you let me know when he gets here? You all probably have a lot of questions for him, but I'd like to hear his answers as well. We're running out of time. The police will act on whatever information he gave them, but it might help us to help others here."

Before she answered, Ted joined us. I checked out his tie, a particularly attractive shade of blue with diagrams of what I thought was some kind a molecule scattered over it. A central hexagon had a pentagon hanging off one side and lines to letters on the others. There were lots of Cs, Hs, and an O and an N on it. "How do you find all these nice-looking ties with the geeky stuff on them? And by the way, what is that?"

He gave me that winning grin. "I find them on the Internet. Then Jen tells me which ones I can and can't wear."

"I totally had to nix the Cthulhu one." Jennifer grinned at him and a little buzz went off inside my head.

Yes, there was something between them, but I wasn't sure either of them had acknowledged it yet.

I raised a hand. "I totally have no idea what a Cthulhu is."

"Some kind of fictional monster," Jen answered. "Looks kind of like an octopus. *Not* a good look for a tie."

"H.P. Lovecraft," Ted said. "It's a classic."

"Still made for a seriously ugly tie. I like this one, though." Jennifer pointed at the tie, but after just a moment, she lifted her gaze to look Ted in the eye. That look confirmed my suspicion that she liked more than just his ties. And "like" might be understating the case. Did Ted know?

"It's nice," I agreed. "But what is it? I recognize that it's some kind of molecule drawing."

"One that's very important to geeks and non-geeks alike," Ted said. "Caffeine."

"Oh. That would make it one of my favorites," I said.

"I'll bet you can get a tee shirt with it on, too," Ted offered.

"I'll look into it after the show's over. Have you heard anything about what made Larry suddenly decide to leave town?"

"Not yet—"

A buzz from my phone broke into the conversation. I glanced at the screen. "I think I'd better take this," I told them. "Please, let me know when Larry gets here. I really need to talk to him."

They promised they would. I moved away from the booth and said, "Hi, Sandy. What's up?"

She drew a breath that sounded like a sob before she said, "Heather, please. I don't know what to do. The police are here searching the booth and won't let me in it. Plus, they took Drake away to their office and I think they're going to arrest him."

"I'll be there in a moment," I told her. My next call was to Janelle. "Did you know the police are searching the RTX booth? I'm on my way over there now. Sandy said they took Galloway away."

"I'll meet you there in five minutes."

It only took me a minute or so to get there, but I couldn't get into the booth since yellow "crime scene" tape surrounded and blocked it off. A small crowd of gawkers had gathered to watch two police officers moving things in the booth while a third was doing something with a brush and powder on the backdrop.

I felt someone tap me on the shoulder and I whirled around to face Sandy. Her eyes were puffy and she looked scared. I nudged her away from the booth a couple of spaces down the aisle.

"Janelle will be here any moment. In the meantime, what happened?"

Her voice sounded breathy as she said, "I'm not even sure. I came in a bit late this morning, and when I got here this is what I found." She pointed at the booth. "I tried to ask those officers what was going on, but they wouldn't say anything. Then Drake came out of the back with that detective who was here before and one other officer and said he needed to go with them. I asked if I could do anything, but he just shook his head. He looked sort of...dazed, I guess."

"So you don't know what they're looking for?"

"No, and I don't know what to do now. Can we find out when I'll be able to get back in?"

"I can try—" I broke off as I saw Janelle approach.

She stopped at the booth and summoned one of the people searching. I couldn't hear the conversation, but I figured out fairly quickly that she was asking if they had a warrant. The tech went behind the curtain and returned with a piece of paper. Janelle read through it, then came over to join us. "What do we know?"

"Probably less than you do right now," I answered.

Sandy repeated what she'd told me, ending with the question of what to do now.

Janelle looked at me. "Which one of us calls Gilmont?"

"He likes you better than he likes me," I said.

"Yeah, but he respects your intuition more."

"Not gonna help us here," I reminded her.

"Right." She pulled out her phone and found the entry for him. It took a while before he answered. She said, "Pete, this is Janelle. What's going on with Drake Galloway and the crowd at the RTX booth?" She listened for too short a time before saying, "That's not particularly helpful." Another pause. "I understand you can't talk about an ongoing investigation. Are you arresting him?" Pause. "That's not very helpful, either. I'm sending our lawyer back there."

She ended the call and immediately rang another number. The lawyer apparently didn't give her as much grief about going back to the police station as I would've expected. We must pay them a nice retainer. She ended the call and sighed. "He's not saying much."

I raised an eyebrow at her. "*Pete*?"

"What? You're the only one who's allowed to have a social life?"

"Well, no, but… With him?"

"We're both uncommitted adults."

"He is rather good-looking," I admitted. "But maddening."

"Good at his job," Janelle said.

"What did the warrant say they were looking for?"

"It wasn't very specific except for something about ethernet cables and cell phones. Otherwise, it was anything related to the business and personal relationship between Drake Galloway, RTX Inc., and Charles Markham."

"Cell phones? Isn't that like searching for a piece of straw in the haystack?"

"I think they're looking for one that's been used. Have you talked to Larry Barnes?"

"He was still at the hotel sleeping it off when I dropped by earlier. They promised to call me when he came in."

"Make sure they do. I want to know what he told the police." She turned to go.

"I guess I'd better stay here until they finish and decide what to do with the booth," Sandy said.

"Let me know when they release it and if you need any help." I'd probably regret making that offer, but Sandy looked so lost and distraught, I had to do it.

I didn't have any messages on my phone and wasn't ready to go back upstairs, so I spent the next few minutes walking the aisles, thinking about Chase Markham and the events of Monday, before he'd been murdered. I knew he'd had words with Larry that morning, urgent words, but not necessarily an argument. With Ted, on the other hand, he'd had a definite argument, witnessed in part by Drake Galloway. Since Sandy had thought Chase was in the back when I first tried to talk with him, it was safe to assume she'd talked with him, and probably Galloway, too. I still couldn't fathom the very public argument with Hovey. Had he just learned something that caused him to lose his temper and go after the man or was there some other purpose? All of his other confrontations had been semi-private, but that one was very public.

As I passed by the eleven hundred aisle, I stopped for a moment to watch the light show and the big wheel at the Schwartz-Mann Booth. Dieter was in a front corner arranging flyers but looked up and saw me. He smiled and waved me over. "Heather," he said, only mangling my name slightly. "We owe you thanks. We did not know we had this problem and made trouble for others here. We would not do it with intent. The lights and noise were to attract attention, but the other thing was a great problem we did not mean to cause. We're very grateful for your help and to that man who helped us fix it. We would like to know if there is something we can do to show you and him how much we appreciate it?"

"Thanks, but I can't really think of anything you can do. We're just grateful that you were willing to co-operate in getting it fixed so quickly."

His smile was the most genuine I'd seen so far. "We are grateful for your help. Wait." His eyebrows rose and smile deepened as an idea struck him. "Wait here a moment." He disappeared to the far side of the booth and came back a moment later with what looked like a stack of tickets. "Drink vouchers for the bar at the banquet to-night. We buy many of them to use for clients, but I think you and that man… Ted?…can use some." He handed me a stack of the coupons. "Our pleasure if you use these. Will you give some to Ted?"

I agreed to share. I probably wouldn't use more than one myself and if I knew Scott he would stick to soft drinks, but I imagined that Ted would be happy to stand his coworkers to a round.

As I was turning to leave, Dieter said, "I almost forgot. Martin found this phone sitting on a display a couple of days ago." He held out a smart phone, then turned it over to show it had no markings to identify the owner. "I was going to call your office to tell about it, but we put it aside and forgot. Perhaps you know if anyone has lost a phone?"

"People do it here all the time," I said. "You're sure it doesn't belong to one of your people? Can you turn it on and check the contacts?"

"It has no charge," he said. "I've asked all our people here. No one knows of it. We don't use this type and we don't have a charger for it."

I took it from him. "I'll put it in our lost and found. We hang onto them for a while to see if someone will claim them."

"Is good," he said.

I said goodbye, and put the phone and the drink coupons in my pocket. My own phone buzzed with a message about a couple of issues to take care of. I was on the second of those when I had a brain flash. Chase had had three phones. The police could only account for two. Was I carrying the missing third phone in my pocket? The only way to find out was to get it charged enough to run.

Who would recognize the brand and have a charger that would work with it? The obvious answer was Ted, but I'd already put enough on him with the interference quest. And in truth, I wasn't sure it was a good idea to ask him about it since he or his friends at Gryphon-Loyall had been involved in whatever led to Chase Markham's murder. I needed someone who had chargers for a number of different kinds of phones, but didn't have any involvement in the crime. The answer hit me quickly.

But as I was making my way toward that end of the show floor, my phone buzzed again. I saw Ted's name displayed. "Larry's here," he said. "He's with Ross right now. Bit of explaining to do there. No idea how long that will take, or what kind of mood he'll be in after. He still looks pretty wrung out, even with the extra sleep."

"I'm sorry to hear it," I told him, "but I still need to have a talk with him."

"I understand. But he's still worried. He'd rather no one know he's around. So, he's asking if there's some way to do this privately. Is there a conference room we could use? And could we not go there all together?"

"Give me a minute to check on what rooms are available and I'll buzz you back."

I knew the room I wanted. An almost hidden, fairly small conference room was tucked away in a back corner off a far hallway. The room we'd used for the confrontation with Galloway. It was well away from all the other meeting rooms and approached by a hallway that wasn't used for anything else, so it offered extra privacy. A quick call confirmed it wasn't scheduled for use today. Janelle had a meeting and couldn't make it, but Scott promised to get there as quickly as he could. On the way, I checked in at the kitchen and asked for coffee and water service in the room as soon as they could get it there.

Jennifer and Larry came in moments after I arrived and closed the door behind them. The latter wore a base-ball cap that covered his distinctive red hair and went oddly with the dress shirt, green tie and jeans. He sat down without saying anything.

"Ted needs to cover the booth for a bit," Jennifer said. "I'll fill him in later."

"Scott Brandon will be coming in a few minutes. Also coffee and water are on the way." A rattling at the door suggested one or the other had arrived. In fact, it was both. Scott held the door for the server pushing the cart. All of us got coffee in silence.

When we sat back down, Larry didn't even wait to take a sip. "The first thing I have to say is I'm sorry. I shouldn't have run out the way I did. I got spooked and panicked. I really regret all the fuss and worry I caused. The second thing is that I did *not* kill Chase, and I don't know who did. I'm not sure why he was killed, though I have my suspicions."

"What made you take off the way you did?" Scott asked.

"A piece of paper. One that disappeared. I probably need to back up a bit to explain. A few months ago, I got a call from Chase. He had a business proposition for me. He had an idea that he'd patented that didn't belong to his employers and he wanted me to be his agent and negotiate the deal for him to sell the rights. He had a lead on a buyer, but wouldn't tell me who it was. He asked if I'd be interested in being his agent for a ten percent commission."

Larry took off his hat, put it in his lap and ran his fingers through his hair. "I needed some extra money at the time, so I said I'd do it. A month or so later, he told me it was a go and who he was selling the patent rights to. I freaked out a bit, told him we needed to have a lawyer involved. He said he already had a lawyer who'd draw

up the contract, but he needed a salesman, me, to negotiate the terms."

"So who was he selling it to?" I asked.

"MegaComp." Larry took in our surprised expressions. "I know. That's how I felt. But it was true. He
gave me a name and number to contact and told me what
his bottom-line terms were. I called the number, nego-
tiated the best deal I could and both sides agreed. I got
him most of what he wanted. We drew up the contract
and it was signed by both parties. I got my ten percent
of a very nice haul, and I thought that was the end of it."

He drew a deep breath and sighed. "You know he
came to the booth Monday morning and we talked. He
told me then that he wasn't happy with the deal. The
money was nice, but he'd really wanted the one thing
I couldn't get him…employment at MegaComp. I reminded him that we couldn't make that part of the contract. It didn't work that way. They gave him a verbal
commitment to try and that was it. Apparently it didn't
work out and he was really unhappy. I told him there was
nothing I could do about it. After a while, he seemed
to accept that, but then he had his huge argument with
Hovey in public and I couldn't figure out what the hell
he was doing. How could he accuse them of stealing
something he'd sold to them himself? Or was it something else he sold them and this was a separate issue?"

He shrugged. "I tried to find him later to ask him,
but couldn't run him down. He didn't return my calls or
Skype requests."

"What happened yesterday morning?" Scott asked.

"My copy of the contract disappeared, and I got a note
from Drake Galloway. I don't know for sure those two
things are connected, but I think they are. Anyway, Gal-

loway wanted to meet with me. He didn't give details, but I'm guessing he found out about Chase's deal with Mega-Comp and wanted to know exactly what he gave them. And maybe he wanted more than that. I don't know."

That explained why the police had wanted Galloway to come in and talk to them. It wasn't enough for an arrest, though, so obviously they knew something else. "How much do you know about what Chase licensed to MegaComp?" I asked.

"Not much. I'm a salesman, not an engineer. Chase and MegaComp's people knew what it was and what it did, so I just helped work out the terms of the deal."

Scott beat me to the first question that came to mind. "The deal was executed months ago. Why did you have the contract with you here?"

"Chase had asked me to bring it. He'd misplaced his copy and wanted to make another copy from mine."

I followed up with a couple more questions. "Who did you negotiate with at MegaComp? And how did you know them?"

"The name is Kellin Farraday. Chase gave me the name. Apparently he'd gotten it from someone he knew who knew someone at MegaComp. I'm not even sure what this Kellin's position is in the company. Some kind of manager, I guess."

"Is he here at the show?"

"You'd have to ask the MegaComp people, but I don't think so."

"But he signed the contract?"

"No, he just worked out the terms."

"Who did sign it?" I asked.

"Hovey, of course."

That silenced us all for a moment, until Scott asked,

"But the copy has disappeared now? You realized it was gone yesterday morning, but do you have any idea when it actually disappeared?"

"Not exactly. After Chase died, I…" He stared at Jennifer and shrugged an odd apology. "I had it in my briefcase, but I was so shocked that I didn't even think of it again until a couple of days later. I saw it while I was looking for something else. Then yesterday morning I got that note from Drake Galloway, and it shook me up again. It occurred to me that the contract might be related to Chase's death and I should probably give it to the police. When I tried to find it, it was gone."

"No one else saw anyone going through your briefcase?"

Larry shook his head.

"You left it in the booth overnight?"

"One night. I forgot about it and left it in the back."

"You think Galloway took it?" Scott asked.

"I don't know. But who else would have any reason to?"

EIGHTEEN

Saturday

"HE HAD A point about who else would have had any reason to take it," I said fifteen minutes later, when Janelle, Scott, and I, joined by Craig, gathered in a corner of the food court for a late lunch.

Scott picked up the turkey wrap from his plate, but set it down again without taking a bite. "Galloway certainly seems to have had the motivation. And he'd have the means and the opportunity."

"To kill Markham?" Craig asked.

Scott nodded and finally took a bite of the wrap.

I stared at the hot dog on my plate and found it didn't make me as happy as I'd expected. Hot dogs had always cheered me up before. "I'm still not sure it makes sense, though. Why would he be so upset that Markham had licensed something to MegaComp? I mean the guy worked for him, but Galloway didn't own him. And if he developed it on his own time, didn't he have the right to do whatever he wanted with it?"

"There may have been something in his employment contract that specified anything he discovered or developed while on the company's payroll belonged to the company," Janelle suggested. "I think that's fairly common with researchers and engineers."

"So maybe he was cheating his employer with this. Galloway found out and was so angry he killed him?"

"It's one possible scenario," Scott said.

The fry stuck in my throat and I had to take a drink to wash it down. "But then why did Chase pick a fight with Hovey and accuse him of stealing the idea from him?"

"Cover his tracks? Divert attention?" Craig suggested.

"Hovey could've just said, 'Look, you idiot, you signed a contract' and ended it right there. Why didn't he?"

Craig snorted. "I'll bet he signs dozens of things a day. You think he reads them all?"

"That's what he has minions for." Scott's tone was so deadpan, I had to cover my mouth to keep from spewing soda.

"But I read this article on Hovey a while back, and it sounded like he was this total control freak. He was all about the details and making sure his product was perfect down to the last button. Would someone like that sign important agreements without even looking at them?"

Scott said, "It doesn't mean he'd remember every detail."

My phone buzzed. Sandy said the police were letting her back into the booth, but they'd left it a mess. I told her I'd be there in approximately ten minutes, but I'd get a crew there to help with the clean up.

After I made the call to maintenance, Janelle reminded Scott and me about the Awards Banquet that night. I promised to be there and on my best behavior. Scott said he'd dig out his suit. I could hardly wait for that. Scott's tall, lean body did really nice things for a suit. His wink and the small, wry smile he threw toward me said he'd caught both my stare and the drift of my thoughts. Even Janelle raised an eyebrow and grinned. Scott said he'd pick me up at six-thirty since the dinner started at seven. The show floor closed at five rather than the usual six today since it was Saturday.

My face felt hot as I headed for the RTX booth. The area didn't look quite as bad as it had the morning of the reported vandalism. I found Sam already there, using a cloth to clean powder off various boxes and things.

"Mark's gone to get the vacuum," Sam told me. While we waited for him to return, I helped Sandy straighten piles of boxes and sort sell sheets and other items. We replaced a piece of the backdrop the police had removed. It had never occurred to me that something might be hidden within the backdrop itself, which was possible only if it were fairly thin. If anything had been there, the police had found and removed it.

"This has been nothing but a nightmare!" Sandy exclaimed, anger and sorrow combined in her words. "Chase is murdered, the booth trashed…not once, but twice!…and now Drake's been arrested for murder. I don't believe it!"

"Don't believe he did it, or don't believe they arrested him for it?"

She gave me a wide-eyed look before she said, "Both."

"We don't always know people as well as we think we do," I ventured.

She waved it off with a slashing hand gesture. "Drake didn't kill him. I'm sure of it."

"Can you prove it? Can you verify where he was when Chase was murdered?"

"No." She drew a quick breath. "But I've worked with him for three years. I've seen him get angry. He has a temper, for sure, but things blow over and he gets over it. He doesn't hold grudges."

"He could've done this in a temper. We think he'd just learned that Chase had betrayed him in a very major way."

"He's been unhappy with Chase for a long time," Sandy countered. "And think about this. Why would he trash his own booth?"

I handed her a stack of flyers and straightened up. "Okay, I tend to agree with you. But that doesn't help us figure out who did kill Chase. And that's Drake's best defense. Figure out who really did it."

We were just about done and I was eager to get away. A quick glance at my phone showed it was almost four. Time was running out. A lot of people would be leaving early in the morning, letting lower level staff handle the few stragglers showing up for the morning session. I told Sandy goodbye and headed for the five hundred aisle.

Mimi waved at me as I went by and said, "Hey, I got some more pens I gotta get rid of. Want a couple?"

"Sure. Can I stop by tomorrow to get them?"

"You come by about eleven and you can have any that I still got."

I went on by to the booth behind hers, now much neater and better organized than the first time I'd seen it. Joel Hallaway was there, with the first guy I'd talked to. Both smiled as I approached.

Hallaway spoke first. "Thanks for recommending for this. It's worked out great."

The other guy, Bob Something, said, "It's been a big help."

He started to say something more, but I cut him off. "I need help. I've got a phone that's been lost, but it has no charge so I can't get any information from it. I hoped you might have the right charger."

Bob took it from me and looked at the sides and bottom. "It's an XPZ. They've got funky connectors. I'm afraid we don't have that kind of charger. I'm sorry."

"Any idea who might?"

He thought about it a minute. "There are a few guys around who are selling software for lots of different kinds of phones. One of them might."

"Right. I know one of them." After a quick thanks I took off, heading a couple of aisles down near the end of the show floor.

It took Vanessa Connelly a moment to recognize me. "You're the lady who works for the Center," she said. "I heard you caught the guy who took the MegaComp unit and we'll be compensated for it. You have no idea how much of a relief that is. I really appreciate it."

"The Center does everything we can to keep things like that from happening, and we try to make it right when it does. But for now, I need your help with something." I went through my spiel about the phone and needing a charger as I handed the unit to her.

"An XPZ. Not many people have them in the U.S. It's more popular in Europe. But, yeah, I have a display model and a charger." She went to a corner of the booth, reached under the table, and rummaged in a box. When she pressed the power button, the unit fired up and showed a screen with a green background and a group of icons.

"There's usually an icon for settings that will show who the phone belongs to," Vanessa said. She pressed a button and swiped to the side a couple of times. "Ah, here it is." She stumbled a bit pronouncing the last name. I didn't recognize it.

My heart sank and disappointment clogged my throat. I hadn't realized how much hope I'd pinned on this being Chase Markham's missing phone. I thought I'd had the key to unlocking the mystery of his murderer. But I had nothing.

Vanessa picked up on my disappointment. "I'm sorry," she said. "I think you were hoping for something else? That it belonged to someone else?"

I told myself it wasn't the end of the world. Maybe the police were right and Drake Galloway did do it. I managed to assure Vanessa that it was fine and I appreciated her help. I made a note of the name and took the phone back from her.

It was almost five by then. I had one more stop before I went upstairs to check out. At the Gryphon-Loyall booth I found Ted and Jennifer manning the area. No sign of the others. Traffic in the hall had dwindled to almost nothing by then. No one wanted to hang around late on a Saturday afternoon, with the big award ceremony coming up later that evening.

I gave the drink tickets to Ted, explaining that they were a thank you gift for fixing the problem with the wheel. He accepted with enthusiasm and gave Jennifer a smile that held more than a touch of steam. I tamped down on a small curl of jealousy. Scott had looked at me the same way once or twice, but our relationship still had a lot of complications and I wasn't entirely sure it had a long-term future.

"How's Larry doing?" I asked.

Ted and Jennifer both looked more serious. "Okay," Jennifer said. "I guess. This has really zapped him. I think it's going to take a while before he can get beyond it."

"I can imagine." Actually I knew all too well. And then I thought of something that had been niggling in the back of my mind. "Larry said Chase had asked him to bring the contract because he'd lost his copy. But apparently Larry still had the contract a couple of days ago. Didn't he give it to Chase?"

Ted made a harsh noise that might have been a wry chuckle. "I asked him about it. He said Chase just wanted to see it then. Said he'd come by later to get it and make a copy."

"Odd that he just wanted to see it. I wonder if he wanted to check the exact wording?"

"No idea," Ted said. "Are you coming to the banquet tonight?"

"It's a command performance for me."

"Great. We'll use one of these to buy you a drink. Are you allowed to drink at these things?"

"Technically I'm off duty, but I still represent the Center, so I'm careful about it. I'll usually have one glass of wine and make it last for the evening."

"Good. Come and see us first."

"Will anyone else from the Center be there?" Jennifer asked.

"Janelle will, undoubtedly."

"The Director? Are you bringing someone? A date?"

I raised my eyebrows. "One of the Center's security people will be escorting me."

She gave me a hard look, then the grin returned. "The hunky blond guy! Scott, right?" She apparently saw confirmation in my expression since she turned a triumphant smile on Ted. "I *told* you there was something between them."

"We've dated a few times, that's all."

"Right."

Around us other exhibitors were closing down their booths, so I told them goodbye and headed upstairs. Scott texted a message to meet him at his car at five-fifteen and he'd drive me home.

I couldn't stop thinking about Chase Markham on the way upstairs. I tried to work out in my mind what he'd done the morning he'd been killed. It sounded like his first stop had been at Gryphon-Loyall to see Larry and look at the contract. But all he'd done was look. Then he'd accosted Jennifer, who'd brushed him off. Was that before or after he'd seen Larry? I wasn't sure. It was certainly before Chase had words with Ted, who tackled him about his faulty hardware as well as harassing his co-worker. Actually, what I'd just seen pretty much confirmed she was more than just a co-worker for Ted.

That was when Drake Galloway had possibly learned that something about their latest and greatest release might be faulty. But Chase had said it was fixed, so why should that bother Drake? Then Chase had that very public argument with Tom Hovey, and I still didn't get what the point of that had been.

That argument had a different feel to it than the one with Ted earlier. The one with Hovey seemed more like a show. It seemed likely Chase had been trying to make something public. The fact that MegaComp was using technology he'd developed? Why would he even want that to be public knowledge? They'd bought that technology from him, legally. More likely he was trying to squeeze more money out of them. He'd wanted to work for them, but clearly that wasn't going to happen, so more money was the obvious goal. But what was the leverage? Threat of a lawsuit from his employer? Why would MegaComp even care? That would be like an elephant worrying about a mosquito. It didn't make sense.

Something niggled at my brain, but it refused to come into focus. It wasn't until I was passing through the lobby upstairs and saw a couple of magazines on the table that I remembered.

"Control freak," I muttered to myself. Pieces started re-arranging themselves in my mind and began to fall into place. By the time I'd got my purse and checked out, I was pretty sure I knew who'd killed Chase Markham. It was logical and fit all the facts I had.

Problem? A nice, logical fit wasn't the same as evidence. The police weren't likely to be impressed by it. But it could start them looking in the right place.

NINETEEN

Saturday-Sunday

I DECIDED NOT to wait for the elevator and called Detective Gilmont as I headed down the back stairs to the parking lot. And of course, I got his voice mail. How much to say? Just enough to get his attention. After his message I identified myself and said, "I think I know something interesting about who killed Chase Markham. Can you give me a call back as soon as possible?"

Scott walked up as I was talking and listened shamelessly. Once I hung up, he unlocked the door for me, and I got in. He got in the driver's side and turned on the engine before he said, "Explain."

I told him how I'd reviewed what I knew of what Chase Markham had done the morning he was murdered and my assumptions about Chase's motive for the argument with Hovey. He followed my chain of reasoning, nodding frequently but not interrupting. When I finished he said, "It makes sense, but it's not a slam dunk."

"And I'm reluctant to make an accusation like that without any evidence to back it up. But it makes everything fit. And I'm just telling Gilmont. Maybe if they know where to start looking, they can find something."

He drove north toward Bethesda. "I think you're probably right," Scott said, after negotiating a couple of tricky turns. "But proving it won't be easy. Hovey's got an army of the best lawyers in the country at his beck and call. I don't see anything clear-cut enough to be probable cause for a warrant. If the phone had turned out to be Markham's you might've had something."

I laughed harshly. "I probably would've had that slam dunk. More likely the killer has the phone now though. Or maybe not."

"What?"

"Why did someone trash the RTX booth?"

"Looking for the contract? At that point Hovey probably didn't know Markham didn't have it. In fact, searching the Gryphon booth was probably a case of trying to cover all the bases. We know Hovey's a stickler for detail."

"Hmm… Maybe. But the contract could be a smoking gun, too, depending on the wording. If the police can get hold of it."

My phone buzzed. A check of the screen showed it was Gilmont returning my call. When he asked "What's up?" I explained what I thought had happened and why I thought Hovey was behind it, if not directly responsible. The detective was quiet for a few long moments after I stopped talking. So long I wondered if the call had disconnected. When I prompted him, he said, "Don't do anything stupid."

"I wasn't planning to, but I'm not sure what you mean by something stupid."

"You know exactly what I mean. No approaching killers on your own."

"Geez, you really don't have a high opinion of my intelligence!"

"I honestly do respect your intelligence. Some of the same things have occurred to us, too. In fact, we were approaching the same conclusion ourselves, though we were having trouble with the motive. Yours makes sense, to some degree, though I have to doubt that bad publicity would cause Hovey to do something so drastic. That isn't to say we're ready to make an arrest. There needs to be a lot more evidence for that. And it should be noted that we could all be mistaken."

That stopped me for a minute. He was right. My reasoning made sense. Most of the pieces fit. But there wasn't a shred of hard proof for it. And there was always the possibility I was wrong, that there was another way to look at events.

I suppressed a sigh. "I get it. But this show is over tomorrow. People will be leaving in the morning. What are the odds that we'll get closure on it once they're all dispersed?"

"I understand your feelings," Gilmont said. "You think we don't share your frustration? But we've got to have something more substantial than gut feelings and hunches. That's the way the law works."

"I hear you. If I think of something—"

"Buzz me," the detective said, and ended the call.

"He wants evidence, something concrete to connect Hovey to the crime," I said.

The light changed and Scott tapped the gas pedal. The blobs of street and traffic lights ahead began to melt and run together. I put my head in my hands and pressed on my eyes to push back the tears.

I wasn't sure which was worse. Knowing who committed murder and having no way to prove it, or not knowing at all.

I'm pretty sure the awards banquet was lovely, but I can't remember that I actually noticed the decor, tasted the food, or heard the music and speeches. I saw and talked to the Gryphon-Loyall people, except Larry, who'd elected to pass on the event. Ted and Jennifer bought Scott and me drinks. I was distraught enough to accept the offer of a second glass of wine. Scott gave me a surprised look, but since I wasn't driving, he didn't say anything.

Even the second glass of wine couldn't cut through the frustration and anger. A murderer was going to go free and another person might well be blamed for the crime if no evidence turned up very soon. Working on auto-pilot, though, I said and did the right things.

I tossed and turned that night before I finally settled in and got a few hours of sleep. I'm not much of a morning person, but I tend to wake early anyway, especially when I'm upset. Sunday morning was no exception. I had no trouble getting a seat on the near-empty Metro train at seven that morning. However, my favorite coffee stop didn't open until eight on Sundays. Feeling bad and stuck with office coffee was not a good start to the day.

As usual I was the first person there, so I flipped on lights in the office and set up the coffee maker before I went to my desk. The useless phone Dieter had given me yesterday still sat on top of a stack of papers and notes, so I grabbed it and took it down the hall to the cabinet that served as our Lost and Found box.

I put the phone in, but my heart skipped a beat as I set it down. There were two others sitting in there now. There hadn't been any phones when I'd checked for the missing glasses earlier in the week, so these had been added since then. They must've been given to either se-curity or maintenance people. One of them was an older flip-style phone. I couldn't imagine Chase Markham would've kept that as a toy. But the other one was a smart phone, a well-known and quite recent model.

My hand shook as I reached for it. Hope rose and I swallowed it down. Hard. The odds were against this being Chase's phone.

I picked it up carefully, holding it by the edges and pressed the button to turn it on. Nothing happened. Of course. But Joanne, our marketing director, had one of the same kind and I'd seen a charger in her desk. I took the phone to her cubicle and shamelessly rooted around in her drawers until I found it. The phone buzzed and flashed a battery image when I plugged it in, but didn't come on right away when I pressed the button.

I made myself count to sixty, flip on my own computer and pour a cup of coffee while I waited, then tried again. This time the screen lit up and opened to a communications app. A heading at the top indicated Skype.

What to do next? Was this Chase Markham's phone? How could I figure that out? A row of little icons sat at the bottom of the screen, offering the only options. One of them brought up a list of contacts. There weren't many, but my heart hammered harder when I found Larry Barnes's name there. The most recent entry on the list of calls made used an ID of "TheBigDGuy," which didn't tell me much about the target of that final contact.

I tapped on the ID, hoping it would take me to a page that included a name. Instead a message popped up. "Connecting with TheBigDGuy." I knew I should disconnect right away, but I couldn't bring myself to do it. Hell, I wasn't sure *how* to do it. The phone shook along with my hand. Then an image popped up on the screen and I almost dropped the little machine. A face I recognized. Not the face I expected to see.

"Ah, Miss McNeil, I believe?" he said.

Crap! In a blind panic, I pressed the button to turn off the phone. I had no idea if that would break the connection or stop it showing my image, so I raced back to the lost and found cabinet, shoved it in, and draped someone's abandoned sweater over it. Then I slammed the cabinet shut.

He was in the building. I'd recognized an aisle of the show floor behind him during that brief glimpse. He shouldn't be able to get inside the building so early. But he was inside, and he might've seen enough of the background behind me to guess where I was. And I was alone.

My brain was making the final connections. I'd almost had it right, but I'd missed one key thing. Why the contract itself was so important. The realization snapped into place. It made a lot more sense if Hovey *didn't know* his signature was on the contract.

My own phone was still in my purse, which sat on my desk. I raced back there, yanked the phone out, and pressed in Scott's number. What to do? *What to do?* I listened carefully as I waited for him to pick up. Did I hear the elevator moving? Footsteps on the stairs?

"Heather?" Scott's voice had never sounded so wonderful to me.

Words tumbled out of me too fast to organize into coherence. "I found the phone. Chase's. The third one. But I think he knows. And he's here. In the building."

"Whoa," Scott said. "Slow down. Who's in the building?"

The elevator had rumbled to life. "The killer. Not Hovey. Driscoll. Can't slow down. He's coming. Got to hide. Don't know where."

"Can you get to the security office?"

"I ran that way but the door was locked and I'd left the keys in my purse on my desk. Too late for that now." I looked around wildly. "Bathrooms?"

"No, he can corner you in them. Janelle's office locks, doesn't it?"

"I don't know. I think so."

"Get in there. Now. If it doesn't lock from the inside, barricade it. Move anything you can in front of it. I'm on my way. Almost there. I'm calling for help so I have to get off but I'll call you back in a moment."

"Okay." I raced to Janelle's office, praying it wasn't locked. Mercifully, it wasn't because the elevator had just pinged as it stopped on this floor. Doors swooshed open. Heavy footsteps sounded in the corridor as I pushed the office door shut behind me.

I fumbled with the latch and searched for a lock. There was no deadbolt or other obvious way to secure it from the inside without a key I didn't have. *Shit. Hell.*

Scott had said to barricade it. I grabbed the nearest loose piece of furniture I could move, a small table that I pushed against the door, then added one of the armchairs that flanked the desk. Neither of those would stand against a strong and determined killer, but they might buy me time. Enough time, if I was lucky.

As footsteps came down the corridor, I had an inspiration. I turned the small table on its side, and wedged one edge under the door handle. Rather than knobs, we have the kind of latches where you have to push down on the handle. The edge of the table should keep it from moving down and letting the door open. Nonetheless, I dragged another chair to the door and pushed that against it too.

My phone rang. "I'm in the parking lot. Where are you?" Scott asked.

"In Janelle's office. Can't lock it, but I've got a table wedged under the handle. It won't hold forever." I lowered my voice to ensure the man approaching wouldn't hear. "By the way, in case you don't make it in time, the phone's in the lost and found cabinet."

Scott swore. "I'm in the building. You only have to hold him off for a few more minutes. Tell him other people know and are on the way if he does get through."

The footsteps hesitated briefly in the hallway. Probably the killer was looking into other offices for me. Then they resumed and got closer, stopping just outside the door. I held my breath.

"Heather, are you there?" Scott's voice from the phone sounded desperate.

The door handle rattled. The table below it quivered but held. It wouldn't last long if he gave a solid heave or started to kick.

"I'm here," I whispered into the phone. "He's here. I need a weapon." Did a quick survey of the office.

My heart pounded so hard I could hear it and feel it. Sweat trickled down the side of my face. A bead dripped into my eye and stung before I wiped it away with my shirt.

I set the phone down and grabbed the nearest substantial object, a heavy, porcelain vase Janelle kept on a shelf. The door shook as a *thunk* resounded against it. The kicking had started. A piece splintered off the table. It held but wouldn't survive another assault like that. I slid to the side of the door, back to the wall, vase raised over my head.

Another kick smashed the table. The door slammed back, pushing the chair aside, and Jim Driscoll rushed in, looking nothing like the cool, collected MegaComp chief technology officer I'd talked to before. He saw me as he blasted past, stopped, and turned. I swung the vase into the side of his head. The porcelain connected and shattered, spraying shards all over the room. The man's eyes widened and he staggered sideways, tripping over the wreckage of the little table and falling backward. A soft whooshing noise came from him as he landed on his back, staring up at me.

I hadn't hit him hard enough. His eyes remained open, staring coldly at me, as he surged to his feet. I leapt over the wreckage of the table and dashed out into the hallway.

The squeal of a door opening and a hubbub of voices came from the lobby. Footsteps rushed toward me, though I couldn't see them yet. I headed toward the noise.

"Heather!" My name had never sounded so good as it did right then, coming from Scott and not too far away.

Footsteps sounded behind me too. Close. Too close. An arm snaked from behind over my shoulder and fingers dug into my throat.

Blind panic nearly took hold of me. But stubborn determination fended it off. I refused to co-operate in my own murder. Before he could tighten his hold, I ducked, scrunching down far enough to force him to either release his hold or be dragged to the floor with me.

He let go. I rolled over in a forward somersault, then another, and only stopped when I heard people approaching from the other direction.

Scott and two police officers in uniform leapt over me and surrounded Driscoll, taking him down to the floor. One officer pulled out handcuffs and put them on the man's wrists. Then the other pulled a bandage packet out of one of the multiple holders on his belt and held it to the bleeding cut I'd left on the side of Driscoll's head.

I struggled up to my knees. Arms went around me again and I started, almost jerking away, before I recognized the fragrance of Janelle's perfume. Nothing had smelled that good in a long time. I turned and buried my face in her shoulder, trying to catch my breath as my pulse finally settled down.

"Are you okay?" she asked. "Sounds like you made a heck of a mess in my office. Jim Driscoll? I didn't figure him for it." Words came out in a steady stream that was probably meant to calm me. It worked. After a moment I drew a deep breath and straightened up.

The police officers, one male, one female, had Driscoll on his feet and were escorting him from the room. They stopped in the hall to look at Scott. "Are we charging him with something?" the female officer asked.

Scott looked at me and so did the others.

My voice wasn't as steady as I would've liked when I answered. "He killed Chase Markham. And he would've killed me."

Driscoll's look of outrage was well done. "I just wanted to talk to you. What the hell was that all about?"

I directed my gaze to his pocket, where the end of what I now knew was an Ethernet cable and not a phone cord, had slipped out and hung down his hip.

"You were planning to talk to me with that?" I asked, pointing to the cable. "And what are the odds there are disposable gloves in one of your pockets as well?"

Scott reached into the man's other pocket and dragged out several items—a wallet, handkerchief, and a set of latex gloves. He held the last up. "Odd thing for a tech executive to be carrying around with him."

Driscoll's fear and desperation came through in a sour smell, though he kept his expression blank. "We work in messy circumstances sometimes."

"Right." Scott looked disgusted. "Murder is definitely messy work. You were prepared for it when you met Chase Markham on Monday, too."

"I have no idea what you're talking about. Why would I be bothered with that worm?"

I resisted the urge to scream as I said, "Because you had licensed technology from him in a way you didn't want anyone else to know about. And though it wasn't in the contract, you hadn't come across with the one thing Chase wanted most. A job at MegaComp. So he was putting the pressure on, threatening to tell Hovey that you'd forged his signature on the contract."

Driscoll went alarmingly pale and seemed to fold up. Scott and the two police officers caught him and lowered him to the floor. Once of them spoke into the microphone at her shoulder. "We need an ambulance at the Market Center," and added the street address.

Two more officers arrived, with another man in plain clothes right behind them. I blinked a couple of times before I recognized Detective Gilmont. Unshaven, in jeans and a polo shirt, he looked nothing like the laced-up detective I was used to. Actually, he looked surprisingly good. Okay, right then anyone who wasn't Jim Driscoll looked good to me.

"Someone want to explain what's going on?" Gilmont asked.

They all turned to me, but I suddenly found myself gasping for breath.

Scott looked after the officers who were holding

onto Driscoll while waiting for directions. "Who is Jim Driscoll?"

I'd forgotten he'd never met the man. I had to close my eyes for a moment until I felt steady enough to talk. "Chief technology officer at MegaComp. And the man who forged Tom Hovey's signature on the contract with Chase Markham."

"So it wasn't Hovey." Scott turned to Gilmont. "It sounds like Heather has something that will tie this man to the murder."

I nodded and told the detective where to find the phone. While he and Scott went off to get it, the EMS and a couple more uniformed police officers arrived. It got kind of chaotic for a while then, with people coming and going, and lots of different conversations going on at once. Eventually they took Driscoll away, handcuffed to a gurney, and Gilmont left with the phone in an evidence bag, leaving me, Janelle, and Scott alone upstairs. Now I was glad it was Sunday so there wasn't a crowd of curious people in the office.

Janelle went to find better coffee than the office pot would provide, while Scott and I did our best to set her office straight. The table and vase were both goners, so we gathered up the remains and dumped them in a trash bag we found in a closet, then we put the chairs back where they belonged. Maintenance would need to bring a vacuum for the smaller bits. Janelle returned just as we finished. A wonderful aroma preceded her and my mouth watered in anticipation.

She had indeed found the good stuff. I got in a few appreciative sips before Janelle said, "Okay. Spill it."

I managed one more long pull before I started talking. "I kept thinking about what Chase did the morning he got here. He was a busy guy and it was clear he had some kind of plan. It just took me a while to realize what it must've been. I couldn't make sense of his having that public argument with Hovey when he had sold them that technology. And the arguments, or discussions, with Larry and Ted from Gryphon-Loyall didn't seem to fit in with some kind of plan. Of course, the one with Ted wasn't part of his plan at all, and even it didn't fit until I remembered Ted mentioned that Galloway had overheard it and looked shocked. In fact, Ted had instigated that quarrel and just wanted to warn Chase to stay away from Jennifer, but it ended up revealing to Galloway that the technology in his primary product might be flawed. My guess is Galloway already knew there were problems with the product. This just confirmed to him that Chase was *aware* of flaws in his designs. Galloway *didn't* know they'd been fixed, which suggested that the RTX products weren't using a repaired version. Worse yet, Chase's later argument with Hovey had Galloway wondering if Chase might've sold that improved version to MegaComp. It made a definite motive for Galloway to want to kill him.

"But then the RTX booth was trashed, and the only explanation that made sense was that the killer was searching for something incriminating that Chase might've hidden. That third phone seemed like a good bet. Which pointed away from Galloway, since he wouldn't have to trash his own booth if he wanted to search for it. He could easily do it quietly and much more efficiently in spare, quiet moments. Plus, we found out Galloway was stealing those MegaComp products to find out what technology they were using. That didn't strike me as what someone would do after he'd killed an employee in revenge or annoyance. Surely if he'd committed murder, he wouldn't risk another crime that might draw more attention to him. Not that he was incapable of killing Chase. He almost certainly planned some kind of retaliation, whether against Chase Markham, MegaComp, or both, I have no idea, but it didn't seem like it would include murder. He was much more about the satisfaction of revealing Chase for a venal, greedy traitor and getting monetary retribution, probably from MegaComp."

I stopped for another pull on the coffee.

"Chase's argument with Hovey still doesn't make any sense," Scott said.

"Yeah. It was pretty clear Chase had instigated the argument deliberately. So I asked myself why he'd do that. They'd already made it clear they weren't going to hire him. He'd been paid for the tech he sold them. So what did he stand to gain? Then I remembered that Chase had asked Larry for a copy of the contract. Why would he need it? To show to Hovey? But why? I began thinking about what I knew about Hovey. He was rich, well-known, charismatic, and more than a bit of a control freak. He was proud of the fact that his company developed its own technology. Yes, they licensed parts from manufacturers, but they developed all the software themselves. Except possibly Chase's piece. Hovey wasn't buying the story that they'd stolen Chase's technology, but he gave no indication that he knew his company had actually bought it. Which didn't make sense, since his name is on the contract. And he's a control freak, the kind who surely wouldn't sign a contract without having a firm grasp of what it said. At first I thought he was just covering it up, which is why I suspected him initially. But when I saw Driscoll's face, I realized the more likely answer was that Hovey really didn't know about it at all."

Janelle's mouth fell open as comprehension dawned.

"Once I figured out Hovey didn't know, it kind of all fell into place. I'm not sure how Chase knew Hovey hadn't actually signed the contract, but he must have. The argument he engineered was basically meant to confirm that, and to put pressure on Driscoll at the same time. I'm guessing Chase was indulging in a bit of blackmail. The plan probably got a boost in urgency when his boss overheard the argument with Ted. Chase knew he would likely be fired and maybe sued as well. So he wanted more from Driscoll. But he didn't understand the utterly ruthless nature of the man he dealt with. Driscoll wasn't about to risk his own position by letting this upstart reveal he'd forged his boss's signature on a contract."

"And the phone?" Janelle asked.

"That was easy. He had to contact the guy privately somehow. The police didn't find any indication of it on the other two phones, at least I assume they didn't. Everyone discounted the third phone because it didn't have a wireless or data plan. But I saw something recently that reminded me most smart phones don't need a service plan to do some things. They can connect to a WiFi network and you can use some of the same features that way, including programs like Skype that let you make video phone calls. That seemed like the kind of thing Chase would do for a call he didn't want to have on record."

Scott's voice was hard and the spark in his eyes looked like anger. "When did it occur to you to go looking in the lost and found for the phone?"

"It didn't occur to me. It was more of an accident. Yesterday an exhibitor gave me a phone someone in their booth had found, and I did think then that it might be Chase's phone. It wasn't. The last time I'd looked in the lost and found cabinet, a couple of days ago, there weren't any other phones there. This morning I found the lost phone on my desk and I went to stick it in the cabinet and discovered two others already there. I checked them out and one had Larry Barnes's name in the contact list. It has Skype on it, too, and I checked for the last person he'd contacted. It wasn't a name, just an ID, 'TheBigDGuy.'"

"So you decided to try to lure Driscoll to you by calling that ID?"

"No!" The word came out as a shout. "Heck no." I drew a deep breath to calm myself. "It was an accident. I don't really know how those things work. I pressed the ID, thinking it would show me a name, but it called him instead. I didn't expect it to do that. I wouldn't ever have done it if I'd even guessed it might actually put through a call."

The lines in Scott's face relaxed.

"I'm a ditz," I said. "And I hadn't had any coffee. My brain wasn't in gear yet."

A smile broke through the coldness of Scott's expression. "I get the coffee thing. It seems like your brain did manage to work well enough to get you through the confrontation afterward in one piece, thank God."

"More than I can say for my office furniture," Janelle added dryly. "And that vase was a gift from my favorite niece. She made it herself."

"Oh my God, I'm so sorry! I had no idea."

Janelle's mouth crooked into a wry grin. "Never liked it much, in truth. Now I can tell her it got broken in a good cause."

Her phone rang and we listened as she responded in her "soothing" voice, scribbled a note, and said, "Someone will be down to check on it in a few minutes." When she hung up, she picked up the note but looked at me and said, "Do you need to go home?"

"And do what? Sit around and think about how close I came to getting myself killed? Through my own stupidity? Kick myself about it, over and over? No thanks." I got up and took the note from her. "I'll check this out."

Scott stood, too, and looked at Janelle. "We only have half a day today, right?"

"Right."

"Good." He stabbed me with a sharp look. "That date I promised you? Tonight. I'll take you home this afternoon and we'll talk about it."

My pulse did a funny little stutter, but I kept my look cool. Almost. Janelle's smirk suggested I wasn't quite as opaque as I'd like to be.

"Sounds good to me," I said.

Based on the look that passed between Scott and Janelle, I most definitely didn't sound as cool as I'd hoped.

Janelle grinned at both of us and said, "There's work to do. Get out of here."

* * * * *

ABOUT THE AUTHOR

KAREN MCCULLOUGH IS the author of more than a dozen novels in the romantic suspense, mystery, and fantasy genres and has won numerous awards, including an Eppie Award for fantasy. She's also been a four-time Eppie finalist, and a finalist in the Prism, Dream Realm, Rising Star, Lories, Scarlett Letter, and Vixen Awards contests. Her short fiction has appeared in numerous small press publications in the fantasy, science fiction, and romance genres.

Karen worked in trade publishing for more than ten years as an editor, managing editor, and senior web editor. She lives in Greensboro, North Carolina.

She invites visitors to check out her home on the web at *http://www.kmccullough.com* and her site for the Market Center Mysteries series, http://www. marketcentermysteries.com.

Get 4 FREE REWARDS!

We'll send you 2 FREE Books plus 2 FREE Mystery Gifts.

Harlequin® Intrigue books feature heroes and heroines that confront and survive danger while finding themselves irresistibly drawn to one another.

FREE Value Over $20

YES! Please send me 2 FREE Harlequin® Intrigue novels and my 2 FREE gifts (gifts are worth about $10 retail). After receiving them, if I don't wish to receive any more books, I can return the shipping statement marked "cancel." If I don't cancel, I will receive 6 brand-new novels every month and be billed just $4.99 each for the regular-print edition or $5.74 each for the larger-print edition in the U.S., or $5.74 each for the regular-print edition or $6.49 each for the larger-print edition in Canada. That's a savings of at least 12% off the cover price! It's quite a bargain! Shipping and handling is just 50¢ per book in the U.S. and 75¢ per book in Canada*. I understand that accepting the 2 free books and gifts places me under no obligation to buy anything. I can always return a shipment and cancel at any time. The free books and gifts are mine to keep no matter what I decide.

Choose one: ☐ **Harlequin® Intrigue**
Regular-Print
(182/382 HDN GMYW)

☐ **Harlequin® Intrigue**
Larger-Print
(199/399 HDN GMYW)

Name (please print)

Address   Apt. #

City   State/Province   Zip/Postal Code

Mail to the **Reader Service:**
IN U.S.A.: P.O. Box 1341, Buffalo, NY 14240-8531
IN CANADA: P.O. Box 603, Fort Erie, Ontario L2A 5X3

Want to try two free books from another series? Call 1-800-873-8635 or visit www.ReaderService.com.

*Terms and prices subject to change without notice. Prices do not include applicable taxes. Sales tax applicable in N.Y. Canadian residents will be charged applicable taxes. Offer not valid in Quebec. This offer is limited to one order per household. Books received may not be as shown. Not valid for current subscribers to Harlequin Intrigue books. All orders subject to approval. Credit or debit balances in a customer's account(s) may be offset by any other outstanding balance owed by or to the customer. Please allow 4 to 6 weeks for delivery. Offer available while quantities last.

Your Privacy—The Reader Service is committed to protecting your privacy. Our Privacy Policy is available online at www.ReaderService.com or upon request from the Reader Service. We make a portion of our mailing list available to reputable third parties that offer products we believe may interest you. If you prefer that we not exchange your name with third parties, or if you wish to clarify or modify your communication preferences, please visit us at www.ReaderService.com/consumerchoice or write to us at Reader Service Preference Service, P.O. Box 9062, Buffalo, NY 14240-9062. Include your complete name and address.

HI18

Get 4 FREE REWARDS!

We'll send you 2 FREE Books plus 2 FREE Mystery Gifts.

Harlequin® Romantic Suspense books feature heart-racing sensuality and the promise of a sweeping romance set against the backdrop of suspense.

FREE Value Over **$20**

YES! Please send me 2 FREE Harlequin® Romantic Suspense novels and my 2 FREE gifts (gifts are worth about $10 retail). After receiving them, if I don't wish to receive any more books, I can return the shipping statement marked "cancel." If I don't cancel, I will receive 4 brand-new novels every month and be billed just $4.99 per book in the U.S. or $5.74 per book in Canada. That's a savings of at least 12% off the cover price! It's quite a bargain! Shipping and handling is just 50¢ per book in the U.S. and 75¢ per book in Canada*. I understand that accepting the 2 free books and gifts places me under no obligation to buy anything. I can always return a shipment and cancel at any time. The free books and gifts are mine to keep no matter what I decide.

240/340 HDN GMYZ

Name (please print)

Address   Apt. #

City   State/Province   Zip/Postal Code

Mail to the **Reader Service:**
IN U.S.A.: P.O. Box 1341, Buffalo, NY 14240-8531
IN CANADA: P.O. Box 603, Fort Erie, Ontario L2A 5X3

Want to try two free books from another series! Call 1-800-873-8635 or visit www.ReaderService.com.

Get 4 FREE REWARDS!

We'll send you 2 FREE Books plus 2 FREE Mystery Gifts.

FREE
Value Over
$20

Both the **Romance** and **Suspense** collections feature compelling novels
written by many of today's best-selling authors.

YES! Please send me 2 FREE novels from the Essential Romance or
Essential Suspense Collection and my 2 FREE gifts (gifts are worth about
$10 retail). After receiving them, if I don't wish to receive any more books,
I can return the shipping statement marked "cancel." If I don't cancel, I will
receive 4 brand-new novels every month and be billed just $6.74 each in the
U.S. or $7.24 each in Canada. That's a savings of at least 16% off the cover
price. It's quite a bargain! Shipping and handling is just 50¢ per book in the
U.S. and 75¢ per book in Canada*. I understand that accepting the 2 free
books and gifts places me under no obligation to buy anything. I can always
return a shipment and cancel at any time. The free books and gifts are mine
to keep no matter what I decide.

Choose one: ☐ **Essential Romance**   ☐ **Essential Suspense**
                (194/394 MDN GMY7)   (191/391 MDN GMY7)

Name (please print)

Address   Apt. #

City   State/Province   Zip/Postal Code

Mail to the **Reader Service:**
IN U.S.A.: P.O. Box 1341, Buffalo, NY 14240-8531
IN CANADA: P.O. Box 603, Fort Erie, Ontario L2A 5X3

Want to try two free books from another series! Call 1-800-873-8635 or visit www.ReaderService.com.

Get 4 FREE REWARDS!

We'll send you 2 FREE Books plus 2 FREE Mystery Gifts.

Harlequin® Historical
books feature passionate
love stories set against
colorful historical
backgrounds.

FREE
Value Over
$20

Get 4 FREE REWARDS!

We'll send you 2 FREE Books plus 2 FREE Mystery Gifts.

Harlequin® Romance Larger-Print books feature uplifting escapes that will warm your heart with the ultimate feel-good tales.

FREE Value Over **$20**

READERSERVICE.COM

Manage your account online!

- Review your order history
- Manage your payments
- Update your address

> *We've designed the*
> *Reader Service website*
> *just for you.*

Enjoy all the features!

- Discover new series available to you, and read excerpts from any series.
- Respond to mailings and special monthly offers.
- Browse the Bonus Bucks catalog and online-only exculsives.
- Share your feedback.

Visit us at:

ReaderService.com